KU-504-681

in a thousand different ways

CECELIA AHERN

HarperCollins*Publishers*

HarperCollins*Publishers* Ltd
1 London Bridge Street,
London SE1 9GF
www.harpercollins.co.uk

HarperCollins*Publishers*
Macken House,
39/40 Mayor Street Upper,
Dublin 1
D01 C9W8
Ireland

First published by HarperCollins*Publishers* 2023
1

Copyright © Greenlight Go Ltd 2023

Cecelia Ahern asserts the moral right to be identified as the author of this work

A catalogue record for this book is available from the British Library

ISBN: 978-0-00-819497-0 (HB)
ISBN: 978-0-00-819498-7 (TPB)
ISBN: 978-0-00-861024-1 (TPB, CA-only)
ISBN: 978-0-00-854105-7 (PB, IN-only)

This novel is entirely a work of fiction.
The names, characters and incidents portrayed in it are
the work of the author's imagination. Any resemblance to
actual persons, living or dead, events or localities is
entirely coincidental.

Typeset in Adobe Caslon by
Palimpsest Book Production Ltd, Falkirk, Stirlingshire

Printed and Bound in the UK using 100% Renewable Electricity
at CPI Group (UK) Ltd

All rights reserved. No part of this publication may be
reproduced, stored in a retrieval system, or transmitted,
in any form or by any means, electronic, mechanical,
photocopying, recording or otherwise, without the prior
permission of the publishers.

This book is produced from independently certified FSC™ paper
to ensure responsible forest management.

For more information visit: www.harpercollins.co.uk/green

in a thousand different ways

South Dublin Libraries

www.southdublinlibraries.ie

Also by Cecelia Ahern

PS, I Love You
Where Rainbows End
If You Could See Me Now
A Place Called Here
Thanks for the Memories
The Gift
The Book of Tomorrow
The Time of My Life
One Hundred Names
How to Fall in Love
The Year I Met You
The Marble Collector
Lyrebird
Roar
Postscript
Freckles

For Blossom

blue

I MARCH TO THE BEAT of the uneaten apple clunking from side to side in my lunch box. Roll, thump, roll, thump. It's been in my school bag since Monday, it makes my lunch look healthy, but it stays there for the week, taking hits and getting more bruised by the day. My little brother Ollie trudges along behind me, head down, occasionally kicking stones that dare to block his path. Our house comes into view and I slow; school is too far away in the morning, not far enough away in the afternoon.

I study her bedroom window. Curtains drawn messily, like they've been pulled roughly and some clips have separated from the rings, leaving gaping holes at the top. The Gangulys next door have tied-back curtains, really fancy, like the ones you draw when you're little and think that's how a house should look. Their front garden is a neat lawn; pretty, colourful flowers around the edges with a red gate that matches the paint around the windows. Not like ours.

Our grass needs cutting, it reaches above the garden wall like it's desperate to see over the top, maybe escape, but at least the jungle hides some of the overflowing bins. Putting the bins out and cutting the grass was Dad's job.

I push our screechy rickety gate open, past the foul-smelling bins to the blue door, the brass 7 of the 47 slightly crooked. I pick up the warm milk on the step and bring it inside. It's nearly 3 p.m. but the house is quiet and dark and smells of stale morning. The kitchen table is decorated in sugar trails, our cereal bowls are in the sink, soggy cornflakes floating in sugary yellow milk. Chairs are pulled at odd angles from the table, the scene frozen from 8.30 a.m.

Ollie throws his school bag on the floor and falls to his knees at the playbox that's filled with mostly broken wheel-less cars from my big brother Hugh and my decapitated dolls with no limbs. He plays with his soldiers and wrestlers, making quiet boom-bash-bosh noises with his lips as they pick up on a battle where they left off. I've never known a child to whisper when they're playing, but he rarely speaks, is always just there, waiting, like the grass and the bins; silently growing and overflowing.

I place my schoolbag by the chair at the kitchen table where I'll do my homework. I wipe the table and scrape the hardened cornflakes stuck to the edges of the bowls before stacking them in the dishwasher. I pull the curtains open; the grey daylight reveals the dust particles floating in the air. I watch them hover, ear cocked to the silence. My brother Hugh will be home soon. He's older and finishes school at four. Everything is always okay when he's home. But he's not here now. A pulsating throb in my temple like Morse code tries to tell me something. Nothing is different, but something feels wrong.

I tentatively peer upstairs, afraid of what I'll find. On the top step of the staircase our usually brown carpet looks blue. It looks like ground fog, low and still, resting at the top of the steps. I sniff to see if it's smoke, but it's odourless. I step onto the bottom stair, and the blue cloud slowly moves towards me. Ollie pauses play to watch me. It's an unspoken rule that we don't go upstairs when she's sleeping.

'Go outside,' I say.

He obeys, then I run upstairs through the blue, moving so fast I send it swirling upward in wisps. The blue hue gushes from under her door like there's a smoke machine inside. My heart is pounding as I place my hand on the door handle. She doesn't like to be disturbed. She has trouble sleeping, so when she's sleeping you don't wake her up. When she's sleeping you're happy she's sleeping, but this isn't any normal day.

I push the door open. The room is completely blue, covered in this odd dawn light. It causes a pain at the back of my eyeballs. I look around for the source of the light, maybe a new device to soothe her to sleep, but I can't find it, plus it's not calming. It feels thick, like I'm stuck in it and it's cold. In an instant I feel so sad, so alone, empty and spiritless, as if I want to surrender, lie down and die right there.

I see her shape beneath the duvet; she's on her side facing the drawn curtains, little pockets of grey light coming through the parts that have been pulled down from the rings. I walk quietly around to her side, her hair is over her face, lank and greasy. With trembling fingers I gently brush her hair back from her face.

'999, please state your emergency.'

'She's blue. She's . . . she's . . . blue.'

'Who am I speaking with?'

'Her face . . . her arms . . . b-b-blue.'

'What's your name?'

'Alice Kelly.'

'Okay, Alice, what's your address?'

'She's blue, she's all blue.'

'Can you tell me your address, honey?'

'Briarswood Road. Finglas. The 47 is crooked.'

'I'll send an ambulance right away. Who are you talking about Alice? Who is blue?'

'Lily Kelly.'

'Is that your mum?'

'Yeah.'

'Are you with her now?'

I shake my head.

'Alice, are you with your mum now?'

'No.'

'Can you go to her for me?'

I shake my head.

'How old are you, Alice?'

'Eight.'

'Okay. Did your mum have an accident, Alice?'

'I don't know, I just got home from school.'

'And where is your mum now?'

'In bed. She's blue.'

'Can you go to your mum for me, Alice?'

I shake my head a final time and hang up.

There's banging on the front door. I can't move. I'm trembling. I put my head down between my knees and hug my legs. The doorbell rings a few times. Banging again and then I hear footsteps, up the stairs. My bedroom door opens, I hold my breath, then there's silence and they leave. They try the next room. Her room.

A knock first, then footsteps. Then—

Screaming. Her screaming?

I block my ears and squeeze my eyes shut, shove my face closer into my knees. I can smell the grass from the stains on my knees from when Hajra rugby tackled me to the ground at playtime. I breathe it in, shuddering, unable to get enough air into my tight chest. The screaming stops and I hear talking. Raised voices. I stay as still as I can. Someone stays in there murmuring while somebody else goes downstairs. It feels like a long time, I was never good at playing hide and seek, would always need to run for a wee. My bladder's full now, threatening to overflow. The footsteps are on the stairs again and my door opens.

'Alice,' a woman says, not angrily. 'Alice, are you in here?'

She comes further into the room.

'My name is Louise, I'm a paramedic. I'm with the ambulance you called for.'

I can't move. If she opens the door then I'm afraid the blue will get me, it must be all over the house now. I took off my shoes to get rid of the blue but some of it got on my hand from when I touched her hair. I hold it upright and away from my body as if it's gushing blood. I don't want it to rub off on anything else, but if she's a paramedic maybe she can help.

'In here,' I say.

The wardrobe door opens and I'm bathed in daylight.

A friendly face comes down low. She's dressed in green and luminous yellow.

'Hello in there.'

I peer out to my bedroom, confused. I'd imagined the blue had spread all over the house, rolled around like hot lava. I was happy Ollie was outside. But there's no blue.

'Hi.'

'Want to come out? Your mum is worried about you. She's fine, but she got a fright when she saw us in her bedroom. That's what all the yelling was about. She was asleep. Want to tell us why you called?'

'The blue,' I say, confused.

'What blue?'

I look at my hand. She thinks I'm offering it to her and she takes it. She has the blue on her now and she doesn't even notice.

'Come on out and we'll talk about it,' she says, guiding me out. We sit on the bed. 'Here, let's wrap you up.'

She pulls my duvet up and wraps it around my shoulders.

'Ollie's grand, he's downstairs playing wrestlers with Tommy, my partner. Kicking his arse, actually.' She smiles.

I relax a little.

'Your mum said she had trouble sleeping last night, so she went to bed today while you were at school. She didn't hear you come in.'

I can hear her giving out downstairs. I'm afraid now for different reasons. How dare you this, how dare you that. Louise looks at the door, hearing it too.

'Is your dad at work?'

I shrug.

'You don't know where he is?'

'He doesn't live here. We don't see him anymore.'

'Do you walk home every day on your own?'

'With Ollie. I collect him at the gate and we walk together.'

'Good girl. And does Mum wait for you here?'

I nod. Sometimes.

Another look at the door, just to check, but we know she's not there because we can hear her shouting downstairs. It's not just playing wrestlers that's smashing Tommy.

'Does your mum have trouble sleeping?'

I shrug.

'Where she has to lie down in the daytime.'

I nod.

'And you were worried about her?'

'She was blue.'

'Ah, I see,' as if it finally makes sense to her. 'When did Dad leave?'

'A while ago.'

'So she's been feeling blue since Dad left,' she says gently.

It's not a question so I don't answer her. The way she is didn't happen after he left, it's why he left. He said he couldn't live with her anymore, that she needed help. But I don't say that out loud.

'Well, you were right to call us.'

I wasn't though. I can tell from Lily's face when Louise brings me downstairs that I'm in trouble. I don't want them to leave, with her this angry at me, but they do leave, waving goodbye and taking their happy cheery voices and my security away with them. I wish Hugh would walk in the door now; maybe he has football after school which means it'll be after dinner, hours away.

Lily watches from the window as the ambulance drives away, pulling the belt of her robe around her waist so tight it looks like she's going to cut herself in half. As soon as the ambulance has disappeared down the road, and the neighbours stop staring, she turns around, comes at me and smacks me across the head.

Hugh and Ollie are already having breakfast when I go downstairs. After the drama of yesterday I was exhausted and slept late. I still feel half-asleep. I pause at the bottom of the stairs.

There are colours around Hugh and Ollie.

'What?' Hugh asks, his voice muffled with toast in his mouth, while he puts his shoe up on the chair to tie his laces.

My breath catches in my throat, for a moment, I can't breathe. But then the air comes again.

'Is it the blue again?'

I shake my head. I'd confided in him about the colour in her room yesterday. He didn't laugh or call me a freak, he'd taken me seriously, but he didn't have any answers.

'Then what's wrong?'

'Nothing.'

He watches me for a while then gets back to tying his shoelaces.

'Toast?' he asks.

'Yeah.'

I force myself to eat, heart pounding, trying not to look at the two of them, but it's difficult because my eyes keep being drawn to them. I watch them, like I'm seeing them for the first time, two exotic creatures glowing in the grey kitchen.

*

She's in the kitchen with two women from Social who've called around unexpectedly. Hugh, Ollie and I are in the TV room with Mrs Ganguly, our next-door neighbour with the tidy garden and perfect curtains. The double doors are closed between us and the kitchen, but we can kind of hear what they're saying and see them moving around through the swirly glass on the doors like they're alien blobs. Even though I can hear the words I don't really understand what they're saying. Adult sentences; same words, different order.

'Did you call them?' Mrs Ganguly asks.

'No. Alice called an ambulance a few days ago,' Hugh says, rescuing me, like he always does, cheerily. 'She thought Mum was sick. I'd say these two are just following up to make sure everything's okay.'

Mrs Ganguly narrows her eyes, assessing the new information. 'You can't mess around with these people. If they think something's wrong, they'll take you away from her, they'll split the three of you up. Send you to different houses.'

Ollie looks up from the floor, his wrestlers frozen mid-attack.

I don't know why she's so angry. Maybe because she's been forced to keep an eye on us while the people are talking, and she has the chicken biryani on because it's biryani night, and she needs to get back to check it before it burns and Mr Ganguly won't be happy. She only came over to give out about the stinky bins and the grass, and they were having an argument when the women arrived and asked if she'd mind keeping an eye on us while they talked to her. Mr Ganguly is nice, he smiles and talks to everyone, but Mrs Ganguly always has her face twisted up, angry, like she doesn't trust anyone.

I look at Hugh, afraid. I don't mind being taken away from Lily, but I don't want us three to get split up. If we do, it'll all be my fault for calling the ambulance.

'Don't worry, nobody's splitting us up,' Hugh says cheerily, with a wink.

In the kitchen Lily starts to shout and Mrs Ganguly turns *EastEnders* up. I can't hear what they're saying in the kitchen anymore but that's okay because it means Mrs Ganguly can't hear what me and Hugh are saying anymore either.

'Have you seen blue on her since Monday?' he asks.

I nod, looking down at my shoes, my laces suddenly interesting. I can barely look at her, can't stand to be in the same room as her. Though that's nothing new but what is new is when I'm too close to the colour around her I start to feel differently and I don't like it.

'Why didn't you say?'

I shrug.

'Can you see blue around me?' he asks.

I shake my head. 'It's a different colour.'

He'd been joking so he's surprised by my response. 'Really? What colour am I?'

I'm not afraid to look at him, to study his colour. His doesn't scare me, it doesn't try to cling to me, it doesn't follow me around the room like hers does, as if it's a big net trying to catch me and pull me in.

'Pink,' I say.

'Pink?!' He wrinkles his nose.

Ollie, who I didn't think was listening, laughs.

'Yuck, Ollie, pink is for girls,' Hugh says, and Ollie laughs. It's so rare to hear him laugh, he's so solemn and serious all the time, only Hugh could do it.

The chairs scrape against the floor in the kitchen as they stand up and whatever it is comes to an end.

'They'll probably want to speak to us next,' Hugh says, looking a little more serious than usual. 'Maybe don't mention the colour thing to them.'

At first it's just the people I live with and every morning I wonder what colours will greet me. Usually for Hugh it's the same colour: a pink warm colour that floats around him like a faint haze. Like the cigarette smoke that sits in the air after she has smoked. His colour is calm, easy, happy, caring, and it stays close to him on different parts of his body, following him wherever he moves, like it's magnetically attached.

Sometimes, when I get over the fear of what's happening to me, I see its beauty. Like a pink sky at night or a pink sunrise.

Hugh catches me looking at him.

'What colour now?' he'll say easily, not freaked out.

'Pink again.'

He smiles, it always amuses him.

'Let me know when it's something buff and strong like black, or blue, or . . .' he thinks, 'or red.' He flexes his muscles and strains so hard his face turns red and a vein nearly explodes in his neck.

I smile but I don't want him to be those other colours he's mentioned. Pink suits him, it somehow manages to keep hers less angry, like the antacid TV ad where the white medicine puts out the flame of the red burning chest. His colour puts out fires everywhere.

'What about Ollie?' he asks.

I watch Ollie. He's sitting at the kitchen table, Coco Pops in a bowl, a messy bedhead and sleepy eyes, crashing wrestlers into each other. I don't want to say, shake my head.

His colour is usually the same as hers. She gives it to him.

'An aura migraine,' Hugh reads from his computer. 'Do you get migraines?'

'What's a migraine?'

'A really bad headache.'

I nod. 'All the time now.' I can't remember a day since these colours appeared when I haven't had a headache. I just want to go to my room, pull the curtains and lie in the darkness, but I don't because I don't want to be like her.

'It's a recurring headache that strikes after or at the same time as sensory disturbances called aura. These can include flashes of light, blind spots, zigzag lines that float across your vision, shimmering spots or stars, or tingling in your hand or face. Does that sound familiar to you?'

'I suppose.'

'It's like an electrical or chemical wave that processes visual signals and causes these . . . what you call colours.'

'Oh.'

'You need to go to a neurologist,' he says, scrolling and reading. 'They'd give you an eye exam, a head CT scan, or an MRI. They recommend medicine, or avoid stressful situations, learn how to relax. Get more sleep, eat better. Drink lots of water.'

'I can drink more water,' I say.

We both smile because it's not really that funny.

'So,' he says, spinning around in his chair to face me. 'That's probably what it is.'

I nod along. Aura migraines. Probably.

I drink what feels like endless glasses of water, trying to flush it out like it's a cold, but it doesn't seem to help. Instead, the colours intensify with each passing week.

Lily says we're not going to see a doctor about a headache and tosses a box of Paracetamol at me.

The colours move from my family to everyone else. It makes me want to stop looking at people. Their swirling colours dancing around, twirling, flashing and flickering, at different paces and rhythms is distracting. It makes me feel nauseous, sometimes dizzy. The brightness, the constant light strains my eyes and gives me a headache. It's like hundreds of people are broadcasting their own radio stations around me. The air around them fizzes then breaches and collides with mine when they come close.

It starts to happen with my best friend Emma. Always fun and exciting, her giddiness used to be addictive but now she exhausts me. Her colours are wild and fast, flashing yellows and hyperactive greens, sometimes zigzagging like lightning forks, as though she's dipped in something toxic. That, mixed with her speed of speech, her high energy, how she always wants to control the games we play, our role-playing characters, what I say, how we play them, drains me.

'Come on, Alice,' she says, pulling my arm roughly. 'Get up. Let's play outside.'

'But we just came inside.'

Has she always jumped from game to game every three minutes? I need her to focus, I need her to be still and quiet. I need calm. I need a friend. But I can't do it anymore. I move further and further away from her. It hurts but I'm actually relieved when she moves on to another group of girls and I escape torturous afternoons of hyperactive controlling girls with headache-inducing power-play colours.

I see a dark murky greenish-black colour floating in the air by a bush. I walk to where the colour hovers, use my foot to move aside a weed and find a dying rat, its leg twitching, the blood on it still wet.

I'm alone on the walk to school. Hugh has gone on ahead with his friends and Ollie trails behind me, even more distant with me than usual after the visit from Social. I don't think he trusts me; he thinks I'm trying to break up the family. School is becoming a nightmare. There are colours all around me, all the time, from every living thing. Thirty people in my class. Hundreds outside at breaktime. Not to mention the people I've to walk past to get to and from school. I dodge every single one of them so their colours don't get on me. It's exhausting. The colours are so vivid and busy I sometimes can't concentrate on what teachers are saying. Colours are quiet but they feel so loud and distracting that I can't hear. It's like somebody constantly interrupting me when I'm in a conversation, a niggly naggy constant tap on the shoulder.

I start wearing sunglasses walking to and from school. Some kids make comments at first, then stop when word spreads I'm special, or partially blind. Then I become so used to them, I wear them outside at lunchtime. It doesn't make the colours disappear, but it does dull everything and makes it less intense. I sit in the quiet area, reserved for kids who aren't feeling well, who have a broken arm or leg, or some sort of special needs. My special need is to be away from everyone. Every single person.

'Breaktime is over, Alice, sunglasses off and in your bag,' Ms Crowley says. She's from Cork and she sings as she talks. Every day she wears a different tea dress and cardigan and large red-rimmed glasses with matching lipstick. She wears a lot of colours, maybe to brighten up the dullness that surrounds her.

'I can't,' I say.

I just can't do it today, I can't take the shades off in class. My head is aching so much I feel my temples pulsating. I wonder if I looked in the mirror would I see them move.

'Why not?'

'It's too bright in here.'

Some people laugh, which does nothing for my defence. It's an overcast day and everything, including the exterior of the school is grey, but this only makes people's colours brighter, or at least more visible to me.

She rolls her eyes. 'Off.'

And she moves on.

I keep them on. She writes on the board and when she turns around and sees my glasses still on, she loses it. A surprising explosion of anger that seems to come from nowhere sparks over her head. As she yells at me to take them off again, a bright metallic red, as bright as her lipstick, flickers around her and it reminds me of one of those fly-killer machines at the local kebab shop that flies fly into and it zaps them and kills them.

I feel Lily before I hear or see her. She has the ability to change the air – and not in a good way like Hugh does. At the sound of a key in the door, Ollie jumps up from the couch, excited. He's been anxious since we came home and she wasn't here. We're not used to her not being here, but unlike him, I was pleased. I don't know where he gets this yearning to be with her and around her.

'Mum,' he says, hurrying to the door.

I'm surprised he isn't flattened against the wall with the force she pushes the door open. And then she slams it so hard it feels like the entire house shakes. Ollie quickly backs away from her and returns to the couch. I try to make myself as small as I can. Maybe the smaller I am, the less angry she'll be.

'I've never had to go to the school for Hugh,' she says, spitting with anger. 'Not once in my life. You're eleven years old and behaving like a little brat. I don't have time for this,' she shouts, and I hold back on the comment I want to make. She has all the time for everything. She doesn't do anything, ever; it's difficult to recognise her without the

just below my eye. It turns a nasty colour as the afternoon goes by.

'Did she do that?' Hugh wants to know, later, when he's home.

I shake my head. 'It was an accident.'

I thought protecting Ollie would go towards him learning to trust me, but it's like the ease with which I do it is all the proof he needs that I'm a liar.

When I wake up, my eye is half-closed, like a peach that I've left in the bottom of my school bag for too long. I tell a concerned Ms Crowley that I have a migraine and she lets me wear my sunglasses in school that day.

'I'm going to open a pancake truck,' Lily says, her cheeks flushed, glowing with health, her brow sweaty from all the egg-beating she's doing.

I don't know who this woman is who claims to be my mother, but I like her. Full of energy and vigour, of business ideas and hope.

'I'll make pancakes at festivals, crêpes. You can fill a crêpe, you see,' she says. 'More diverse. Broadens the market and the opportunity to make a profit.' There's sweat on her chest, under her arms. She's stirring and stirring her third batter bowl.

She makes one for me, folds it into quarters. It's so thin, at first I can almost see through it. It's delicious.

'The filling options are endless,' she says, blowing her hair from her sweaty face. 'Savoury or sweet. Or just with icing sugar. Banana, caramel, strawberry, Nutella . . . Then the savoury: cheese and ham, Mexican . . . Here, taste this.'

She places another one down before me and starts making more. It's still delicious, but by the fourth I don't think I can take another bite. They keep coming, one after another on to my plate and I pass them to Ollie. She keeps breaking eggs, measuring milk, sifting flour, pinching salt. Using four pans now to make them in multiples, working out how many customers she can serve at once, and in an entire day or night.

I can't eat any more, and as she turns around to place another pancake on the top of the pile I can no longer eat, I prepare for her to lose her temper, but the new pancake lands on the old pancake without a word. It continues: eight pancakes piled high on my plate. I quickly realise it doesn't matter if I comment or not, if I join in with the conversation or not. It doesn't matter if I'm there or not. She's talking but not conversing, she's in the flow of something, something is happening in her head, something great and grand and life-changing. My excitement fizzles a little. She is manic in her thoughts and movement, behind the eyes there's no great connection with her.

Her colours are fascinating: deep purples and indigos appear to mimic her movements. They swirl and mix, changing consistency as if they're in the bowl with the eggs, flour and milk.

She lists the festivals she can go to, talks about the different types of vans, what equipment she'll need inside the van, where she can get one, who she knows. Van costs against ingredient costs; the numbers of eggs, the weight of flour and sugar. All that against the profit. She talks and talks, a mile a minute. Breaks more eggs, mixes more batter, greases more pans. Beads of sweat drip from her forehead and chest.

I've stopped licking the bowls, I've stopped tasting the pancakes. It's midnight on a Friday; Hugh is out working, Ollie is pinging off the walls, high on sugar. She begins a fresh batch, opens another tray of eggs. Ollie and I back out of the kitchen. Ollie has a stomach ache and falls asleep on the couch. I sit beside him while she continues, talking to herself, making lists out loud. Then all of a sudden, as fast as the frenzy was seemingly whipped up, it finishes. She abandons everything, the utensils and pans, and goes to bed at 3 a.m.

I assume she will have a long lie-in, but I'm wrong.

On Saturday morning Ollie and I are sent out to the back garden and she locks the door behind us. If we're going to behave like animals, we'll be treated like them too, is her reasoning. I wouldn't have minded being sent outside if I'd been able to go to the toilet first. I sit down on the cold concrete step, my back to the door, legs folded, trying to squeeze it up inside.

Ollie kicks a football against the back wall, over and over again.

'Can I play?' I ask Ollie, needing some way to pass the time before I pee my pants.

'No. This is your fault.'

He thinks that because she said it, and he believes everything she says.

What kind of eleven-year-old didn't know how to make herself useful, she'd ranted and raved at me. She was annoyed I hadn't cleaned up the kitchen after her. The abandoned mixing bowls in the sink, the whisks covered in globs of batter, the eggshells, the flour spattered everywhere, the batter on the floor and walls as though there'd been a violent mass pancake murder.

I'd actually intended to clean up later in the morning. She never gets up early, especially on Saturdays, and especially after a night like she'd had last night. I didn't think she'd surface at all. But up she popped, out of the woodwork, and caught me out. Now she's banging around the kitchen with a load of reds spinning around her like washing machines and tumble dryers as she mutters to herself, having an argument with somebody in her head. Domestic duties always irritate her. Ironing, the little she does of it, makes her hot and irritated, red comes off her like steam. Red, red, red: the domestic devil.

She chucks the pancakes straight in the bin, along with the elaborate business plan that she'd hatched.

Ollie brings her hot red angry colours outside with him and so I stand back and let him work it off, hoping the breeze will take it away. Increasingly, her hate becomes his hate, her fears become his fears, her rage becomes his rage. Her sadness, his sadness. It always transfers to him, and he sucks it up greedily, consumes every last particle. Her loss today is his great loss. Last night she had sold him a dream, pulled back a secret curtain and given him a glimpse into a new life, a new world where he would be in a pancake truck by her side, at music festivals, at the seaside, sprinkling chocolate, chopping strawberries, spraying cream, and melting cheese on hot pancakes before handing them to customers, and taking their money. Playing shop is one of his favourite things and he would have been in his element.

He'd lived it all out in his eight-year-old head in a rush of sugary excitement, bouncing off the walls before crashing on the couch. He'd probably dreamed about it and leapt out of bed eager and excited for it to begin. Instead, it's gone, taken from him, chucked in the bin without another thought, because that woman from last night stole away from the house in the middle of the night when he was sleeping. I allow him his anger.

I walk with Hugh and Ollie to the park. Ollie loves the playground, could sit on one of those spinning things for hours, going round and round with his face down watching the ground whirl by at a million miles an hour. Watching him makes me feel sick. I'm happy to be with Hugh now. Happy to be hanging with him; pink hues all round. We don't talk about Ollie and me being locked out that morning, or about the pancake truck idea the night before. There's no point. We rarely talk about anything that happens at home, because talking about it doesn't solve anything. We're just relieved to be out of it and away from it. Ollie is spinning round and round, head down, one foot doing all the groundwork, when we hear a 'Hey.'

I look up. A pretty, smiling girl walks over to Hugh.

'Hey,' he says, a new tone in his voice. 'Alice this is Poh, Poh this is my sister, Alice.'

She stands close to him, her shoulder in his pink zone, like they're sharing a girlie fuzzy sweater.

'I've heard all about you,' she says. 'The school warrior.'

She says it nicely. Almost like a compliment.

'If she doesn't watch it, she'll get kicked out,' Hugh says. 'One more strike and she's out.'

I roll my eyes and look back at Ollie, but I still pay close attention to Hugh and Poh from the corner of my eye. This isn't an accidental meeting; this is planned. They're holding hands. Then they start kissing. She's a bit shy in front of me and he tells her not to worry, that I'm not looking, which is kind of like a direct order to me. And then I see a new kind of colour on Hugh that I can never un-see. A deep red swirl around his crotch that makes me embarrassed. It builds up to a throbbing hot red.

I have to look away. Sometimes seeing people's colours is like seeing them naked.

I watch Mr and Mrs Mooney talking in the car park. He teaches History, she teaches English. They drive to school together every morning. They're married. All around her is pink, she's a nice person. She sends all the pink from her chest to him as she talks, and she makes more for herself. It stops at him, and hangs there, as though there's a forcefield all around him, blocking everything from entering. With nowhere to go, it hangs in the air between them. He gives her a quick peck and leaves her standing there in the car park, as a cloud of unrequited pink works its way back to her.

We go to Wexford for a few days in the summer with my Uncle Ian, Aunt Barbara and my cousins. I sit on the warm sand, feet and toes wriggling in the sand, listening to the waves crashing, and watch happy near-naked people, lighter and brighter without their clothes and the weight of the world's problems on their shoulders.

They breathe in light, and exhale darkness.

She's with Ollie in the kitchen. I can hear them both laughing. It's the sound that draws me in, a peculiar, alien sound in this house. Unapologetic happiness. I watch them from the door, I don't want her to see me or she might stop, the spell broken. They're baking. Not a manic pancake-making session, this is a calm moment.

'Just tap it against the edge and pull it apart,' Lily says calmly.

He breaks the egg and stirs it. He puts his finger in and steals a lick.

'Hey you, batter thief!' She dips her finger in and puts a dollop on his nose.

He giggles.

Both of them are rose pink.

As soon as the colours arrive around her, he sucks it all up, his body like a vacuum cleaner, taking it all from her and keeping it around him, wrapping himself in it like a blanket.

She has moments of kindness, but she is not kind. She has moments where she cares, but she is not caring. One good moment with her doesn't make her a good mother, which is why I will never call her that.

*

'I hear you've got a girlfriend,' Lily says to Hugh one day, and the tops of Ollie's ears go pink so I know it's him that told her. Hugh would know that too, not that it was a secret, but it makes life easier when you don't tell her anything so she can't use it against you. 'Neighbours saw you wearing the faces off each other, said it looked like you were trying to eat her head off.'

This is not true. Her crooked smile, not just her colours, tell me this.

Hugh lobs a load of jam on a slice of bread, squashes the other slice on top, then takes the biggest bite, half the sandwich at least, while looking at her.

'When were you going to tell me about her?'

He points at his full mouth. Can't talk.

'Are you afraid of her meeting me? Are you embarrassed of me? Of where you live?'

He shakes his head, keeps chewing.

'I need to check she's all right, seeing as your dad fecked off. Someone around here has to show her who's boss.'

As she's talking, he takes another bite.

'When can I meet her?'

He swallows, I wonder what he's going to say, but he's been thinking about it. I can see him, calculating it all.

'When do you want?'

I'm surprised by this. So is she. She was looking for an argument. Always looking for an argument, so defensive of imaginary attacks, and when they don't come it's like she's floored even more.

'I'll have to think about it,' she says, on the back foot.

'Whenever suits you,' he says.

'What's her name?'

'Poh.'

'Poh?' she says, crooked smile back. 'What is she, a Teletubby?'

A metallic flicker of red across Hugh's chest, like a fork of lightning, then gone. 'I knew you'd say that,' he says, with a smile.

This sets her back too. Even her insults are predictable. He's impenetrable, his every response like a bucket of water over her flames. I can hear the hiss coming from her.

He throws the last bite into his mouth, and it's finished; three man-bites, all gone. He takes his study folders out and covers the kitchen table with them. 'Let me know when you'd like to meet her.'

She never comes back to him with a day, of course.

Hugh and his tactics.

Hugh brings Ollie and me out to the park more regularly, just so he can meet Poh. I've always wondered what it'd be like to have an older sister and she's nice. We never complain, but even though I'm with Hugh, I'm not with him at all anymore. Poh has his complete attention. All the rosy pinks go in her direction, and all the reds, the hot reds, are still outside his pants. I'm too old to play on the swings or slide and Ollie is almost too tall for everything now. He goes off spinning on his own while I sit alone on a bench or a swing and just watch.

I try not to stare at Hugh and Poh, but it's hard not to.

I don't know many people who are in love. I thought I did. I know lots of people who are supposed to be in love but they don't look anything like Hugh and Poh, who are giving and taking colours all the time. The same amount, no one is selfish, no one blocks, it's back and forth. It's relaxing to watch them. Sometimes it's just enough to sit and watch somebody else be happy.

Ollie and I are playing tag in the park, Ollie gets annoyed that he can't catch me, that he's always on. He's frustrated and irritated and I don't blame him. Hugh and Poh have joined in, and I like when they stop kissing to pay attention to us. Ollie gets angrier as we dodge him, the joyful adolescent innocent pinks turning to angry blood-red. I can see it coming. I let him catch me before it flashes metallic and it ruins the game. As I chase him, I step on the back of his shoe by accident. It comes off and he runs on in the wet grass in his sock, soaking it. He pulls his sock off and hops back to his shoe, all the while yelling at me for nicking his ankle. He loses his balance and his bare foot lands on the grass. The angry red mist starts at his head and starts to work its way down his body, but as it hits his foot, it turns brown. Then the brown starts working its way back up his body, dominating the red, and I stand and watch, my mouth agape at this beautiful balayage effect taking place before my eyes. Brown sweeps across the red like a tidal wave, almost the same colour as the soil beneath the grass, like he's rooted to the ground, sprouting. When it hits his head, he looks down at his foot, in the wet grass. He wriggles his toes in the mud. And he laughs.

The next time he loses it, or starts to, I encourage him to go outside and take his shoes off. He walks around in his bare feet, head down, watching his toes disappear in the long grass and squelching in the mud before coming up again.

She watches from the window, it's open and she's smoking. I hope she'll say something nice but she throws her cigarette out and bangs the window closed. The cigarette lands on the wet grass and sizzles as it's extinguished.

I find myself being drawn to happiness. Not the obvious kind, not a room filled with people laughing aloud – no, too many bodies with too much going on beneath the laughter. But the quieter moments, the private ones. I skip school a lot, go to the local park and watch a mother push her daughter on a swing, singing songs, making jokes, the swishing of the purest of happy colours, the ebb and flow from one to the other, so relaxing, like watching the tide. A toddler with her toy, the pink and gold love for a comforter she won't let go of. I want to sidle up to her, bury my feet in the bacteria-infested sandpit as she is doing, and immerse myself in her light.

Until I realise.

That when I do that, I am stealing it away. And you shouldn't steal someone else's happiness.

You have to make your own.

On account of my unacceptable behaviour in primary school, the community secondary school will not accept me. Only one of the four schools in our catchment area agrees to accept me, pending a behavioural evaluation.

I'm polite to the behavioural assessor, and think I do a good job, being kind and asking after his family and if he's going away on summer holidays and stuff like that. Hugh told me this was really important, and to behave myself. Not that I needed reminding. I only misbehave when someone is teasing me, when the headaches are bad, or they put their colour on me and I can't help it.

'Do you think your mum is coming?' he asks.

'No. I didn't know she was supposed to.'

'She was sent the paperwork. Right, well let's get started with your side then.'

He takes out some sheets of paper. The real behavioural test is on paper, with boxes to tick, which seems wrong to me when I turned up, and she didn't.

'Where were you?'

It all starts as soon as we walk in the door. I'd been out with Hugh and Poh, like a gooseberry but loving every second of their company and not feeling in the way at all. She's sitting down on the couch, too calm, facing the door, waiting for us. The joy, the fun, the easiness of being out with Hugh and Poh all day Saturday comes to an abrupt end as soon as we open the door.

Red mist around her head, spitting like a volcano.

It flies towards Hugh and I move to block him, protect him, but it's lightning speed and before I get to him it bounces off his chest as if he has a forcefield around him, and goes right over his head.

How did he do that?

'You were in bed, I didn't want to disturb you,' he says.

He drops his bag down on the floor and goes to Ollie. 'Hey Ollie, have you eaten yet?'

It's four o'clock. Ollie has been up since seven this morning, watching TV.

'I had some toast,' he says, never one to land Lily in trouble.

'There's no bread,' I say, to help him out, it's okay, he doesn't have to lie, we know you're hungry, but he looks at me angrily.

'I was going to go to the chipper,' Lily says with a superior sniff of her nose. She's defensive around Hugh, as if she doesn't want him to think badly of her, because she must know too that he's better than all of us put together.

'That's a good idea,' he says. 'Do you want me to go out and get it?'

'Okay.' The red mist starts to disappear back inside the crater it escaped from. He's done it, he's managed to change her colour, how does he do it? Green emerges, like a green dye dipping in water. Splurge. Splurge. Bacteria-shaped. A dark green, almost black, but not black. Definitely not black. Black has threatened to come but never arrived, I can't imagine what will happen the day it arrives, but the fear of it looms large.

'Can I come too?' I ask Hugh, feeling nervous about what's to come.

'No.' She speaks instead. 'Take Ollie, though. Here,' she hands him a twenty-euro note. 'I'll have a batter burger and curry chips.' I expect her to go upstairs, back to bed, but instead she stays on the couch and changes the channel from cartoons to a quiz show. Ollie glares at me as he leaves, jealous that I'm staying and that he's been sent away. He doesn't sense like I do that there's a reason I'm staying, and it can't be good. I awkwardly sit on the other end of the couch, sitting rigid.

Mustard yellow. Snotty green. I anticipate sarcasm and spite.

'You got a letter from your new school,' she says, waving at a torn envelope on the chipped table by the front door. No one thinks to move the table; it just keeps getting walloped every time the door opens.

'Which school?' I ask, hopeful that my behavioural test has meant I can stay in a normal school.

'The boarding school for freaks,' she says, and lights up a cigarette. 'You start in September.'

Watching the colours of her mood swings can be beautiful. If it's not directed at me. Or if I can somehow extract myself while it's happening, in my head. I can kind of be in the front row of this magical performance, watching her go from mustard yellow to a metallic red. The transformation. The beauty of the shades of light. But the sound of it is never beautiful, the feel of it, the face of it, the energy behind it. Nothing about that is beautiful.

On the second-last day of school before I never see my classmates again, I am a little sad. True, I have been in physical fights with most of them – given Jenny a black eye, thrown a Coke can at Faraj's head, and other things – but it was all in self-defence. Even though they warned me, Hugh more than anyone, if I had really understood that it would all come to this, that I would be taken away and put somewhere else, like a prison, then maybe I would have tried to ignore the bullies. But I know what happens when you ignore things and don't defend yourself. The situation gets worse. People think you can't stand up for yourself and they use you as their punch bag. You've got to show from the beginning that you won't put up with it.

I wish I'd done that at home with Lily, only I can't remember when it started, it's just been always. I never wanted school to be like being at home. This was my time, to be me, only I'm not sure I liked the me that came out here either. I'm grateful they can't see my watery eyes behind my shades.

I can't keep my eyes off Ms Mooney and the colours around her today.

When we're leaving class, I pass Ms Mooney at her desk and say, 'Congratulations.'

She looks at me in surprise, and confusion, and I realise she hasn't a clue what I'm talking about. She doesn't know yet. But the next day, our last day before the summer holidays and my last day forever, she asks me to go outside the room with her. The class all oooh as I walk out. James makes a face at me. I throw my compass at him. It stabs him through his jumper and he looks like he's going to cry.

She closes the door, sits down on the bench outside and speaks really low, almost like a whisper.

'Why did you say congratulations to me yesterday?'

'Because you're pregnant.'

'How do you know?'

'I just know.'

'You can tell me, Alice. Tell me how you know.'

35

'I think I heard someone say it.'

'I didn't even know yesterday, Alice,' she says gently. 'You can trust me.'

I do trust Ms Mooney. She is one of the rare teachers who allow me to wear sunglasses in the classroom, because her brother suffered terribly with migraines.

'I can see the baby's colours.'

Gold. Pure shimmering gold around her belly, like it has a crown. No one ever has gold, at least no one I've ever seen. I've only ever seen it on babies, newborns only days or weeks old when they're pushed by me in a buggy. Swirling nuggets of gold like halos around their crowns. I imagine maternity wards to be like Fort Knox.

It takes Ms Mooney a while to process what I've said.

'I have this thing where I can see colours,' I say quickly, already regretting I've said it. 'Which is why I prefer to wear shades.'

She studies me. 'Who else have you told about this?'

'My brother Hugh.'

'You're beginning in Clearview Academy in September, aren't you?'

'Yeah. The school for weirdos.'

'You can't say that.'

'That's what Faraj called it,' I look into the class. 'Which is why I threw the Coke can at his head.'

'That's not what it's for. It's a therapeutic boarding school, Alice. It helps those with conduct disorders, yes, but you're different. I realise now that you're finding yourself in trouble because you're gifted.'

'I'm cursed.'

'I think it's a gift,' she says, with a smile that actually

makes me blush. 'I wouldn't have taken the test until you said it yesterday. I've wanted this for a long time.'

'Oh.'

'I think the academy will be able to give you all the special attention you deserve to help you deal with it, so you don't get angry with everyone else who's stupid enough not to understand. I'm sorry nobody here has understood you properly.'

I don't know what to do with this. Apart from the eternally understanding Hugh, I don't think anyone's ever said sorry to me in my life. Or pretended to understand. It gives me insight into a world that could possibly exist for me, people who actually listen to me, people who actually understand. It frustrates me that not everyone can be like Ms Mooney.

She sits back on the bench, smiling, enjoying this. 'Well, do you see anything else?'

I think about it.

'He doesn't love you,' I say.

'What?' Her smile fades.

'I see you giving Mr Mooney all your pink, and he doesn't take it. It bounces right back to you.'

Maybe, from the look on her face, I shouldn't have said it, but it's true and she probably knows it deep down. Better for her to know now, before the twins arrive.

Hugh holds the letter from the school in his hand.

'This is outrageous!'

Red mist surrounds the top of Lily's head as though she's a volcano sprouting hot lava. I watch Hugh. The red comes towards him. It bounces off him and moves to me. I duck and dive, I dodge it. I watch Ollie. He absorbs it; her anger now his anger.

'It'll be easier with her gone,' Ollie shouts at Hugh, joining in.

'There's nothing wrong with her!' Hugh pushes.

Hugh rarely argues with her. He doesn't seem to think much of her, give her space in his life. He's always busy, has got better things to do than pander to her, whereas she's the biggest thing in my world, she's my obstacle to everything. I step around her, go sideways, suck myself in, try to make myself smaller, try and make my own space. As for Ollie, she fills up his entire world, not even enough room in there for himself.

But I've never seen her this colour before. Apart from the predictable angry lava red, there's a storm building, a sludge so dark and murky it doesn't know if it's green or brown or black. It's slow and mucous-like, and twists like a tornado. Its slowness is unsettling. It appears to pull in all the colours from around, the minority colours hidden in the larger mass, flecks of colours and light, promises of happiness and good humour are sucked into this cyclone. As it pulls the colours in, it picks up speed.

'Hugh,' I say, a warning in my voice.

We're in the kitchen. She's cooking dinner. Something is on the hob in a saucepan bubbling. She has actually tried today. She's out of bed. Of all the days for Hugh to challenge her, maybe today isn't the day. We should be congratulating her, making her feel like it's worth her getting up every morning but Hugh isn't in his usual peaceful mood. He's defending me, but it's not worth it, something is brewing within her and I don't want it to be unleashed.

Hugh can block it.

I can dodge it.

But Ollie will absorb it.

'They spoke to the teachers, they spoke to her. That's how they decided. Don't be angry with me.'

'Who's they?'

'The doctors.'

'There were no doctors involved.'

'The psychologists, whatever they are,' she says, embarrassed for not knowing, angry at being caught out. 'The school organised the tests.'

'Did they speak to you?'

'Yeah.'

'No they didn't – you didn't show up.'

'Well they rang me, didn't they?'

'Who's *they*?' he raises his voice.

'A man, I can't remember his name, can I?'

'What did you tell him?'

'I told them to listen to whatever the teachers said. They know best, don't they?'

'They don't know her at all. You're supposed to defend her, that's your job. She's only eleven.'

'She's almost twelve,' she says, stirring the pot, looking inside it as though it suddenly holds all the answers to the world. 'She's violent, you know. Not your sweet little baby sister you're always protecting. She gets into fights with people at school – she punched one of those Ward girls, and you don't mess with that family. She'll get us all in trouble.'

'She was defending herself. And what about Ollie? Do you know that he threw markers at the wall because he coloured outside the lines? Did you know that? I was called from my school to help calm him down at the principal's office. Because they knew if they called you, you wouldn't come. What about him? Do you even care? Do you even notice? Do you ever wonder why this is happening?'

The cyclone turns a purplish colour, with grey. There's a storm a-brewing and I don't like it. It's at her torso but it's on the move. It winds its way up, spiralling around her body and spreading.

'*Clearview Academy, an alternative school facility,*' he reads the letter. '*For the education of students with challenging behaviour arising from severe emotional disturbance or behavioural disorder. Behaviour modification,*' he says, waving the letter in the air. 'There's nothing wrong with her,' Hugh says, incredulous.

She smiles. A nasty one, showing her yellow banjaxed teeth. 'You're just panicking now, because, with Alice gone, you're afraid you won't be able to move away to university. Have you told her you're going away yet?'

I look at him in surprise and she loves it. Other people's sadness and loss feeds her. You can see it in the way the colours pick up, gain momentum and power. Her laughter is cruel, and the cyclone wraps itself around her, snakes around her head, back down her chest, her body, her stomach, all the way around her legs and feet. She is immersed in this tornado.

'I haven't had time to.'

'Hugh's moving to Cardiff, Alice,' she says nastily. 'In Wales. Won't be home on the weekends either.'

'You're leaving?' I ask Hugh.

I should have known. Of course I should have known.

He's eighteen, he finished school this summer and, even though she wanted him to go straight to work, he's been studying so hard to get into university, and working at a bar too, saving money, his brains are his ticket out of here. While I've been self-sabotaging, he's been working on an escape plan. Without me.

'I'm going to get you and Ollie when I can,' he says, his voice low as if he doesn't want her to hear his plan.

She laughs. 'Pull the other one. Your dad said the very same thing and you've barely heard from him since he left, have you?'

My mind races, I can't imagine a life without Hugh. Even with the threatened behavioural school, I thought I could come home to him on the weekends, and he could visit me, but if he's not here, if he's miles away, and won't even be able to visit me? I feel panic swell in my chest. She's laughing, stirring it up, loving that she's not the centre of his anger anymore, that she deflected it. She took control and moved it all to us. Now that she's completely consumed, the cyclone starts to reach out to Hugh as though it has grown tentacles. I watch in horror.

'We'll talk about this later,' he says to me, trying to be gentle, but he's made of anger. His orange is red, his pink being eaten up by it, all his own emotions, not hers.

I don't know what's happening to her but it's unlike anything I've ever seen before. She's like an octopus with eerie grey, smoky black and purple tentacles, and they're feeling all around them. It's terrifying. I'm trembling, I think I might puke. She doesn't look real, she doesn't look human. And Hugh continues arguing, his kind voice, sweet diplomatic Hugh, he hasn't a clue she's brewing something.

The tornado tentacle licks at his face.

'Hugh,' I say, concerned now. 'Move.'

'Why?' he asks, seeing my terror. 'What's wrong?'

'Look at her,' I whisper.

The tentacles whip and lick at his face like a flame.

I move quickly, knocking over a chair and flatten myself against the wall.

'Alice, what's wrong? Is it the colours?'

I stand against the wall. Back flattened, eyes wide, terrified.

'Alice, relax. Take deep breaths.'

'Nothing wrong with her, you say?' she says.

They're everywhere, long black-purplish bruises of tentacle flames licking at me, all around me. They know about my dodging tricks, they've covered every angle.

'Oh Jesus,' she says, and starts laughing. She lights up a cigarette, stirs whatever is on the stove and puffs, then turns back to me, one hand on her hip, the other sucking her cigarette like it's a straw. 'What's wrong with her?'

'You're scaring her.'

'Boo,' she says and the tentacles whip.

I scream and cover my face with my hands.

'I've never seen her like this. Alice, look at me.'

'You're telling me there's nothing wrong with her?' she says.

They lick at my face, and I feel it. For a moment, an insight into the twisted dark madness that pervades her thoughts. A hundred thoughts race at once, nothing making sense. Too fast and overlapping, echoes of words chattering in my head. Not one moment of space or clarity, it's noisy, too much, too fast, too much, too fast, on and on and on and on. Swirling thoughts and no dead ends, no conclusions or solutions, no end to the looping thoughts on top of thoughts, on top of thoughts, on top of thoughts.

Ollie walks into the kitchen. 'What's for dinner?'

'Out Ollie, now,' I say.

'No. I'm hungry.' He walks right in anyway, straight over to the stove. The tentacles embrace him, wrapping themselves around him tighter than she ever physically has.

'No!' I shout and dive after him. He won't be able to live with this, she will suffocate him. She will consume him and he will let her.

I dive for him, push him to the floor, to cover and protect him. As the tentacles grab a firm hold of him on the ground, he screams as they tighten. I'm screaming too, feeling the sting in my back from her colours. Until I realise I've whacked against the handle of the saucepan on the stove and it has sent boiling water over us both.

'How do you do it?' I'm lying on my bed, on my stomach. My back is raw, after the boiling water incident. I caught most of it. Ollie received splashes on his hands, a little on his face. It's wrapped up in dressings from the A&E. I have to lie on my belly for I don't know how long. Until it stops hurting, I suppose.

'Do what?'

'You block her colours. You don't let them on you.'

'Really?'

'Yeah, every time. Her colour comes for you, but it bounces back, or goes over your head, or goes straight back to her.'

He shrugs but thinks about it. 'I don't want to let her in. I don't want anything to do with her. Why, what do you do?'

'I dodge them.'

'What happens to Ollie?'

'He takes them all. Sucks them into him when she's not even trying. It's like he wants them.'

He ponders this. 'Is that why you jumped on him?'

'Yeah. I wasn't trying to hurt him. Is that what you thought?' My back stings as I try to sit up to look at him.

'Alice,' he says, rubbing his eyes and face tiredly. 'No one's going to believe this.'

'Sorry.'

'No. I'm sorry. I'm sorry this is happening to you.'

I feel the hot tears drip from my eyes, as if I soaked up all that boiling water and I have to get rid of it myself, through my tears, through my sweat.

He lifts my shades up, looks into my eyes.

'Do you hear me?'

I nod and wipe the tears away.

'Try to . . . try to find a way to live with the colours. You can't keep fighting people. And you can't keep avoiding them either. I'm sure it's difficult, I don't know what I'd do . . . but you can't keep going like this. You're young, you've got the rest of your life. Maybe they'll go away, maybe they won't. But you won't always be here, with her, you've got to start thinking of yourself now. It'll only be six years,' he says, trying to lift his voice, but I can hear that it's forced, and it feels like a prison sentence. 'Then you can come and live with me.'

'Fine, I'll stay out of trouble.'

'No, that's not enough. Education is the way out.'

I roll my eyes.

'Hey,' he says sharply. 'You want to get away from here? Start your own life? Not be depending on her?'

'Of course.'

'Then study hard. When you get out of there, you're going to university.'

'I'm not like you, Hugh.'

'Then start thinking like me. You have to play the long game, Alice. Plan for the future.'

'I can't look that far ahead. Most days, I just try to make it to bedtime.'

He looks at me then, sad. 'Okay then, just take it one day at a time.'

'How is she even paying for this place?' I flick through the prospectus. Happy teenagers with happy teachers in clean colourful classrooms. I know it's not true, just like a Big Mac is never like the Big Mac in the posters.

'You have a grant,' he says. 'The government are paying for it.'

'How did that happen?'

'The school organised it.'

'Wow. They really must have wanted me gone.'

'Or some people really cared. But there are conditions,' he says. 'They'll only pay if you attend every day.'

'So if I don't go, then they won't pay for it and I get to come home?'

'Yeah, Alice, you come home, you stay here with Ollie and Mum, but mainly it'd just be you and Mum all day every day because no school around here will let you in, so you'll have no education, no job, no money and it'll be just the two of you at home all day. How does that sound?'

'Fine. I'll go.'

'What colour is she?'

He asks me as we're walking home from the park after he's introduced me to Poh for the first time.

'Green,' I say. 'Like moss. Like a forest. And solid yellows.'

'Is that good?' he asks.

'Yeah,' I say. 'It's good.'

'Good.'

We walk in silence.

'You'd tell me, wouldn't you, if there was something else there?'

I think of the throbbing, messy, flaming red around his crotch and her privates and I smile.

'What? What are you laughing at?'

'Nothing,' I say, my cheeks heating up as I get giddy and awkward. I take off.

'Tell me,' he says, chasing me all the way down the street.

'Synaesthesia,' Poh says. She's excited. She came across something in a book, she's as bookish as Hugh, and I've been summoned to his room. She's been coming here the past few weeks as they prepare to leave.

The contents of the room are mostly boxed up, leaving Ollie's stuff looking lonely. Hugh's been working all summer and I've barely seen him during our final weeks together. I get a pang of loss and a lump in my throat when I look around.

She sits cross-legged on his bed, he's sitting on his

swinging desk chair, and I sink into the beanbag. The room smells of Lynx deodorant and mint chewing gum. He chews it all the time before he sees her and that's how I know they're kissing.

'*Research in Spain has found that at least some of the individuals who see the so-called aura of people actually have a neuropsychological phenomenon known as synaesthesia, specifically emotional synaesthesia,*' Poh reads aloud. '*In synaesthetes, the brain regions responsible for the processing of each type of sensory stimuli are interconnected. Synaesthetes can see or taste a sound, feel a taste, or associate people or letters with a particular colour. This is the first time that a scientific explanation has been provided for the phenomenon of the aura, a supposed energy field of luminous radiation surrounding a person, which is invisible to most human beings.*'

She looks at me, eyes wide. Hugh is on the edge of his seat, a grin on his face.

'This is it, isn't it Alice?'

'Maybe,' I shrug. He's always been so desperate to put a name on it. Give it a reason, a justification, but it doesn't change anything for me. It might be that, it might not be. Just as it might have been an aura migraine. Whatever it is, I still have it, still have to deal with it. A name won't make it go away.

She continues: '*Synaesthesia is thought to be due to cross-wiring in the brain, leading to links between brain areas that are not normally connected. New research suggests that many healers claiming to see the aura of people might have this condition.*'

Might.

'Wait a minute,' Hugh stops her. 'Healers?'

Poh reads back over what she read. 'Yes. People who are aura-seers are healers.'

He looks at me and I know what he's thinking.

No.

I say it out loud. Firm. Loud.

'No.'

She's asleep on the couch. It's three in the morning and the TV is still on. Back-to-back episodes about people finding treasures in abandoned storage units have been blaring for hours. I've been listening to it from my bedroom. I leave tomorrow. My suitcase is packed, standing upright by the door. Hugh left a week ago and it stopped feeling like home as soon as we waved him off.

I know that he was sad to leave but he couldn't lie about the excitement he was feeling, the relief to be leaving this place behind, all of his plans coming together for him just as he deserved. I could see it in his colours, and it was for all those reasons that I couldn't cry when I hugged him or watched him leave. Like a mini firework display all around his torso and head, pops of bright colours: pinks, yellows, oranges, greens, indigo, blue, silver. All the warm tones, nothing sludgy. A little bit of sad blue inside them all, in the centre like the stigma of a flower, that I selfishly hope was in there for me, while around the edges the colours burst and popped. Ollie had hugged him tight. I had to pull him off, just so Hugh could leave; always the cruel one, taking Ollie's happiness away from him. She didn't wave him off, I don't think she did it to be cruel, I think she couldn't. She stayed in her room, the blue hue threatening to seep out from under the door, so I stuffed the gap with a blanket. Ollie and I have enough of our own grief without being given hers too.

As soon as I went to bed and closed my door I heard her moving about in her room, as if she'd been waiting for me to go to bed. She went downstairs, sniffing.

Now she's asleep on the couch. Purplish-blue all around her, wearing her sadness and self-pity like a cloak. I'm wearing Hugh's old football gloves as I approach her. They're enormous, far too big for me, tattered and covered in dried mud from who knows how long ago, but they're thick, impenetrable. I don't want her colour to get on me, or to feel the depth of her sadness. The cold, icy, painful sting of loss.

I'd googled healers and looked into what I should do. A lot of nonsense and weird talk, it was hard to understand, but I'm basically supposed to clear the colours. I don't know how exactly to do that, but I'm thinking the colours move, so maybe I can just, with gloved hands, waft away the bad ones, in the opposite direction, maybe out the front door into the air. I pity the bird they may float up and get stuck to, or the person out walking this late, but at least they will be off her. I'm doing this for Ollie, who will be left alone with her. Hugh made arrangements for him to walk to and from school with a neighbour who's in his class, but I'm worried about him. What about the rest of the day, and the nights. And the weekends. He's nine years old and he can't protect himself from her, not in the way he needs to.

I place my big, gloved hands over her head, so they hover inches above her. I don't need to worry about not being able to see the colours in the dark; they glow brightly, like she's rolled around in a nuclear disaster. I start wafting the colours away, towards the door.

'What are you doing?' Ollie says loudly.

Startled, I spin around to find him sitting in an armchair in the corner of the room, in the dark. I can only make out the shape of him, a single-layered purple-blue glow around him, the very same as hers, as though he's been sitting in the dark, watching her, and charging himself with her energy. His presence feels eerie. Lily wakes at the sound of his voice, eyes widening with fright at the sight of my big, gloved hands over her head.

'What are you doing?' she asks, her sleepy voice filled with panic.

'Nothing.' I pull the gloves off, feeling stupid.

She scurries off the couch, clumsily, stumbling in her quest to get away from me as quickly as she can.

'What the hell were you going to do to me?' she shouts, metallic red sparking over her head like lightning. Zap. Another fly dead. It disappears as soon as it appears.

'Nothing,' I repeat, unable to explain this one.

She looks from me to Ollie nervously, then back to me again, thinking we're both in on it, everyone against her. She backs away from me, then pulls her dull grey and muddy yellow blanket through the room like a child with a comfort blanket, and drags it up the stairs behind her. When she locks the door behind her and half the blanket remains on the other side of the door, I realise it isn't a blanket at all but the colour of her fear of me.

*

'This might be a good thing,' Hugh says, the night before he leaves, the letter from the school in his hand, as he reads it over and over again. He's taken it worse than I have. 'I'll be gone, you won't be stuck here with her. I'll still be worried about you, but at least you'll be with responsible adults.'

Neither of us mention how we're leaving Ollie behind, all on his own, defenceless against her.

'Here, I got you something,' he says, handing me a gift bag. 'For good luck.'

I open the tissue-lined bag, and discover a new pair of sunglasses.

He wraps me up in a hug and as I squeeze him tightly I think about this being the last time for a long time that I will allow anyone to touch me. We'll all be home at Christmas; four months until my next hug. I breathe in his Lynx and Hugh smell, trying to magnetise his colours of hope and excitement for the escape and adventure that lie ahead of him.

Lily visits me once at the academy. Once in six years, during my final few months of the academy, without an explanation as to why. I watch her outside, having a cigarette before she enters the school, and search her for signs she's dying. If anything, she looks better.

'So,' she says, when we sit down in the family room reserved for Sunday visits. She's nervous. Shifty. It's weird seeing her outside of her territory, beyond enemy lines. 'You hear from Hugh?'

'Yeah.' He calls me almost every day. He's started teaching English at a secondary school but I can't think of anything to say to her about this. There's a more than uncomfortable silence, as the families around us can't stop talking.

'And . . . Ollie, you hear from him?'

'Once.'

The foster family he's with forced him to call me. I think they thought a chat with his sister would help settle him. Little did they know I've never been able to comfort him.

'He's all right,' I say.

He'd threatened to burn his foster home down if someone didn't take him out of there. Fifteen years old and he thinks he's twenty-four. Living alone with Mum, his behaviour had been getting increasingly worse and he was no good at hiding his new-found riches, flaunting stolen goods around the place for everyone to see and know exactly what he was up to. It was decided his home was a toxic environment for him and he had to be put in social care.

'I came to tell you that I'm, eh, I'm getting myself better,' she says.

I sip sugary tea because I don't know what to say. Getting better is the very opposite of a terminal illness. I had been prepared for the latter.

'When Ollie was taken away from me, I went to a terrible place. Terrible.' She shudders. 'I tried to kill myself.'

'How?'

'Pills. Mrs Ganguly found me outside in the garden.'

I picture the long grass, the overflowing bins, her on the ground beside them.

'They've diagnosed me with bipolar disorder. Do you know what that is?'

I have an idea from some people in here, but I shrug.

'They say it's when you have extreme moods. Extreme highs and extreme lows. They gave me this for you.'

She reaches into her handbag that she's been guarding and slides a Health Service leaflet across the pine table. *Living with Bipolar: For people living with someone with bipolar.*

No one lives with her. She lives alone. Chased us all away. I flick it open. I'm not sure if she wants me to read it now or not, so I scan it, hoping that nobody around me can see it. A family at the table behind her, in front of me, are playing charades. The dad's turn. Film. Two words. He puts his hands on his cheeks and looks shocked in a silent scream.

Home Alone, I guess it straight away. They're idiots, they don't get it, while over here I'm looking at a Health Service pamphlet.

Formerly known as manic depression, bipolar is a mental disorder that causes unusual shifts in mood, energy, activity levels, concentration and the ability to carry out day-to-day tasks.

Yep. I'd say they got it right. I place it down on the table.

Scream, they keep saying over and over. No, it's two words, he said two words, didn't he? *Scream 2* then, *Scream 3*, they guess, while he shakes his head wildly.

'They've given me pills to treat it.'

I can already see she's on pills, I recognise it from the other students here. So many on medication for ADHD, ODD, OCD, depression and anxiety. Her colours are still there but they're muted by the calming colour of the pill. It surrounds the mood, suppresses it, clings to it like white blood cells attacking bacteria, only the problem is the pill doesn't know what's a good colour and what's a bad colour, it hugs every colour she has, even the good ones, dulling everything down, making meh her primary emotion.

'If I stay on course, then Ollie can come back home. They need to see that I'm trying.'

Hugh left first, then me. Then Ollie. It took the third child being taken from her, and all of us gone, for her to take a look at herself. I wonder if it's because she misses us or because she just can't stand to be alone.

'The doctor said that I probably got this,' she says, looking at the pamphlet, 'from having kids.'

I don't know how something so horrific could come from something so beautiful, something so stormy and dark come from something so pink, so tranquil and peaceful as Hugh.

'I got postnatal depression from you. I didn't know it until I spoke to the doctor recently, but that's what it was. And then it got worse after I had Ollie.'

She sips her tea, while I look at the pamphlet on the table, the letters blurring, not seeing them. My heart pounding at her revelation. What I hear is *it's your fault.* I try to figure out if that's what she means, if she's playing games with me, her hands wrapped around her cup for warmth and hunched over like a crackhead. I'm tired of her and her games; being here is a relief, like being at a spa. I don't miss this mind-scrambling. I realise how much she drains me, trying to constantly figure her out, work her out. How her very presence bothers me more than anything bad that anyone else could say. I remind myself that she'll be gone soon, she'll leave this building and I'll be free of her, so I breathe. But I'm not letting her get away with it.

'So it's my fault.'

She has the nerve to look annoyed. 'That's not what I said. Don't twist my words.'

'Maybe say it another way then. Maybe with all the time you had on your own over the past few weeks and even in the few hours it took you to get here in the car, you could have found another way to say it. A kinder way.'

'Never mind,' she says, grabbing her bag and standing up. 'I knew this would be a waste of time. I told the counsellor you wouldn't understand.'

This place started out feeling like a prison and then became a kind of haven. I will have to leave soon, as I've watched everyone before me, some with hesitancy like a deer finding its legs, others with full-blown Andy Dufresne blueprints in their suitcases. I'm in Andy's corner. I'm making plans, I'm moving in with Hugh and Poh until I get myself set up. I have no intention of going home to her. Not ever.

It would have been easier if she'd said she was dying.

Lily keeps her promise. She makes the necessary changes in her life to get Ollie home from the foster family. She takes her pills, her symptoms are successfully managed with medication, she 'behaves' and she's rewarded by his coming home. She has a job. She works nights at a Chinese take-away, answering the phone, taking orders, arranging deliveries, serving customers. I would have thought dealing with the public, particularly the drunken public late at night, would not be conducive to her leading as stress-free a life as possible, but she seems to have patience with the unhinged. She has something to talk about, a new world of her own outside of the house, even if it is bitching about customers, the chef, the filthy kitchen. She has a flirtation with the delivery guy.

Despite her sacrifices for him, Ollie is constantly in trouble. She can't manage him, she can't handle him. They're toxic for each other and yet always, always together. He won't leave and she won't throw him out. Blazing rows that go late into the night, into the early hours of the morning that Hugh has to referee.

To give her credit, she worked hard making changes in her life for Ollie to come home, but Ollie never really came home.

But I do.

rust

A T THE VERY BEGINNING I used to see just one
prominent colour around a person.

Blue for Lily.

Pink for Hugh.

But gradually, the number of colours around an individual
grow and appear like layers. Everyone walks around like
fluorescent onions, shedding layers and growing them again.
Over the years the colours intensify, and with them, my
instincts adapt. Not all at once, but a slow evolution, and
I have to keep learning how to decipher what they mean.
I emerge from my six-year stint at the academy thoroughly
modified, though not in the way they think. With the
limited abilities of my youth, I had only a basic understanding of people, but now as an adult I'm more in tune
with their layers. Whether I like it or not.

'I didn't come here to talk about my periods,' I finally snap
at the GP. 'I'm not here because I'm bloated, I'm here
because I see *colours* around *people*. Colours. Dancing round
their heads and their bodies. Do you understand? Happy
colours, sad colours. And I feel them, when they get close

to me, it rubs off on me and whatever they're feeling, *I* feel. Do you get it? I explained it in quite full detail already.'

I'm shouting. I don't care. It took me a lot to come here. I'm finally free of the academy and this has been on my mind for some time. Find a doctor. Tell them the truth. Get better. Give me the magic pill that makes it go away, anything, I'll take it. I didn't sleep a wink last night; I lay in bed imagining all the things they could do to me as soon as I say the words aloud. *I see people's colours.* Have me sectioned, for one, put me on a 'do not employ' list.

'These intense migraines and what you're describing as levels of high sensitivity can be symptoms of hormone imbalance or PMS—'

Aura migraines, synaesthesia and now PMS. I don't let him finish. It's a waste of time. I stand up and storm out, slamming the door shut. 'I'm not paying for that,' I say to the receptionist as I pass. 'He's a shit doctor,' I add to the startled people in the waiting room.

Poh leaves the room when I return to the apartment from a day's work at a coffee shop. Lowering her gaze and barely making eye contact, she closes the bedroom door behind her with a gentle click. I look to Hugh suspiciously.

He pulls a chair out from the table, motions for me to sit. Before me are a selection of college courses, degrees, diplomas and certificates.

'Humour me,' he says.

'Paddy Englishman, Paddy Irishman, Paddy Scotsman are at a swingers' party—'

'Alice,' he says, firmly in the adult no-nonsense Hugh voice.

'I already told you, I don't want to go to college.'

'There's too many people,' he says, repeating my much-repeated words. 'New places, new things, horrible teachers and lecturers in positions of authority, telling you what to do. You hate being told what to do. You like the familiar, you want things to be simple, you like to be in control, you like the café you work in,' he says, airing my very real fears.

He lets that all hang in the air for a moment. He understands, I get it, now it's my turn to listen.

'But you're eighteen and you can't live like this forever. No one ever stays on a stepping stone, Alice. Colleges are nothing like schools. You're an adult, you can come and go as you please, you can sit alone in lectures, you can disappear off campus for lunch, you can do whatever the hell you want, you can still work part-time in the café – in fact you'll have to – but you go to class, you do the work and you get your qualification.'

'And then what?'

'And then you go.'

'Where?'

'Anywhere. Away. Out of here. The qualification is your ticket to wherever you want to go. The world is your oyster.'

'Oysters are rank.'

'You've never even tried one.'

That's the difference between me and him. He'd try one. He'd see if he liked anything. He's open, I'm closed. He calls this a stepping stone, I call it a safe house. He's worried about me, he's always worried. I'm not ambitious like him, I don't have drive. I don't have hobbies, I don't have passions,

I don't have friends and I don't have a clue what I want to do or who I want to be. I'm better at hiding, at staying in, at staying away. Keeping to myself, keeping it all in. Slithering along the side in the shadows. He wants me to be the best I can possibly be when it's hard enough just being. I look above his shoulder at a new colour that arises. It's not one of his usual colours and moves differently. It's like concrete mixing, slow and thick, a sludgy porridge-like consistency. It must be heavy; a growing weight on his shoulder.

He looks to where I'm looking, at thin air above his shoulder, then back at me. 'What?'

'You need a massage.'

'I know, my shoulder's killing me,' he says, starting to manipulate it roughly himself. 'Can you see it?'

'Yeah.' I pick up a leaflet at random. I don't want to be a burden. 'Fine. I'll look at these.'

'Maybe you could be a masseuse,' he says, rolling his shoulder around.

'Yeah, one who doesn't touch people.'

'A masseuse's assistant, or better yet, the boss. You make them do the physical work, you can pinpoint the pain.'

He's being playful but his insight into my ability to distinguish pain stings me. 'How about a job where I can pinpoint joy.'

Neither of us can think of one.

Ollie arrives home at 3 a.m. to find me sitting in the dark on the couch watching the door, waiting for him. Lily had called the flat, upset, to put it mildly, Hugh was out with

Poh. She'd wanted him to come over, comfort her, to talk to Ollie, be the referee again. I came instead, reluctantly. He's wearing a Canada Goose jacket and trainers. The jacket costs over a thousand euro, and it's identical to the one he got for Lily on Christmas morning, along with a wad of cash stuffed in a box of Quality Street.

He gets a fright when he sees me, then covers it up with the usual bravado.

'Hi freak,' he says.

'Hi drug dealer,' I reply.

He snorts and goes into the kitchen, bangs around. As he brushes by me, I shudder. The hairs on my arms stand up, goose pimples rise. My baby brother has induced a cold fear in me.

'What did you do?' I hear the tremble in my voice. So does he. He appears at the door, eyes dark, feasting on my fear as he does with the packet of lunch ham in his hand.

'What are you talking about, freak?'

'Ollie,' I say, trying to appeal to his human side, not this monster energy that's coming off him like steam. He's on a high – not a drug high, something else, something visceral and cruel, a wicked adrenaline.

'Anyone asks, I was home all night.' He stuffs the ham into his mouth, eyes black, and goes upstairs to bed.

I sit in the front row, beside Hugh, where I've sat every day of Ollie's trial and watch the hypnotising woman before me who has colours like a lava lamp. Great big blobs of royal blue move slowly up and down in a haze of logical yellow. The blobs drift upwards, shapes changing ever so slowly like mutating globs and then travel back downward again. I've never seen anything like it before, so precise and controlled, it's captivating. One each side of her head, they move at the same speed but in alternate directions, always meeting exactly in the middle at the same time, like a see-saw. The royal blue is a colour I have learned over time to trust in natural leaders who are keen on fairness and equality, and I recognise the shade of yellow that surrounds it from seeing students hard at work, applying themselves. The royal blue blobs' movements may be fluid and change shape, but they are thoughtful and measured. I feel that this is an energy searching slowly and methodically for truth. The scales of justice. Which make sense as the host of the blobs is Judge Catherine Radcliffe, who is presiding over Ollie's trial.

Lily doesn't come. It's too much for her fragile state; she's never been one to sacrifice a little of herself for the sake of someone else.

'What do you think?' Hugh asks me from time to time. He isn't referring to the words being argued back and forth from lawyer to lawyer, which is its own language that he can understand. My job is to watch everybody's colours as we cling to each other in hope for our brother's life.

'She's fair.' I decide this early on, and we share a look of foreboding, because we both know that means Ollie's doomed.

Ollie and an accomplice had forced their way into a house and threatened the two occupants with a baseball bat before subjecting them to a 'terrifying and sustained attack.' Ollie had done the attacking while his accomplice went around stealing from the property. It wasn't his first crime. Not by half. The judge said he was a risk to the public, and it was such a serious crime there was no option but to send him to juvenile prison for two years until he's eighteen, when he will then be transferred to the men's adult prison. The jail time, she says, reflects the seriousness of the crime and the effect it has had on the two victims since the events.

Her fairness decides that Ollie be sentenced to a total of six years and nine months for aggravated assault and burglary. I don't know. I suppose it was fair to the other side.

Ollie is staring at the floor. The tips of his too-big ears are pink, his cheeks flushed. He's tall and skinny, he hasn't yet grown into himself, physically or mentally. He doesn't even know who he is. He will be serving his time for the acts of a passing version of himself. He doesn't react when the sentence is announced. I wonder at first if he's heard her, but as he processes it his colours reveal the stormy swirls. None of the good colours; flashes of metallic anger, a proper rainstorm. Nothing to suggest remorse or regret, though I search for it, I hope for it. There's just anger and a different kind of regret: that he didn't get away with it.

It's only when he's cuffed and taken away that he glances over at Hugh. When I see his face, I see the little kid playing on the floor with his wrestlers, desperate for attention and love. Then he looks at me and his face hardens. He toughens up as he's taken away.

I could never give him any comfort. Or, in this instance, an alibi.

*

Lily complains of lower backache, initially blaming the hard stool at work. It's around the time of Ollie's arrest and the stress is getting to her, it's getting to us all, so we put it down to that. We ignore it, ignore her for a while while we focus on the most important thing. She has a tendency to put herself first in the middle of somebody else's drama and we have more important things to worry about. It's only afterwards, when he's sent away and she's still complaining, that she goes to the doctor. She has to visit a few times before they really listen to her and start referring her for appointments that she joins waiting lists to attend.

They diagnose a spinal infection, which turns out to be a tumour so big it's wrapped around her spine like tinsel around a tree trunk. Colour-wise it's like rotting fruit, a bruised banana, a rusty brown.

They discover Burkitt lymphoma, a type of non-Hodgkin's lymphoma, after spinal surgery.

I question why I didn't see it more clearly. I was concentrating on Ollie, yes, I was concentrating on Hugh, yes. I was even trying to keep my own head above water. But Lily . . . I'd stopped looking, and I'd stopped listening. It was like she'd become so loud in my head I had learned to live with the white noise. What had I become to be able to recognise everybody else's pain but hers?

Ollie is in prison, Hugh has accepted a teaching job in Doha, I'm here.

*

She has ten rounds of chemotherapy, ending with a spinal tap in three spots, plus chemo in her tailbone area, up the spinal cord around the brain cavity. It's followed by months of physical therapy to crawl, to sit. I nurse her, I care for her. The first time I haul her into the bath to bathe her, she cries. It is not an effortless, seamless job; it is flawed and awkward. I hurt her when I accidentally pinch her, when I grab her in the wrong place, when I bang her against the side of the bath and the wall, and the pointed corner of the toilet roll holder.

It's hard on us both. At night, I cry too.

'I can't do this to you,' Hugh says, looking harassed, hair messy on his head as though he's been in a fight with himself.

He's getting married tomorrow to Poh, something quick in the registry office, because they can't live together in Doha if they're not married. They both got jobs in an international school in Doha, teaching English. They'll be living on an oil refinery in a townhouse with a swimming pool, getting paid triple what they'd get paid here, saving up enough money to move back and buy a house and start a family. They've dropped the wedding on us at the last minute, though they must have known for a while. It will just be me, Lily and Poh's parents and brothers. I go shopping with Lily for something nice for both of us. Trying to manoeuvre her wheelchair through shops and department stores makes us both hot and bothered. Finding something that will fit her changed body sends her over the edge. I feel like I'm shopping with a hormonal teenage girl. It's painful for both of us.

'I feel like I'm abandoning you again.'

'You're not abandoning me. You have a job in Doha waiting for you. Ollie is in prison.'

He flinches at that, unable to bear it. I bet he doesn't tell anyone about Ollie.

'I'm here, Hugh, it's the only sensible option. This is my decision.'

'But this shouldn't be happening, Alice, it's messed up. You should be studying.'

'Please don't tell me the things I should be doing now,' I say firmly.

'Sorry.' He slowly turns his pint around on the table. 'You got the details I sent you about the remote learning?'

'Yeah, I'll see.' Right now I'm so tired by the time Lily goes to bed that all I can do is sleep. I can't imagine studying.

'We could get a carer,' he says. 'It doesn't have to be you, full-time.'

'We've already talked about this. We can't afford it. She has no savings and I have less.'

'You're nineteen. No one has savings at nineteen.'

'You had.'

We smile.

'Yeah, well. No normal person has savings at nineteen. So Poh says. Nobody organises themself this much. I drive her crazy.'

'She's crazy about you. Anyway you had to do it. You had to organise yourself or you would never have left here.'

'The plan was to take you with me.' He's tormenting himself, over and over. I can only take so much before it starts to penetrate into me. I need him to lift me up, to tell me I can do this, not the opposite.

'And what would I have done? Dig for oil?' I joke.

He takes some forms out of his backpack and places them on the table. His fingers are shaking. 'You qualify for benefits. I've researched it all. Sign these forms and post them with some form of ID. A carer's allowance. It's officially your job because you're alone and doing it full-time. I've applied on Mum's behalf for a grant for the home adaptions. You can't keep carrying her around, you'll do your back in.'

'What kind of home adaptions?'

'A ramp, a shower, grab rails, a stair lift. She's entitled, she has a medical card, essential items of equipment are free. She could apply for a house swap, get on the list for a ground-floor flat or something, she's entitled, but I doubt she'll leave the house.'

I agree. She'd never leave.

He places another form on the table. 'You need a copy of her passport for this one, and proof of address, this one for you, this one for her. I've put Post-its on the pages explaining what you need to do, these yellow sticky things are where you've to sign.' No one can say Hugh has never cared, never worried, never felt responsible, never felt the burden. He feels it all and he doesn't deserve it. He deserves to live.

The words on the forms are all swimming in my eyes. I won't be able to do this. Grants and application forms are not my strong suit. I take them all and hug them to my chest, knowing I'll probably leave them to collect dust on the kitchen counter for months. I'd really love it if Hugh stayed. That would be the perfect thing, the ideal. Him and me in the house, it would be so much easier. With her new mood-stabilising medication, she had been having less manic episodes, but the chemo has messed with everything and she has to find new levels again. Plus she's physically harder to care for.

I wish he didn't have to leave but it's less of a waste of a life if I stay.

I judge people so quickly by their colours, by their true hidden selves; I make a decision instantly whether to move forward with them or not. I never try to learn anything more about them, get to know the outer part, try to help them or even understand the reason for their inner part. Even with more insight than most, I recognise that at eight years old I became lazy with people, with actual human interaction, and growth has been stunted. It is the opposite to everyone else; most people begin knowing somebody on the surface level and spend time gaining trust, getting to know what's beneath. The fun part, perhaps. Only when they get in there and discover what's inside do they decide whether they like it or not. Takes them a year or two, maybe a decade or two. But I know straight away.

There are lovely parts to people too, always such lovely parts that can draw you in. They can radiate happiness and contentment, strength and solidity from their core. People who'd be good for you. Daria at the coffee shop who writes positive messages on the take-out cups, Mr Ganguly next door who sings Tom Jones when he's doing the garden. Their granddaughter, who looks like a wobbling dumpling, giggles and laughs as she discovers everything for the first time. And the conversations between the two of them is the stuff of joy.

That's what you want to be around, be a part of. People who make you want to be with them, and be better.

But you can't just observe, stand by idly like a spare part. They have to want you too.

One month after Hugh has left, one month caring for Lily completely alone, and I feel like I'm drowning. Drowning, not in her colours but in my own. Drowning in the drudgery, the routine, the loneliness, the giving, the giving, the giving.

Caregiver.

Caretaker.

Care grabber, care snatcher, care monster.

I must look like those blank-faced, staring, zombie parents who are there but not there when standing at a playground, looking but not seeing a thing while their kids could be rolling in dogshit for all they know. So unaware of their surroundings; following, not leading, turned into lemmings, live agar in a Petri dish, some social experiment.

I'm nineteen years old, Lily is forty-nine and she's in this chair for life. She's doing physio but the odds are against her. Hugh is in Doha, Ollie is in prison, I am here. If the first month is like this, I won't last the year, never mind ten years, or more. Looking forward into my future is what sends me into a panic. I can't keep doing this forever. I can't catch my breath at the thought. I can only focus on the moments I'm in, to truly cope. And then when those moments, like cleaning her, dressing her, are too much to cope with, my mind travels to the future: a silent hope that this will all end soon. But I know it won't. And then I panic.

I start making a routine. We get up. I wash her, dress her, we eat and then no matter what the weather, we go out. We go to the local parks every day – Johnstown Park, Mellowes Park, Griffith Park, Tolka Valley Park, National Botanic Gardens – but over time they are not enough. I know every lane, every curve, every route, and we have all day, every day, so why not venture further? We get the bus to the Ormsby Estate and Private Gardens and, though we have to pay for entry, it's worth it. Suddenly there's a new place to explore.

My energy is restored by the vibrant colours floating around from nature, exotic trees brought in by grand lords and ladies from way back when, but also from people I don't know, people not from my area. I think that Lily feels the same way because she doesn't complain, not even when it's windy, or cold, or starts to rain. We both want to be out of the house, away, distracted, doing something.

The first day we're there it's mid-June. It's a warm day but cooled nicely by the shade and cover of the trees. We don't talk. We rarely do.

I can feel my chest start to loosen and it's only then I realise how tight it was. My body uncoils, starts to release, my shoulders relax, my hands stop clenching the wheelchair so tightly. I can breathe. I lift my face to the sky and breathe. I open my eyes and smile and when I open them we're at a bridge. There's one step up to the bridge which means I can't bring Lily, or I could if I turned her around and pulled her up the step as I sometimes have to do, as though she's in a buggy, but that's difficult with such a heavy wheelchair and I don't this time. A space she can't enter makes it all the more attractive. My eyes are pulled to the sight before me. A rose garden in full bloom, bathed in glorious colours.

The blooming flowers have a blooming effect on my heart. I wander through the maze and walkways of rose beds, under the arches of the climbing roses. I don't know anything about flowers, but I know they are pretty. I know that they are alive, that they're healthy, that they're beautiful, that they are pure, that they are proud of their beauty, gurus of nature, raising their heads to the sun, reaching tall.

It's not just the colours of their petals, it's their auras too that are sublime. I weave my way through them all, reaching out and touching the velvety petals with my fingertips, wanting their energies.

Lily gives side-eye from across the bridge, letting me know she thinks my expression of joy is weird.

'Do you want to come over?'

'No. You're all right.'

On the way home I buy a bouquet of flowers at the petrol station. I realise that this is the energy our house is missing.

I can't see people's energies when they're on television. Lily teases my reactions; how I howl so loudly with laughter I can't breathe, and cry so hard my chest hurts and my eyes sting. Even though the acting is a deception in itself, there are no colours around them to distract, or to suggest they are deceiving me. I can believe them. It's both an escape and a trap.

It's a Sunday, Lily is in front of the TV watching a football match. I'm in the kitchen trying to revive a plant that insists on dying even at the window and with me watering it every day. It's the third plant I've killed.

'There's your friend,' she calls.

I ignore her.

'Alice!'

'What?' I snap. It's not me that's killing these plants, it must be her and her bad vibes.

'Your friend is on telly.'

'Who?' I walk in carrying the plant pot, it dribbles dirty soil water from the base onto the carpet. I curse.

'That lad from school.'

It's a football match, I assume she's referring to someone in the stand. I scan the crowd for a familiar face, not seeing anyone. I finally listen to the commentator: 'Gospel Mkundi. Dublin native. Only his third appearance on the first team, but his recent debut revealed that he's Crystal Palace's shining new talent.'

'Absolutely,' the second commentator agrees. 'Gospel has shown himself to be a very gifted player, with a blistering pace and remarkable dribbling capabilities. Certainly one of their most promising players and I predict great things for him.'

Gospel runs across the pitch in his blue and red kit, fixing the waistband of his shorts to his position as a centre forward. He looks around, finding himself, rooting himself, a little glance to the stadium with twenty-five thousand people watching. He blinks a little, once, twice, nothing like before, no twitch of his head or shoulders. No one but me would even notice.

*

'Girls, you three will be sharing this room. Nice one, it's over the kitchen, smells of freshly baked bread every morning,' Gloria says the first morning I arrive at the academy. 'You'll meet Chef Alan, he's a wizard. Cakes, doughnuts, pies – you name it, he bakes it.'

We all look out the window as if expecting to see them lined up, but we just see the ugly flat roof of a kitchen and pipes.

'I'll leave you to settle down and get to know each other. The principal will be greeting everyone in the dinner hall in an hour, so relax until then.'

We all look at each other.

'What are your names?' the Indian-Irish girl asks. 'I'm Saloni. Can't remember names for shit.'

'Me neither,' I say, laughing. 'I'm Alice.'

'I'm Grace.' She's small and birdlike, with a spattering of freckles over her nose and cheeks. She looks like she'd blow over in a breeze.

Saloni chooses the bottom bunk, Grace takes the top, which leaves me with the option of either top or bottom of the second bunk bed to myself. I choose the top. No arguments, no drama, no psychos – yet, anyway.

During the night there's a thump and a crack as Grace lands on the floor between the two bunks. Saloni wakes up and screams when she sees Grace lying on the floor at an unnatural angle, groaning.

'Oh my God,' Saloni says. 'Get the light.'

I try to get down as quickly as I can, feeling like I'm moving in slow motion as I fumble and try to find my way down the ladder. I feel along the wall for the light switch, and it takes me a moment to adjust to the light and find Saloni on her knees beside Grace's dislocated body.

'Call for help!' Saloni says, and I hurry down the quiet corridor to where the dorm manager is sleeping.

I don't sleep the rest of the night, not for one second. Nor was I asleep when Grace fell. I had been wide awake, getting used to the new sounds of the building when I'd heard the creak of Grace's bed as she sat up, then stood up and threw herself off the top.

I watch Grace being showered with kindness and attention in the canteen. Someone offers to carry her tray, a table of girls invite her to join them, everyone instantly knows her name. She seems to revel in the light.

'I bet she broke her own leg for the attention,' a voice says, behind me.

I turn around to find the source of the voice and come face to face with a cute guy, huge brown eyes, never-ending eyelashes, tall and broad. Then he blinks once, twice, twitches, then throws his head back and grunts, like a horse tossing its head. The move is so violent it looks painful. Then he's back to normal again. He doesn't explain anything about what just happened and his colours don't suggest any kind of anger or malice. With no apologies or an attempt to address it, he continues to watch Grace.

'What's she going to do when her leg heals?' he asks.

'Break the other one,' I say.

He laughs, then twitches, his shoulders moving in quick shudders, then one blink, two blinks. He throws his head back again and grunts. 'Want to sit together for lunch?'

*

Gospel tells me to meet him behind the pottery prefab. Ceramic-making is supposed to have a calming effect on the students; they stick a glob of clay on a spinning wheel and watch us transform into a zen-like state of focus, in the hope that a cognitive metamorphosis takes place. It doesn't work for everyone. Not for Josh Dabrowski, who had a tantrum and threw his vase that looked like an ashtray at the window.

No one ever comes here. They gather in plenty of places where they're not supposed to, but this is just one of those places that's ours. It looks out over a neighbouring field with cows, not owned by the school. Gospel, depending on his mood, tries to fire missiles at them and I ignore him because when he's in that mood, there's no getting him out of it. It's also where he smokes weed – and it works, a green surrounds his other colours, calms him down, stops his tics.

He makes his way across the playing fields, carrying a box. He has good energy and we became instant friends. Gospel is Irish-Zimbabwean from Tallaght. His dad is from Zimbabwe, and is a computer analyst. His mum is a nurse in Tallaght hospital. He loves his family, they sent him to Clearview to help him, he came here to be helped, which feels the opposite to my situation. I was sent away. I feel I was disposed of. I meet his parents on the weekends when they visit; they've even invited me out with them for meals at the local carvery. I like to listen to Gospel talk about his life rather than speak about my own, but he knows enough to know that, unlike him, I didn't exactly come here of my own free will. And now that I'm here, I don't want to go home.

'Hey, sorry I'm late, I had to empty this box first and Nigel wouldn't let me put my stuff on the desk because of his OCD, so I had to put it away in exactly the right place and in order of the visible light spectrum so he wouldn't freak out. I thought cyan was like coral?'

I laugh. 'You brought comics,' I say, reaching inside.

'Don't touch them; some of them are special limited editions. I will explain, but first I need this.'

He puts the heavy box down, sits on the grass, and lights a spliff.

I sit further away so the smoke doesn't cling to my clothes, and I watch him. It's hypnotising, watching his anxious yellows mellow as the CBD starts to take effect. He's found the right balance now, Nigel his roommate supplies him. Agoraphobic, OCD Nigel, who will barely leave his room unless he's had CBD. Even though Tourette's is a part of who Gospel is, I can see who he is when he's like this; the mellow Gospel who tics less, the one more in control of himself. Cannabis isn't like the pills I've seen Lily on, or the other depression or anti-anxiety pills I've seen other students on. It doesn't surround the mood with a relaxing haze, disguising it to trick the person; instead it removes the mood altogether, the anxieties literally fade away – for a short time at least, giving them just enough respite to catch their breath. I've never been tempted to try it because I need to be in control. I couldn't imagine being so relaxed that I'd walk straight through colours that might cling to me and alter my state, but it's relaxing to sit and watch a friend transform for the better.

'It's working,' I say, smiling as he becomes a grounded, rooted earthy brown. I've always wondered why people say they're getting high when in reality it looks like the opposite.

He leans his head back against the cabin and closes his eyes for a moment, enjoying the feeling of being free, not a captive in a body that won't obey him.

'Okay, let's get to work. I'm a comic fan, you learn something fascinating about me every day. X-Men, Spider-Man, Superman, Batman, the Avengers – all the obvious ones, and there's lots there you don't know. We won't get into them all, but basically there's a superhero logic, like an algorithm, and they all follow it.'

'Okay,' I say slowly, confused as to why he's telling me this but appreciating him sharing a secret part of himself with me.

'What is a superhero?' he asks, as though beginning a lecture. 'It's a character that possesses abilities beyond those of normal people. *Just like you*. Someone that uses their powers to help the world become a better place, to fight crime and protect the public. *Just. Like. You.*'

'Gospel! I'm not a superhero.'

'Did you or did you not, in the first month I met you, hit a paedophile in the cock with a bicycle helmet, at the playground.'

I laugh. 'Yes, I did.'

'Well then.' Blink, blink, twitch, throws his head back, and grunts. 'We shall continue. Every superhero has three characteristics: their superpower, their weakness, and their nemesis.'

'I can tell you who my nemesis is straight away: Mr Battersby.'

I'm joking but he's taking this so seriously. 'Wait, we're not there yet.'

'So, the superpower. Spider-Man, well he has genius intellect, he's a scientist and inventor, superhuman strength, speed, balance, endurance, precognitive spider-sense and webbing ability. His weakness is ethyl chloride pesticide and his nemesis is the Green Goblin.'

I watch his face, so animated, as he launches into Superman's traits. I thought his concentration face was the greatest, but perhaps it's his enthusiasm, his passion. The honey-coloured energies flow like liquid around him, I picture a cartoon Winnie the Pooh with his pots of hunny.

A bell rings for lunch, we ignore it.

'Why are we doing this?'

'Because I've been thinking about you. A lot.'

My heart pounds, butterflies swirl in my stomach.

'Your superpower is seeing people's colours, reading energies and moods. You know if someone is lying or being truthful, if someone is,' Blink, blink, twitch, throws his head back and grunts, 'Sick, messed up in the head, pregnant or whatever – you know it. You might know it before even they do. You know people's secrets. Everyone is completely transparent under your gaze.'

'I don't know how it's a strength,' I say.

'It's leverage, for a start. Your weakness is . . .' He looks at me as if expecting me to know the answers.

I shrug. 'Seeing colours? They give me migraines, force me to wear glasses.'

'No. Your weakness is being afraid of getting the energies on you. You won't touch anyone, won't let anyone touch you.'

Those eyes again, that soothing honey voice.

'Which leads us to the nemesis. A hero is only as good

as the villains they face, so the greatest superhero in the world would have to have the greatest arch-nemesis. Lex Luthor is Superman's mirror reflection and that's what makes him one of the greatest villains. So I was thinking about your mirror reflection. You have empathy, you understand people, you feel what people feel, even when you don't want to. The opposite of that are sociopaths, psychopaths. Somebody with no empathy, no compassion, no remorse, who manipulates and charms, and who uses others for themselves.'

Despite my embarrassment, I'm all ears.

'Superheroes are drawn to their arch-nemesis. The war is a lifelong one: they will continuously battle it out and the hero will win, but the nemesis is in their lives forever.'

'Okay, I get it. So the academy is like the X-Mansion and all of us kids have special powers.'

'I'm not a superhero. I have a chronic tic disorder. I'm not even here for that, I'm here because it makes me so angry I throw furniture against the wall.'

'I meant your alarming good looks and football skills.'

He smiles but is unaffected by my attempts to deflect.

'You have to hear what I'm saying, Alice. I'm serious about this. If your nemesis is a mirror reflection of you, then in a way that makes them part of you. You'll be pulled towards them for life, constantly facing the battle with them, maybe winning the battle but never finishing the war. They are charming and they are smart, they are master manipulators, and they will play with you time and time again, hoping that evil will triumph over good, never giving up until it does. They will be so clever that you may not even know that's who they are. And right now you don't care because you don't even know the power you have. You hate your powers, you want them to be gone. And you'll let a nemesis do that to you because you want to destroy your power and you want to self-destruct.'

I'm not smiling anymore. Neither is he.

He's so concerned about me, he has barely ticced in that entire speech. He's in his football gear, his legs are long and muscular, his shoulders are wide, his eyes are deep and dreamy. He genuinely cares about me, has carried a box of stuff that means something to him across the pitch because he thought of me. I move closer to him, breaking the natural distance I keep from people.

Just sitting beside him feels intimate. I touch his face.

The feel of someone's skin beneath my touch is new and dangerous. But I trust him.

I run my finger over his lips, he kisses my finger, then waits. Waits to know that it's okay, and then we kiss.

My heart pounds watching Gospel on the pitch. A striker for Crystal Palace. He's done it. His parents must be so proud, I picture them in the crowd somewhere, cheering him on as they did on the sidelines for every match at the academy. His little mum, his tall dad, there every Sunday for him. He looks handsome, muscular, strong. Beautiful. Striking, as he always was.

She's looking at me.

'What? What did you say?' I'm back in this room, in this house, with her. In the wheelchair. With a dripping dying plant in my hand. The washing needs to be ironed and the bed linen needs to be changed. I need to call a plumber about the blocked toilet. Maybe she sees something in me die.

She thinks about it, then says, 'Nothing.'

I buy another plant at Tesco. It's an aloe vera. I'm determined not to kill this one. I don't like floral bouquets; they look beautiful but as soon as the flowers are snipped, their nutrient supply is severed and they're already dying. Their rotting energy hangs around the house like a bad smell. I've tried with them, but I cannot display and admire death in my home. Plants on the other hand are in soil and they're alive, living and breathing.

I place the new plant on the windowsill in the kitchen.

'Hello. I'm Alice and I'm not going to kill you,' I say, more of an affirmation to myself.

An orange energy appears around the leaves, like a bud quickly opening then closing before fading completely.

'Oh,' I say in surprise. 'You like me talking to you, don't you?'

The orange is stronger, larger, opens like a large flower then closes again.

I try something else. 'You're a beautiful plant. Such lovely, um, leaves, what do we call these?' I run my fingers gently down its long pointed leaves.

More bursts of orange floral blooms. They open and close, a time-lapse of flowers blooming before disappearing again.

'Holy shit,' I whisper. I lean down to the plant's level. 'I'm going to call you Vera.'

*

I try something later that day, a kind of experiment.

Lily is watching TV. She hasn't smoked since chemo-therapy. She said it affected her taste buds and the smoke was disgusting.

'How long without a cigarette now? Almost a year?'

'Yeah, probably.'

'That's great. You must be proud of yourself.'

She looks at me suspiciously.

'I mean you've smoked all of my life, that I can remember, and now look: you're cigarette free. Well done you.'

I mean it, but it's coming out robotically. We're not used to speaking like that to each other.

'Fuck off, Alice,' she says, and turns back to the TV.

I watch her colours for time-lapse flourishing blooms, for pops of pinks, for a grand firework display, for the fan of proud peacock feathers.

Nothing.

I laugh to myself and get back to the ironing. Cheered me up anyway.

I learn how to keep Vera alive by listening to Vera. When I think it's time to water her, it's usually not. She's a hardy plant, she enjoys her place in the sun and only seldom requires a drink, as if she's too busy for such things, too busy looking out the window at our dingy garden. It doesn't seem to put her off as it does me; she grows towards it, as if reaching her long leaves to paint, to touch the glass and say, look, look out there.

She makes me look out there. At the patchy too-long grass, balding in some places. The weeds, the hedging growing over from the perfectly constructed Ganguly side. She points it out to me and I see it. Which makes me want the view for her to be better. So I start work on the garden. Lily watches me from the door, thinking I've lost it. She's heard me talking to the plant, which I do now without embarrassment. Good morning in the mornings, comments on the weather, all kinds of chat directed at Vera while Lily rolls her eyes. Sometimes she includes Vera in her conversations to get at me, like: 'Oh Vera, I think someone got out of the wrong side of bed today,' or 'See this, Vera, looks like we're eating old leather boots instead of steak again today.'

Gardening is expensive and it takes time and patience, none of which I have. I concentrate first on the grass, focus on bringing the soil back to its full health. We finally get the house modifications that we need. Lily hasn't been in the back garden for over a year and even then I don't know what she was outside for; smoking, probably, but she did most of that inside. The new ramp means she comes outside and watches, makes annoying comments mostly.

At first I hated her company in the garden. I did this to get out of the house, to get away from her. Her presence is less than calming: shuddering at every breeze like it's going to blow her over, swatting at every flying creature that comes near her as if they're going to kill her. She wasn't made for being outside. She points at things I've done wrong and at gaps I've missed.

The birds eat the seeds for the new grass and it remains as bog-like as it was before, but I eventually get there, focusing on it with an almost obsessive amount of attention. By the end I have a vibrant lawn, greener than green, almost radioactive and unreal looking. Each blade is of perfect and equal length, as though I'd gotten down on my hands and knees and cut it with scissors. Even Vera, who has grown, touches the windowpane with the tip of her leaf and seems to say, 'There.'

Lily surveys the garden, her face scrunched up from the sun.

'Well?' I ask her. There is no fault in my lawn, she can't pick at anything. There are no gaps, no bare spots, no bogs, nothing to pick at.

'It needs flowers,' she says.

I see Dave around the place most days. The supermarket, in the park, at the bus stop. Sometimes it seems as if we're the only people utilising public spaces while everybody is at work; the invisible daytime layer of society made up mostly of mothers with babies, the elderly and the unemployed. He's a carer too and always with his brother Christopher who has severe autism and needs twenty-four/ seven support and supervision. Dave is always so jolly it can't be real and yet his colours don't suggest otherwise. In fact his colours don't suggest much, which makes him quite an enigmatic figure. He has mainly one colour, grey, but at least four shades. I've seen grey in people, positive and negative. The negative being depression or dishonesty. Grey is common but his shades are new to me. What I learn is that this positive grey that surrounds him is a kind of neutrality. He's adaptable, he compromises, he'll be whatever it is that you want him to be, he can blend into the environment and just be there without making a fuss.

Dave's dad passed away when he was young and his mother died very suddenly of cancer when he was eighteen and it fell to him to care for Christopher. There's much I can relate to about Dave and yet that grey just hangs around him like a shield and he's impenetrable. I can't catch his eye and share a look over Lily and Christopher's heads, I can't bond with him in that way. He will never say how shit it is, how unfair it all is, if he's had a bad day, if he ever resents Christopher. Instead it's always positivity, which I should be grateful for, considering the atmosphere in my house, yet it feels like a blockade, a denial. But who am I to criticise a coping mechanism?

'Sad,' Lily says one day as we leave him and Christopher on the street after an awkward conversation about the weather that went on longer than any conversation about the weather should go.

'What's sad?'

'For the young lad.'

It's an unusually empathetic comment from Lily and it surprises me. I wonder if she thinks it's sad for me.

'No more than it's sad for me,' I say, testing her.

'I'm nothing like him,' she says, insulted. 'You get to stay home, you don't have to work, you're having a field day compared to that.'

My anger at her inability to acknowledge my sacrifices for her is immediate but I chomp down hard on my lip. She can't though; she has to keep going, snapping and snapping until it's all out of her and uploaded to someone else. 'I did sometimes wonder if you'd turn out a bit like that lad, Christopher.'

I don't speak to her for the rest of walk back to the house

– or for the rest of the day for that matter. I stew in my rage. I pull her up from her wheelchair more roughly than I should, I throw the sponge at her with more strength than I should. She can wash her bits herself.

For a woman like Lily, who has never seemed to want to work, has never seemed to have any ambition, then yes, it would seem as if I have won the jackpot. I'm not sure what I would be doing, if I wasn't here with her. Maybe I chose to stay with her not because I was a saint but because I was afraid of all the things that Hugh said I should be doing, things I knew I couldn't do. Maybe I'm more like her than I realise. Maybe she knows that, that this is helping me to hide away from the fact that, without being tethered to her, I have no idea where I would float. If I would float at all or if I would choose to stay, drowning with her.

Lily enjoys the walks in the park even if she never says so. We stick to a routine. The fresh air is important to me, the sunlight, the trees, they lift me. Though the house is a far more positive place now than it ever was.

Today, something feels wrong. I don't get the usual lift that I feel when I go for a walk. My soul is not being fed by the environment. I stop walking and look up. A tree is emitting an orange brown colour, as though it's on fire, but there is no fire. It's not the usual earthy brown that you want to inhale into your lungs; it's rust-coloured, and it's not the only tree on metaphorical fire. I look around and find the same rust colour above other trees in the woods.

'Are you still there?' Lily asks, unable to turn around to see me.

I continue walking, faster now I'm on a mission. I head straight for the park warden's office.

'Where are we going? Bus stop's the other way.'

'There's something wrong with the trees,' I explain.

She tuts and sighs.

The park warden answers the door with a cup of tea in his hand. He puts his hat on.

'Hiya, love.'

'Hello, could I speak to the person in charge of the gardens?'

'Lose something, did ya?' He puts his mug down and grabs a set of keys. 'Lost and found is just down here.'

'No, I'd like to speak to somebody about the trees.'

'That'd be Laurence Metcalf, the head gardener.'

'Where can I find him?'

'He's not here. He has a team of gardeners though, they're dotted all around the park. Do you've a question about the trees, love?'

He's beginning to view me as a simpleton.

'It doesn't matter,' I say, reversing and moving away with Lily. 'Thanks.'

'What's going on, Alice?' she asks.

'The trees aren't well.'

'What do you know about trees?' she says with a snort. 'Honestly, Alice.'

I write to Laurence Metcalf, who, to be fair to him, responds that he has carried out an examination just three months ago of the trees in the area that I'm describing, and they're healthy.

I write back and tell him to examine them again. I'm no tree surgeon but the trees are sick. I can't hear them moaning in pain but I can see their pain. The rust runs from their roots to the tips of the tree, twisted around each other like braids. They're sick to their roots and it's billowing out from the top like fire.

Despite the energy that particular park sucks from me, I continue to walk through the grounds with Lily. I press my hand to the bark of the sick trees, hoping to give them some comfort.

'You look like a right wally, Alice – stop it, someone's coming,' she'd say.

Until one day, probably six months later, we can't walk down our usual path. Pedestrians are being diverted due to the felling of infected trees.

I see orange ribbons on surrounding trees.

'Ash dieback,' Lily reads the sign. 'A fungal disease.' She looks up at me in surprise. 'Well.'

Then a chainsaw starts up.

'They're cutting them down,' she says. 'Ah Alice, you've only gone and got them cut down.'

'They couldn't be helped,' I say. 'At least they'll be out of pain.'

'Cut me down.'

A fierce growl wakes me up. I fell asleep on the couch watching a marathon of *Homes Under the Hammer*. She's suddenly beside me, in my face; how she managed to get so close to me, I'll never know. She must have pulled herself along like a slug.

'What?'

Her breath reeks of alcohol.

'Cut me down,' she says again. 'Put me out of my misery like you did with them trees.'

I look at her, wide awake now, and see her colours spiralling.

'Please,' she says, nails digging into my skin.

'Did you forget to take your pills?' I ask, standing up and trying to regain control of the situation. The two I placed on the table are gone.

'I did.'

'What about the lithium?'

If she doesn't take that then her manic episodes can worsen. The lithium is the mood stabiliser. It's happened before. The last manic episode was brought on by the antidepressant and they had to prescribe an anti-psychotic medicine to manage the mania. But I don't want it to get that far. I need to put the fire out now.

The lithium is gone too.

'Stop it,' she says, grabbing my arm, gently this time, almost massaging me, pleading with me. 'Please, Alice. End it for me. End it for both of us.'

I reach out to Dave the following day. He talks endlessly of support groups for carers, tea and coffee mornings that I don't have the remotest interest in joining, but maybe I'm failing as a carer. When the person you are caring for no longer possesses the desire to live, surely it means you're not caring enough. I can recognise the pain in a tree more than I can in my own mother. I'm blind to it; the very pain that brought my senses to life is now the only pain I no longer see.

There's a carers' meeting in the local library. Coffee and

chocolate muffins, he informs me with lots of exclamation marks in his text message. Lily's right, it's sad that chocolate muffins have a young man so excited.

'Where are we going?' Lily asks as I turn into the library and wheel her up the long winding ramp.

'In here for a minute,' I say. I have decided not to give her warning because she has just as much interest in this kind of thing as I do.

'What for? A book?'

We take the lift to the second floor and as I push the door open into the gathering and we see the gang in front of us, she throws me a look of loathing.

Dave is super welcoming; it makes me cringe, and I don't know why I can't open up to his genuine warmth. It makes me fold in on myself in the same way a sales assistant in the Disney store makes me feel. Is it because it's not real, or is it because it really is?

He reminds me of a children's TV presenter, so upbeat and full of cheer, so innocent, so kind and simple, and yet his life is anything but simple. He cares for Christopher with such confidence, reaching into his eye socket to remove sleep, taking fluff out of his hair like they're two gorillas. Christopher is hugely overweight, and I don't know how Dave physically does it, but I watch the colours between them, transferring and mingling more than I've ever seen with two people before. It's fascinating, so intermingled it looks like they're conjoined twins.

Dave's base colour is grey, but with Christopher he sends his pink energy out. It throbs like a heartbeat, a living, breathing entity. Christopher takes it, adds his own pink mist to it, makes the throbbing heart bigger and sends it back. Dave adds to it and passes it on. It's the opposite of a game of pass the parcel; when the music stops, an extra layer is added at each turn.

Christopher wants to hug me. 'Christopher loves hugs. Is that okay?' Dave asks, not expecting me to say no.

But I don't love hugs and Lily knows this. She watches with a twisted smile on her face, curious to see what will happen.

I take a few steps back. 'No, I'm sorry, I . . . don't do hugs,' I mumble, and find myself face to face with a young woman named Beatrice, who's caring for her aunt and who launches into a militant rant about how under-represented and underappreciated carers are. Her stress is coming out of her in buckets, and droplets of colours hang around her, like rainbows caught inside the rain.

Christopher's energy colour movements are like a jellyfish, the smooth in and out movement. Perhaps it's awareness coming and going, Christopher moving from knowing himself to drifting to another space. It has no rhythm, just in and out at its own tempo, then it holds for a moment. Christopher is here; he's engaged with Dave, with the chocolate muffin, he eats it, attention solely on the muffin, then slowly but surely the jellyfish flexes and he's gone again. Though who's to say whether he's gone or whether he's merely arrived someplace else that we don't have access to. Perhaps I should have hugged him, to figure out where that place is, or what it feels like.

By the time we leave, my head is hot and I'm sweating. I can smell my armpit sweat and I hope no one else can.

'Sorry about that,' I say, pushing Lily out. 'We won't go there again.'

'I wouldn't mind going back again,' she says to my surprise. 'He was a nice man, Gregory. His wife has dementia. She didn't say boo. Just sat there with a smile like she knew what she was doing, but you could tell she hadn't a clue. Were the muffins free?'

'Eh yeah, I think so.'

'Good,' she says with a cackle, one appearing from inside her hoody.

'Hey, Alice,' Dave says behind us, out of breath. Christopher isn't with him. He looks different without him. Like a teacher outside of school, a police officer out of uniform, or seeing anyone you know in their swimwear.

'Sorry I didn't get to talk to you.'

'That's okay.' I thought we did talk. 'Sorry about the hugging thing. I just don't do it.'

'That's all right,' he says chirpily, as if I'm the tenth person he's met that day who has a phobia of hugs.

I look to Lily and away again, wishing I could have a moment of privacy.

'I was wondering if we could meet up again? Just you and me? Christopher has a day centre on Wednesdays. He goes at noon for two hours a week, if you want to catch up then?'

His face is flushed, he's so bright and eager. I can't bring myself to look in Lily's direction even though she's got her back to me. I can only imagine the look on her face. If I let go of the chair she could roll down the ramp, all the way down, onto the path, out onto the road.

'Eh . . .' I look down at the back of Lily's head. 'Yeah, I just need to check that out first,' I say awkwardly.

'Sure, yeah. No problem. You've got my number so just text, yeah?'

'Yeah.'

He grins, baring two dimples in his cheeks. 'Cool.'

I don't like to touch people. I don't like people to touch me. Which makes sex difficult, but not impossible.

If they want me, really want me, I can get lost in their desire, confuse theirs for mine and touch becomes okay. But if their desire is desperate, as Dave's is, sad and lonely and desperate, hungry and greedy, panic-stricken and conscious of time, then it does not spark joy in me. Like somebody breaking a diet to wolf down a slice of cake. That sad, lonely want comes through to me and leaves me feeling every morsel of it. Not an aphrodisiac; it's like I'm doing them a favour as opposed to being desired.

It matters.

When you're naked with a stranger, allowing them to go to places only you can allow them to go, those things matter.

He kisses me a few times hungrily, greedily. I let him touch me a few times. He grabs and pulls, pinches and squeezes as if he's running out of time. Then when the touching has brought it to where it needs to be, I explain the rules. No more touching.

He nods and lies back, hands to himself. I take over.

'I want to start rehab,' she announces the following day, suddenly.

I have a thousand questions but I don't ask. She did a minimal amount of rehab at the beginning, enough to learn to crawl. I suppose that was no small feat, but while they said she would never walk again, the physio wanted her to continue. He was a young positive lad who insisted nothing was impossible – apart from actually getting her to continue to do rehab, it turns out. I'm happy she's made this decision, because if she wants to walk, it means she wants to live.

I receive a letter from Laurence Metcalf, the head gardener at the Ormsby Estate and Private Gardens. He thanks me for letting him know about the trees. He says they re-examined them and found ash dieback, a highly destructive disease of ash trees caused by a fungal species known as *Hymenoscyphus fraxineus*. He tells me that the gardens have been accepted for an ash dieback replanting scheme and they have begun the process of clearing the ground, removing all leaf litter, and replanting an alternative species to ash. He thanks me for my recognition of the trees' disease and wonders how I knew at such an early stage, even before the experts? He encloses a membership card to the Ormsby Estate and Private Gardens, which allows me five years' free access as a token of his sincerest gratitude. A thank you from the trees, he says.

Green potted plants line every windowsill of the house. I haven't killed any. Vera lives on, watching the empire grow, and my slow, increasingly competent progress in the back garden.

'Feels like we're living in a jungle,' Lily says, on more than one occasion.

She never forgets birthdays. For all her shortcomings over the years, her dark moods and disappearances, she would always remember our birthdays. Usually it was a birthday card with a fiver inside. But this year, on my twenty-fourth birthday, she surprises me.

When I come downstairs, she's already up and dressed, in her wheelchair, sitting with the front door wide open.

'What are you doing? It's freezing in here.'

'Waiting for Ian. He was supposed to be here an hour ago,' she says, fuming.

'Are you going somewhere?' I glance at the kitchen table: there's no envelope where there usually is one for the birthday person to collect. I genuinely believe that she has forgotten my birthday, and then I remind myself I should be too old to care.

'No. Ah, here he is!'

Uncle Ian pulls up outside in his minivan.

'Late as usual,' she shouts out the door as he climbs down, flustered.

'Sorry, sorry,' he says. 'Where do you want them? Outside?'

'No, in here.'

'In the house?'

'Yeah, would you hurry up? I told you eight o'clock.'

'Traffic, Lily – Jesus!' he says, opening the back doors of the van. He walks towards us with a tray of flowers and sees me. 'Hiya, love.'

'Give them to Alice,' she says. 'They're for her birthday. I'm putting the kettle on, want a cuppa?'

'Yeah, go on. Happy birthday, Alice.'

'They're not from him,' she calls from the kitchen. 'Ian, come in and fill the kettle, will you?'

He rolls his eyes at me and scurries to the kitchen. 'I thought you asked me for a cuppa and now I'm the one making it.'

'Well, I can't reach, can I?'

'You should get lower counters.'

'Want to pay for them for me?'

They bicker back and forth while I stand in the living room with a tray of beautiful red and pink flowers.

'Geraniums,' she says suddenly, and I look up to see her watching me. 'For your garden.'

'Thank you,' I say, through the lump that's formed in my throat.

On Sundays we visit Ollie.

He's in Mountjoy Prison with over five hundred inmates. He's filled out over the years, moved from gawky teen to young man, lean and muscular because his favourite thing to do is to work out at the prison gym. His acne is bad, nothing he can do about the quality of food. He's had opportunities to learn by having access to classroom learning, but he's avoided all of that since moving to the men's prison, saying what could be worse than school in jail. He has coped well in prison and this concerns me.

He talks of his current job in the laundry.

'You'll be well trained for when you come home,' Lily says.

'I'm not going anywhere near your dirty knickers,' he says, and they both kind of smile, as ever sharing the same destructive, weird humour.

He asks her about her chair and her back.

She tells him how horrible it is.

They talk about how bad the weather is, so grey and cold.

She never discusses our lovely walks, our routine, our new meetings with new friends, how she's improving with each session at physio, how she can pull herself along on the bars with no chair. She doesn't bring any light in with her for him. You may as well be in here, is the projected message, you're not missing out on anything out there. You could say that she is doing this for him; maybe she would say that if I asked her, but I don't think so. I think they have always bonded over what is collectively crap and dark about this world.

The only thing I can ever think to tell him is about Gospel. How he's playing and how the team are doing in the league. I don't even speak to Gospel, I haven't since the day we said goodbye for good, but I use whatever quotes I can glean from him in the press or on TV, things I hear from commentators, other players, coaches and managers.

Ollie doesn't want books, he's not interested in studying, he's counting down the days until he gets out. I remember visiting him in juvenile prison those first few weeks; he was counting up the days until the halfway point of three years and four months, and then he was going to start counting down.

'He seems all right,' Lily always says when we leave, and she's right. He does seem okay. Prison life seems to suit him. He's with a crew of lads that have his back and he has theirs. He seems to enjoy scheming and planning for the hell of it, concentrating on petty issues instead of seeing the world as a bigger place, or of seeing a bigger place for him in it.

I told her after the first few visits that he was on something, but she didn't want to know about it. 'Stop it, Alice,' she'd snapped.

So I stopped. But he didn't.

I would be happy not to visit Ollie, and he obviously feels the same about me, but Lily physically needs me to go with her. It's not an easy journey in a wheelchair, she would never make it through on her own. I hold my breath inside as much as I can. It's stuffy. It smells. All the bodies clustered together, sad, scared, all the worst and lowest versions of people in the room.

I'm thankful for the physical distancing from everyone, but the fear and despair hangs in the air: who's had a bad night, a bad week, who is dreading the walk back to the cells to hear those doors bang closed and lock. Sometimes there's an air of excitement to see Daddy, sometimes there is so much love in the room you could almost forget where you are. But I don't. The orange-brown coloured fog above the prison doesn't just carry the energies of the men locked away that day but all those who have been incarcerated over centuries. It is a building of bad light and bad energy, of rust and rot.

Ollie attracts the despair around him. He sucks it up. In the visiting room it drifts over to him like a storm cloud. He's not the only one, of course, but I focus on him. I think he's taking antidepressants. There's something numb about him, about his eyes and face. His colours are muddy blues and greys surrounded by an unnatural fog of green. Not a calming green, but a neon green. Like toilet cleaner. I don't know what kind of pills they're giving him; low-grade stuff, probably. It's a synthetic, chemical calm; the real feelings are all still there, they've just been blanketed by an itchy scratchy chemically dyed nylon. I wish I could bring him in a patch of grass to stand on, to put in his cell so he can curl his toes into the soil like he used to and calm himself, root himself, get some perspective, remember that all surfaces aren't hard and rough and non-porous.

Other people's woes in the visiting room move towards him like an army and hang around him, then it mobilises, parts of it break up and attack his energy, but the neon green pills do their work, blocking the soldiers from entering. If it's been a while since he's taken a pill you can see the negative energy start to break the forcefield down and find a way in. Maybe they give them the pills before visiting hours to make it easier for everyone. Sometimes it takes him longer to get from his cell to us, some fight or drama has delayed everything, and the pills are wearing off by the time he arrives.

'What are you looking at?' he asks me, looking back over his shoulder, thinking there's someone standing behind him.

'She always does that, never mind her,' Lily says.

'It's fucking weird, freak, don't do it,' Ollie says.

I take long showers after our visits. I wash it off me. All that misery, all that wasted life. I spend time in the garden. I eat raw carrots and celery, chew on chia seeds, imagine the pumpkin seeds scraping my gut and colon, I drink green smoothies; I want to clean myself out from the gut. She's happy to sit on the couch with the chips we pick up on the way home, watching *Coronation Street*, the melancholy dripping from her like greasy fried chip fat.

*

'You'll be coming home soon,' Lily says.

'Yeah.'

'Got your room ready for you and all. Your Star Wars duvet on the bed.'

'You can burn that for a start,' he says, smiling briefly. I see a tooth missing, at the side, near the back. 'A friend of mine was released yesterday. He was in here ten years. From Cork. He asked us, when they let him out, when he's on the street, does he turn left or right.'

For a moment I think he's being philosophical but then they both start laughing. She snorts.

'Eejit,' he says.

Though I boast of knowing somebody on first sight, it can actually take years to figure someone out. I might know that I don't like them, that I don't trust them, but I won't know why. Sometimes I see a new colour and I can't read it; I don't know what it represents. I need to have known someone with it before, witnessed their character in order to understand. Some colours I've only ever seen on one person and never again on another, and it's the moment when I see the colour again that the first person becomes completely understandable, clear and in focus in my head.

It happens when the doorbell rings and I answer to find a man at the door, surrounded by a harsh magenta, pretty and becoming on a hard man like him, but I know exactly who he is.

I've seen his colour before.

*

I've tried to stay away from Esme, the Clearview Academy reiki practitioner, but this person I'm deeply repelled by also has the power of pulling me close. It's like I sense her before I see her, as though, when I near a corner, I know she's around it. And when she passes by with her pretty smile, she sucks the oxygen out of the room and leaves me feeling depleted. I have never spent so much time and energy on disliking somebody so much. Disliking her, obsessing over her has become a hobby.

I work on a plan for Gospel to attend a session with her.

'Your nemesis,' he whispers, dramatically, knowing about my obsession with her.

But we both laugh, not actually thinking it's true.

Seeing that there's only one of her and hundreds of us, there's a long waiting list, and she won't do more than a few hours a day as the sessions drain her. Despite the waiting list, the school prioritises the worst, so it doesn't take long until Gospel is first on the list. I've noticed that when he's stressed, or mentally exhausted, like during exam time, his tics increase. Gospel has explained that his tics are like having a song stuck in your head, he has to make the movement until he no longer feels the need to. The more someone mentions it or attention it is given, the more he feels the need to keep doing it.

During a History exam, Gospel has such an enormous tic attack that his neck continuously throws his head back and his grunting is rapid fire. He has to be removed from the classroom. Gospel is so mortified and apologetic and requests a new form of therapy with Esme.

For Gospel's session with Esme, I sneak across the playing fields to stand outside the reiki prefab. Gospel knows I'm outside and when Esme's back is turned he winks at me, enjoying the clandestine mission. They have a talk first, about his tic disorder and his moods as a result of it, and I feel bad listening in, so I move away from the window so that he can speak freely. She explains what reiki is and her intention to clear his chakras. He lies down on the bed.

If I was asked to describe Gospel in one colour, I would say honey. It's not quite orange and it's not quite yellow, maybe it's both of them mixed together, but it's warm, syrupy. When he goes into a rage it's all the usual angry colours everybody has, but his personal colour is honey. It comes alive when we're at work in school. He's smart; he loves technology. He excels at football. He is the best player on the field. Because the football field is the one place he doesn't tic, he spends as much time there as possible, finessing his skills and abilities, and because he doesn't tic on the field, he doesn't get agitated, and there-fore doesn't lose his head. It's his escape and he's the king on the field.

The orange is rich and warm, the yellow is clear and sharp, and when they mix it's honey-coloured, like sugar melting in a pot and transitioning to caramel. Watching his colours is like watching his brain at work. Sharp, focused, processing, turning grains into something smooth. Solution-based. Syrupy flowing oozing thoughts.

He's not anxious now. Not really. Now and then I see him jerking his shoulders as his muscles tic, but he's mostly relaxed.

Esme takes a few rounds of deep breaths. Her magenta isn't as powerful as it was when I was in the room with her, she mustn't feel the need to mark her territory as grandly with Gospel as she did with me. I watch her magenta as she takes deep breaths, expecting it to become sharper and more focused, but the opposite happens. Oddly, a grey, maybe more like a misty white appears. Harsh magenta and misty white. I watch the mist, wondering what it is and what it means.

She stands at his head with her back to me, so I've to move to get a better view. She asks him to take deep breaths, she counts to three as he inhales and counts to five as he exhales. Absolutely nothing happens to Gospel's colours. She stands at his head and shoulders for ten minutes, eyes closed, hands out. I look for the colour of the heat she spoke about but there's nothing, nothing between her hands and his shoulders. She moves on to his chest and the rest of his body.

After a maddening twenty minutes of nothing happening, she says gently, 'Now I'm going to seal off the energy.'

All of a sudden she starts waving her hands around as if she's wafting a fly. His colour spatters. Some of it gets stuck on her hands. She wipes her hands, the colours fling off and land back on Gospel. She's breaking them up, honey becoming orange and yellow. The yellow breaks up into different shades of yellow, light, sharp, clear, bright, a brilliant canary yellow, all emerge as she stands over him like a Teppanyaki chef doing an intricate knife skills show. Chop chop chop, the colours are broken up, fly around the room. The same with the orange; now a pale orange blob hovers by his knee. This is confusing. It's like she's a child, carelessly splashing paint. Blobs of it are landing around the room. I have to fight the urge to burst in there and put an end to her freak show.

After her manic fly-wafting, knife-chopping, paint-blobbing outburst, she's finished. She says his name gently, but he doesn't move.

He doesn't move.

His eyes don't open. My heart pounds. I race around the front of the cabin and practically kick the door open.

'What have you done to him?' I yell, at the same time as the door flings open and bangs the wall.

She shrieks in fright.

Gospel sits up. He grins at the sight of me. 'I fell asleep.' He looks at Esme. 'Did I?'

Esme nods, hands clutched to her chest. She's afraid of me.

'What did I miss?' he asks, sliding off the table, looking from her to me mostly amused, not at all bothered, no idea of the danger she has put him in.

I glare at her, feeling a physical repulsion. Nothing but air between us, yet there's a barrier so strong that it won't let me go near her, like two clashing magnetic fields. Not that I want to go near her. I want to be out of this room, away from her.

'Let's go,' I say.

'Well, whatever happened I didn't feel anything.' Gospel hops down and slides his feet into his trainers. He's a bit stiff as he lands on his feet and hobbles a little to straighten up.

I take him by the hand and pull him out of there and across the playing fields back to the school, while he forces his feet into his shoes, laces still undone.

'What's wrong?' Gospel says, amused and not at all worried. 'What happened? I thought you were going to hit her. Did she do something weird?' Blink. Blink. He throws his head back and grunts. 'She didn't touch my cock, did she?'

'No! No way! Nothing like that. How do you feel?' I ask.

'Fine. The same. I just fell asleep. It was relaxing. Look, as much as I love the fact you're my knight in shining armour and that you're holding my hand, I've got football now. I'm over this way.'

'Oh.' I try to let go of his hand but he clings on, a grin on his face. He kisses me, briefly, a light brush of our lips, because we're not allowed to. He finally lets go and I walk back to the school alone.

'Talk later, yeah?' he calls.

'Yeah,' I say, my back still turned.

But my blood is boiling, my heart is pounding at the hot harsh magenta and misty white of a fake guru. I can't control my rage. I don't even try the breathing techniques I've been taught. This time I can't be bothered. I don't want to calm down; there is only one way to get this anger out. I go to the toilet and grab a toilet roll, then I take it to the car park and wrap it around Esme's car. Round and round and round, I use the entire roll while a group of kids gather to watch and laugh.

'Anyone got a Sharpie?'

They are only too delighted to give me one.

I write FRAUD on her windscreen. Nice and big and clear.

I learn later that Gospel didn't play football for long. His knee was sore; the one where she left the pale orange blobby energy hovering.

*

'Hello,' the man at my door says cheerily. 'My name is Howard Higgins.'

He hands me a leaflet, and I smile. I lean against the doorframe. This should be fun. 'That's my business information there. I'm in the neighbourhood, I've just done a job for your neighbour and I noticed you've got some roof damage. We've got the materials here left over from the other job and can do it today at a discount, if you're interested. I'd recommend you do it now, love, before it gets worse,' he says, looking up, concerned.

'Which house were you working on?'

'Twenty-five.'

'The Johnstons'.'

'To be honest, I didn't catch their names, love. My colleague was in charge of that one. What's your name, so I don't get caught out again?' he grins.

'Minnie,' I say. 'What were you doing at their house?'

'The gutters. You see when leaves and other debris clog up your gutters to the point that water is flooding over, you can end up having issues with rot on your roofing, which is what you've got happening up there. Come out and I'll show you.'

I'm quite sure he's making it up: both the claim that he was working for a neighbour and that my roof has problems.

I walk out with him and look up at the roof.

'It's best to clean them twice a year. Once in spring and once in autumn. I know you probably don't give much thought to your gutters, but that's what we're here for. We can do you a deal, a reduced price if we do them today, and then we'll come back in the autumn. The work is urgent, I'm telling you. But up to you, of course, love.'

'How much is it?'

He blows out air. 'I'd do it for one hundred. Cash. Would cost you double that usually, though.'

'I don't have any cash on me.'

'I could go to the machine with you, if you want. I'm going for a coffee anyway.'

I smile. 'No thanks.'

'I'll put you down in my book for next time. Minnie, is it?'

'Yeah. M-i-n-n-i-e. I think you called round here before,' I say. 'You were talking to my mum.' I do admit to her official role now and then.

'Ah right.'

'The woman in the wheelchair.'

'Ah yeah, I remember her. And your surname?'

'Mouse.'

He looks up at me and for a moment I think he's going to hit me, but instead he backs away, angry head on him. He knows I know he's a fraud. I can catch a phoney from a mile away. Charming and calculated, if you've met one you've met them all. They ooze it. He makes his way to the waiting white van and drives off.

After five years inside Ollie is released and allowed to come home. He went in at sixteen and returns as a twenty-one-year-old. The remainder of his sentence is remitted.

I feel a sense of trepidation about his return, about who he will be when he steps in the door. What stranger will we be living with? But I also feel relief that he will at least now be given a chance to live, to have freedom, to go for a walk outside when he wants, eat when he wants, sleep when he wants. I worry for him that employers won't hire a young man with a criminal record, that the world will make it so hard for him to be the best version of himself that there will be a return to business as usual. I want to advise him to be wise, to be careful, to change, to take this second chance of life. To warn him that his prison sentence didn't necessarily end when the prison gates opened.

I want to show compassion for a man who has new-found freedom. I am ready to help him, to be the big sister he would never let me be. While he was counting down his weeks and days, I too was counting down mine, because I wonder if when he comes home it will mark the beginning of my freedom. Two of us here to help Lily means that perhaps I can pursue something else. After all this time, even I don't know what exactly, but I spend my days thinking and hoping.

Scrap that.

He comes home set for a fight. He takes one look at the house, at his room with the Star Wars duvet that she didn't throw out, and suddenly realises the time he's lost. He goes off like a grenade. And he blames me for this lost time because I wouldn't provide him with an alibi. He accuses me of being a scrounger, not working, living off Lily when everyone knows I never cared about her, and he bangs his bedroom door closed, the first time he has closed the door on himself in one thousand eight hundred and twenty-five days.

*

Lily and Ollie sit at the kitchen table looking at me. Two against one.

'It's unfair on Ollie,' Lily begins, 'that both of you are caring for me now and you get all the carer's allowance.'

'Excuse me? He brings you out with him for a few walks now and then, probably as a disguise because he looks less like a drug dealer with a woman in a wheelchair.'

'Shut the fuck up,' Ollie yells, one hand banging against the table, the finger of the other hand pointed close to my face.

It does startle me, and scares me, this sudden level of anger. I got no warning in his colours. He just explodes, a charcoal-coloured eruption, like gunpowder. Not black, I'm afraid of black in people, but it's scarily close.

'All right,' Lily snaps, pulling his hand away from my face, swatting it away like he's merely a silly little boy and not a recently released jailbird.

I swallow, feeling my insides tremble.

'Well,' I say, looking at Lily, unable to give him any attention. 'We can't pretend it's not happening.'

I can't tell by her face whether she knew it or not, what she was being used for. She's not an idiot but he can be quite deceptive. Especially with her; her baby Ollie can be so charming to her.

'I've given him plenty of my carer's allowance already to help him get on his feet,' I tell her. 'Loans which he owes me.'

'I don't owe you fucking anything. Jesus!' he pants, looking disgusted. 'Does family mean anything to you or are you running a bank here?'

'Does family mean anything to me?' I ask him through

gritted teeth, feeling the anger rise. I look at Lily, waiting for her to defend me. I will her to step in. She never has before, but I want her to now. I stayed here. I stayed. I did everything for her for the past five years. In fact you could argue I'd been doing it all before then too. What eight-year-old makes a packed lunch for her five-year-old brother? Not that he's grateful for it now.

'All we're saying is that you should let Ollie have the allowance and you can get a job.'

'This is my job. I'm not sitting around on my arse doing nothing.'

'No one will hire him.'

'He's barely tried.'

'Shut. Your. Mouth.'

'Ollie,' I yell. 'We're having a conversation. You're not some mob boss who gets to shout me down every time I open my mouth. So let me talk. I have been here. While you and Hugh were gone—'

'Hugh chose to leave. I didn't have a choice—'

'Yes, you did. Yes, you had a choice. You chose to break into that house, you chose to beat those people up, Ollie, you chose to steal from them. That was your choice. *Your* choice. And you were punished for it. I've been here. Here!' I slam my fist down on the table just as he did and feel the sting shooting up my arm. 'Taking care of things. You don't get to just come home and mould my world and my life around you. We talk about it like grown-ups in the real world, not like we're in prison. Do you understand?'

Silence.

My throat is raw. I hate that he's made me do that. I continue.

'If I give Ollie the allowance then I can't get another job. It's on file – an employer will see this. I can't be paid twice.'

'You're allowed to get another job as long as it's no more than eighteen and a half hours a week, if you want to be so prim and proper about it. Not that you wanted to do any extra work before.'

Oh, so she has suddenly done her research. This angers me. 'But I don't have eighteen free hours a week to work. I care for you full-time.' I can't believe I even have to tell her this; does she not see me here, doing everything, all the time? 'All the hours are logged in the system with the benefit officer; the information needs to be up to date and accurate. It's how we manage my allowance. And I tried to get a job at night, remember? You fell out of bed and shit yourself, remember?'

Ollie looks at Lily and smirks.

'Shut up, you. She left me. I had to try and get to the toilet myself, didn't I? You could get a job that pays cash,' Lily says. 'A job that doesn't log your hours.'

'What kind of job will pay me cash? Dealing drugs?'

Ollie angrily kicks the leg of the table. We give him a moment.

'A cleaner,' Lily says. 'You can make a good few bob cleaning houses. Sam gets fifteen euro an hour and they need her twice a week. And that's just one house. She does a few houses every day.'

I look from one to the other. They're deadly serious, they've discussed this, they've planned it.

'But I could be prosecuted,' I say. 'Benefit fraud – it's called defrauding the state.'

'Oh come on, don't be so dramatic! No one would know, and you'd hardly be the first one to do it. Why should we follow the rules when everyone else is breaking them?'

I look at Ollie. 'Do you know how much the allowance is?' I ask. 'Two hundred and nineteen euros a week. It comes in and it goes out on household bills.'

'Hugh sends me money,' Lily says, looking down and folding and unravelling the end of her blouse, before flicking an imaginary piece of fluff from her chest. 'She takes it for herself,' she mumbles, barely able to look me in the eye.

'How much does he send?' Ollie asks, euro symbols in his eyes.

'Fifty a week,' she says, looking at me accusingly.

She never had the balls to say this to me when he wasn't here, when she was all alone with only me to do everything for her. It's all coming out now.

'It's no secret,' I say. 'I withdraw the money because I'm in charge of the household bills. We agreed it would be more convenient.'

'I bet you did,' says Ollie.

'And there's my disability allowance, you take that from me too,' she says. 'That's almost one hundred a week.'

Ollie looks at me as if seeing me for the first time. 'You've been nicking all her money?'

'The money all goes out, Ollie, you can check the accounts. Most of it in direct debits for household bills, to you in prison—'

'My allowance pays the gas and electricity,' Lily says in a gotcha way.

'You've been robbing her money,' Ollie says again, not even listening to my reasoning, thinking I'm sitting on a golden throne here. 'You're getting hundreds a week.'

I roll my eyes, giving up. 'Why doesn't Ollie take the cleaning job?' I ask. 'He's the one with five years of cleaning experience.'

The words are barely out of my mouth when I feel Ollie's hand around my neck, crushing my throat.

Lily is screaming at him to stop, hitting his arm, pushing him with all her might, a frantic squeal from her like a pig at slaughter. I pull at his hands around my neck but to no avail, I'm not strong enough. It feels like forever but it's probably only a few seconds. And then just like that, he lets go.

'Say that again,' he warns.

'Get out of there,' Hugh says.

'I am out of there,' I say, pacing the rose garden of the Ormsby Estate and Private Gardens. I'd fled to the rose gardens as soon as Ollie released me from his grip. It was the first place I thought of. My membership card makes me feel like it's home; the fact you have to pay to get in makes me feel safe from Ollie and her. It's November though and there are no roses. It's stark and grey and skeletal, more like a rose graveyard. It doesn't give me the lift I need and I feel panicky again, a tightness in my chest. My throat is raw inside from the shouting and tender on the outside from being crushed.

'I mean get out of the house for good. Pack your bags and get out of there.'

'Then I'd be leaving her with him,' I say. 'Is he going to bathe her, dress her, cook for her? He has no idea, Hugh. She can't even reach the kitchen sink, she can't even make herself a cup of tea.'

'If she wants him to get the care allowance, then she'll get what she wants. How dare they?'

He's so angry I can feel the steam coming through the phone.

'How dare he lay his hands on you. Pack your bags and get the hell out of there.' I can hear Poh in the background asking what's going on. 'Ollie and Mum. What do you think?' he growls in response. But he's not being rude to her, his anger is directed at the thing that stresses him. I bet he wishes he was rid of us all. I bet his life would be so much easier. I imagine they lie in bed cursing us; the bane of his life. 'You've done enough, Alice, you've done more than enough. It's time to go. I'll take care of the rest. Contact your benefits officer, tell them you're no longer caring for her. Cancel that money. They're not getting their hands on your money. You don't owe them a damn thing. Just get out of there.'

Hugh has tried to get me to visit him plenty of times before but I repeatedly refused. Lily wouldn't travel and, even if I left her with her brother Ian, I refused to get on a plane, go through an airport. I avoid mass gatherings and closed environments like the plague, because that's what being in them feels like. Too many bodies writhing around with their messed-up moods and mixed-up emotions, herded together in close quarters like cattle, with no windows or fresh air, no sense of kindness or compassion for others. It's all about them getting where they need to go.

But I also desperately need to get away.

I wear sunglasses, a face mask and gloves. Hugh books two seats in the front row of economy so that there's nobody in front of me and I can have my space. It's a full flight. I manage to keep my distance from people as much as possible while passing through the airport, although I almost lose it with the woman in the queue at the security gate who's standing so close to me I can feel her breath on the back of my neck. At the terminal I sit away on my own in an empty gate beside ours. I avoid contact. I don't want to see people's woes or hurt, I don't want to get sucked into their pain and have to worry about why or how. On board I look out the window as the plane fills and the baggage is loaded. It's my first time on a plane and I've been dreading the flight, but not the destination. In a plane for eight hours with recirculated air. Farts, fears and feelings.

'Excuse me.'

I don't look up. I'm hoping the flight attendant isn't speaking to me. My heart thuds as she tries to get my attention a second and third time. When I'm finally forced to look up by her changing tone, she has friendly eyes, nicely framed in black kohl. Her name tag reads Gail.

'I'm sorry to disturb you, but we have a mother here who is separated from her daughter. These are the only two available seats together. Would you mind swapping? You can choose 14C or 18F.'

The mother's face is crinkled in concern, looking at me with big brown hopeful eyes. Her child stands beside her on the verge of tears. They hold hands tight as if their grip alone won't tear them apart.

'No.'

'Excuse me?'

'No,' I repeat firmly, then look back out the window.

Gail's colours change. 'I'm going to have to request that you swap seats,' she says, tone immediately altered.

'But you were asking me. You asked, and I said no.'

'Yes, and now I'll have to insist.'

'No,' I say. 'My brother bought me two tickets, these two seats. I'm not moving.'

The child, who is not such a child, looks around thirteen, starts to cry.

It's not my problem. They've made their problem, my problem. They've put it on me and I didn't ask for this. I look away, away from her fears and sadness, back out the window again. The man in the aisle seat on my row buries his face in his magazine, wanting nothing to do with it. She didn't ask him to move. Ignore the businessman, pick at the young woman because she'll be easier, more understanding, softer to the needs of a mother and child. Well I'm not.

'These seats are mine,' I repeat.

'I'm afraid it doesn't work that way,' she says, more firmly now. 'If nobody checks in then the seat is available, and it can be used by us for whatever means we wish.'

'I'm not moving.' I raise my voice. I shouldn't. That's a mistake. But I want them to understand that I would rather get off this plane than fly for eight hours beside someone else, their elbow bumping against mine, their personal space and my personal space intermingled. I couldn't do it, I couldn't survive.

Gail shuffles her way into the front row, crouches down closer to my level so that she's not making a scene. She invades my space and I yell. Everything goes momentarily crazy and all the crew gather around. The pilot comes out to see what's going on. The daughter is crying more now and the mother's upset and I wonder at what point are they both going to realise that they caused all of this, that if it wasn't for their own fears and insecurities, then the rest of us would be doing just fine. If they could just manage their own circle, their poison wouldn't pervade mine.

I think I'm going to be escorted off the plane, which is more than fine with me because the air is bad already and the door hasn't even closed yet, when a man and woman seated behind me speak up.

'We'll swap,' he says.

'Thank you,' I say to them both. I'm not a monster.

But Gail has had it with me, she's lost trust in me. She's worried I'll kick up again in the air and all hell will break loose. She stomps around, getting in huddles with her crew and discussing whether we should throw me off, how long it would take to get my bag off and if we'd make the take-off time. As the man leaves his seat behind me, he says, 'She's not doing any harm, she doesn't want to move,' and that's it, I've been saved.

Gail doesn't look at me for the remainder of the flight as she stomps around, slamming overhead compartments closed. I keep my face mask on and try to breathe slowly, closing my eyes against the recirculated stale energies floating around the air.

When we land in Doha, I'm asked to step into a room

beside the passport office. I remove the mask and glasses for the passport queue but replace it in the bright stuffy room. I assume I'm to be given a stern warning about air travel, but after sitting there for an hour without anything happening, I begin to wonder if I'm going to be arrested. I've really messed up now and Hugh will never want me back.

I hear shouting outside the door.

'Did it look to any of you like she wanted to be touched?' Hugh yells.

The door bursts open and I see the flight attendant, and a few members of security.

'Well? Does it?'

There's anger on his face, but it's not at me.

They all take me in. My mask, my gloves, my clothes covering every inch of skin on my body.

'No,' the security guard says, 'it does not.'

'Well, I didn't know . . .' the flight attendant begins.

'We're very sorry,' the security guard says, and opens the door wider. 'You're free to go now.'

'What now?' Poh asks gently.

We're sitting outside in November in twenty-eight-degree heat, she's drinking red wine, Hugh is putting the kids to bed. Again I think of Lily and Ollie mashed in the house together, but with less feeling of panic this time, like I need to go back and check on her. The physical distance surprisingly removes the deep concern I had and the ball of worry that sat in the pit of my stomach loosens and lessens. The further away we flew, the further the problem became. I can understand why Hugh did it.

'I've had five years to think about it, you'd think I'd know,' I say, embarrassed.

'I don't think you've had time to think about anything at all,' she says, understanding. 'Maybe that's just what you need. What do you want?'

I pretend to think about it, but I know, I've always known. I want to learn to shut down the part of me that sees inside people without their permission. Until that happens, I can't see a way through.

Before I fly back Hugh makes a few arrangements with the airport for me to travel home with special assistance, a man who keeps his distance and respects my personal space, only speaking when he is directing me. He has a quiet word with the flight attendant when I take my seat, a polite nod and then he leaves. I'm left alone all the way home.

I remember the punch of Lily's words when she told me Hugh was leaving for college, how stupid and left behind I felt. I'd thought things would always be the same, that people would be static like me, but I was wrong. It had happened again when Gospel left for football, and Saloni left for greater things, when Hugh headed to Doha. I've never known where I'm supposed to be or what I want to do, but I knew there would come a day when I'd have to leap off my stepping stone.

Ollie was right about my stealing. I'd been taking Hugh's weekly household contributions, withdrawing the cash and putting it into a separate savings account in my name. Fifty euro every week for five years. I had never once, not even when we really needed it, dipped into that account, and I now have it all waiting for me, for the moment I'm ready to take my turn.

The Cock Tavern. Liverpool. I order a still water and sit by the fire. A woman in her fifties with rippling muscles in her shoulders and arms has been flying around the bar collecting glasses and banging greasy bubbling buttery shepherd's pie and chips down on round tables as if her feet have wheels. 'Don't touch the plates, they're hot,' she says to everyone, holding them herself with skin like leather. She pours my spring water into the ice-filled glass, then slides the glass along the polished wooden table to touch my hand. 'There's your water,' she says. Her hand is hot as it brushes mine, nothing to recoil from: she's kind, focused, hardworking. A grafter. I realise though, with that gesture, she thinks I'm blind. I'm wearing my sunglasses, perhaps an odd thing to do on a December night in rainy Liverpool, but I'm snug in the corner, beside the fire, being shown kindness.

Three men are playing a card game. I know nothing about cards or how to read them, but I do know how to read people. I can't see their hands, they keep them literally close to their chests, not that seeing them would help me in the slightest.

The man with a large nose with such visible pores it looks more like a giant strawberry eventually sees me watching.

'You want to play, love?' He has an Irish accent, mixed

in with Liverpool. He's wearing a tweed cap even with the heat in here, and his moustache is so bushy you can't see his mouth. It's like an upside-down broom.

'I don't know how.'

'Same as these fellas.'

They all laugh.

'Oh don't go near them, love,' says the woman serving, 'And don't drag her into your dirty tricks, Seamus.'

'Dirty tricks,' Seamus says, in mock wide-eyed horror, which makes me laugh.

I watch them some more, not feeling in the way, enjoying their camaraderie, their intensity, their highs and lows, until it's finished.

'You jammy bastard,' the skinny lad says to Seamus, standing up to leave.

Seamus chuckles. 'Can't be jammy if I win every time. Are ye scuttling away now? Too afraid, or will we go one round more?'

They back away, grabbing their coats, hats and caps, and shuffle out, sharing good-humoured insults with each other. He's left there alone, looking at the cards on the table. He studies them, serious now, analysing the game. It's closing time, I should probably leave.

'You lied,' I say.

He looks up at me.

'About your hand,' I say.

'In poker it's called bluffing. Will you have another drink? Nic?' he calls over his shoulder to the woman.

'Water, please,' I say.

'I'll have another one,' he calls.

'You will not, you've had enough,' Nic shouts back.

He rolls his eyes at me, pulls out a chair opposite him and I take it as an invite. I sit down and look at the cards still laid out where they dropped them. Nic eyes us, figuring out I'm not blind, then probably wondering if I'm not blind, what's with the glasses. Through narrowed eyes that have seen pretty much everything, she watches.

'It's called Texas Hold 'Em,' he says gently, and without my even asking he takes me through the rules, and each move he has just played.

'And this is where you lied,' I say, as we reach the part, the turning point where he raised the bet.

'Bluffed,' he corrects me again, but he looks at me, impressed. He gathers all the cards together, shuffles them, while his eyes don't move from mine, scanning me as if I'm a card hand he's trying to decide whether to play or fold.

He takes a card from the pack and holds it close to him.

'I'm holding a seven of hearts.'

'Lie.'

'Bluff. There's no lying in cards. Thanks, love,' he says as Nic places a straight whisky down on the table for him anyway and a water for me. 'This is Nicola.'

'Everyone calls me Nic.'

'Hi,' I smile.

'Sure you don't want something else?'

'I don't drink.'

'Well now.'

'Every publican's nightmare,' he jokes.

'You're the publican?'

Nic coughs dramatically.

'She's the boss,' he says, smiling.

He puts down the card and randomly selects another. 'Three of clubs.'

I watch the air around him. No flash, no metallic, no tarnished colours.

'True.'

He reaches for another. 'Six of diamonds.'

'True.'

'Jack of hearts.'

'Bluff.'

'Jesus Christ, how do you know that?' he says, finally revealing his feelings.

I shrug. 'I just know.'

'Is it my face?'

'You can barely see your face.'

'Ha!' Nic says behind the bar and chuckles an evil one.

'What is it then?' he asks.

'It's your energy,' I say, thinking he'll laugh, throw me out, call it a night.

'My energy,' he says, watching me. 'My father, rest his soul, knew a fella like you. He worked with him. He used to talk about him. The quare fella, he used to say.'

'Quare?'

'Queer, quare.'

'I'm straight. Not that it's any of your business.'

'No, not that quare. Strange,' he says, shuffling the cards again, one eye on me, one eye on them, if such a thing was possible. 'One of those people with a gift. He saw things. Felt things. He had one glass eye that went that way,' he alters his eyes. 'At least you don't have that,' he says. 'Or maybe you do – can't see beneath the glasses.'

I take off my glasses. Squint a little, even in the dimmed pub light.

He examines my face and his eyes fill with tears.

I'm not the only person in the world to have the skillset that I have. No, there are others who are afflicted with the same poison, only unlike me or society in general, others don't view it as freakishly weird or the poisonous curse that I see it as.

A mother who knows instinctively when a man is bad for her daughter; a mother can always see what's behind the charm, sees the face behind the mask. If she doesn't see it, she feels it. When a police investigator follows their gut on meeting a person, or watching someone, when they hear an alibi and immediately know it's not right, when their head starts reconstructing the words and pairs them with the truth. Or the women who know not to go down the dark, quiet lane alone at night, when they listen to the hairs that rise on the back of their neck when it looks like they're alone but they're not. These natural instincts are there for a reason, we all have them because we need them; since the beginning of time they have been central to our survival. Modern life has made us forget them, but they're still there, more alive in some than others, dormant and waiting to be tapped into.

Or a father when he hasn't seen his daughter since she was seven years old, weeks before her eighth birthday, and sixteen years later when she walks into a room he instinctively knows it's her.

*

'Hugh told me there was something special about you,' he says, dealing the cards, stealing glimpses of me when he can. I leave the glasses off. I want him to see me. I want him to see the time that has passed since we last saw each other.

I'd known Hugh had kept in contact with him over the years, I'd chosen not to.

'I think Hugh is the special one,' I say.

'You always did,' he says, smiling. 'Followed him around like a pup. Wanted to eat what Hugh was eating, wanted to play with what Hugh was playing. And he'd let you; he was always great with you. So patient and kind with you.'

'He hasn't changed.'

'Good. I always knew you were in safe hands with him.'

We leave a long pause, which says what neither of us wants to say. I don't want to do it, to be that predictable, show up after close to twenty years with bitterness and recriminations. But even I am an earthling, after all.

'You shouldn't have done that to him. Left him to take care of us like that. You knew that she wouldn't be able to.'

He looks at me, pained expression like he'd rather talk about absolutely anything else but this.

'I didn't think she'd be a bad mother, Alice. She was a bad wife, a bad person, but I thought me leaving would mean she'd at least have to be a good mother.'

'That's an interesting risk to take, but I suppose you are a gambler.' I don't say it with spite, it's just an observation.

'It's an appalling truth and I'm sorry. I couldn't spend another minute with her. I think we would have killed each other. It was dark. I was supposed to move away, get set up, take care of myself so I could take care of ye, but . . . I don't know, time passed, and nothing I had was ever

127

going to be enough for you. Couldn't have you sleeping on floors, or couches, couldn't find a job where I could care for you full-time. I asked her if I could see you during the summers, some weekends. No, no, no – it was always no. I kept sending you what I could. You got the cards and that?'

I nod.

'She wouldn't let me speak to you when I rang. It always ended up in an argument with her. So I stopped calling.' He takes a moment. 'Hugh stayed in touch. I'm sorry I didn't try hard enough with you and Ollie.'

Seamus deals. 'The idea is to construct your five-card poker hands using the best available five cards out of the seven. The showdown is when the remaining players reveal their holdings to determine a winner. The player with the best hand wins.'

'But you didn't have the best hand,' I say.

'If you don't have the best hand,' he says, 'then bluffing will get you there. But it's always better to have the best hand.'

We play for hours. Then for hours the following night and the night after that. I lose when he has the best hand, I win when I can call his bluff. Every single time.

He likes playing with me, not because he likes to beat me but because he knows he can't rely on his bluffing, which is really his strong point. Playing with me helps him get better at getting a stronger hand. He's frustrated when I call his bluff. It's not just his colours that give it away; his strawberry nose speckled with large hairy pores gets irritated.

He tells me the same thing time and time again. 'It's not enough to rely on a person bluffing, you can't rely on other people's weaknesses, you've got to work on your own strengths.'

'But what if seeing other people's weaknesses is my strength?' I say, frustrated.

He stops and smiles. 'Hmm. Then you're ready.'

'Ready for what?'

I can't play poker, that much is obvious; all it would take is for everyone to play without bluffing and for my hand not to be as strong as theirs, which it never would be as I can't get my head around the strategy of play. But I can read people better than Seamus and, while it's a crime to read cards, it's not a crime to read people. Maybe there's a job in reading people's joy after all.

I go with him to his next card game. I sit in his eyeline, and when I see that sharp metallic flash of lightning as they call or prepare to call, we have a signal. I take a sip of my drink, put it down to the right of a beer mat for honest, to the left for bluff. We share the winnings.

The greatest lesson I take away is that, despite the fact Seamus is a master bluffer, that is not enough. I'm a master at reading people, but that too is not enough. I can't rely on a bluff to win, I need to learn how to play.

'Tomorrow, we're going to make a fortune,' he says, a glimpse of his bottom teeth below his large moustache the only sign of his huge grin.

'I thought we'd already made a fortune,' I say, thinking of the bag full of cash hidden in the bedroom of Nic's guesthouse that makes me excited and nervous just looking at it. He is giving me half of all his winnings.

'Oh you ain't seen nothing yet, baby,' he says, happily rubbing his thick hands together.

Up until this point we've been playing in 'home games', which are often played after hours in the back rooms of pubs, or people's houses, a friend of a friend's garage. The daughter no one has ever met attending with him didn't raise eyebrows as I thought it would; maybe they'd have been suspicious if it was his son, but I'm not the kind of person they distrust. Weird maybe, with my sunglasses and gloves, but that's what makes me blend in; the special girl sitting with Daddy. Only once during a game does somebody suggest I'm cheating: a man who lost a pile of money and blew his lid. But he was quickly quietened by the other players, and his son, who was sitting beside me.

'Da, I can't even see your cards from here, how can she?'

He'd apologised to the simple girl, the odd girl.

'Are we cheating?' I asked Seamus on the drive back to the pub and guesthouse, and where he lives. He doesn't drink while playing, he likes to have his wits about him.

'Reading cards is cheating. Do you read cards?'

'No. I wouldn't understand even if I could see the cards.'

'Then we're not cheating.'

I stay with him longer than planned. I stay for Christmas, deciding I don't want to spend my first Christmas away from home alone. Besides, I like the company of my dad and Nic. I like her four children, who help run the business: one a chef, one the pub manager, one who runs the guest house, and the glamorous youngest who works at reception, screwing things up for everyone, and would rather be in Hollywood than there. They don't need him but they tolerate him, for the sake of their mother's happiness. He makes her happy, I can see that. And I can also see why he stayed.

I call Lily on Christmas Day.

'Where are you?' she asks.

'I'm staying with a friend.'

'You don't have any friends.'

'From school. You don't know them.'

'Oh. Well, are you coming back?'

'Do you need me to come back?' I ask, concerned about her.

'You can come back and sort out the mess you made for us,' she says, with a snap. 'You didn't have to cancel the allowance – they wouldn't have known you weren't even here anymore. Sure, who'd notice?'

'Tell her not to show her fucking face around here again,' Ollie yells in the back.

'Call me if you need me. Happy Christmas,' I say, and end the call.

Seamus has a game set up at the Leo Casino with some big hitters. I don't exactly know what that means or what the stakes are, but I can tell it's big. We're due to attend at 8 p.m. He's excited, thinks he's going to hit the big time, wonders why I don't seem to have the hunger he has, why using my skills for money-making wasn't the first thing I thought of. Someone like him is always looking for a fast way to success, spending more money on lottery tickets than bettering himself. Investing in the easy way out.

I don't know what my aura-seeing is for, but I know it's not for this.

I go to my room, pack my things, leave an envelope with money on the desk, a generous donation towards the cost of my stay. I'm halfway to London by the time we're supposed to be playing.

green

THE NIGHT TRAIN TO London is quiet. I choose an unoccupied table for four so I can put my feet up. A woman gets on the train with a little girl, who I assume is her daughter. The mother practically shoves the little girl away from her and into the chair diagonal to mine, of all the empty seats to use, while she dumps her bag next to her and puts her feet up on the chair in front of her.

I immediately take mine down.

The mother's colours are familiar. So are the child's. The girl's face is sullen, dark eyes, light in colour but dead somehow. Sad eyes, black rings beneath. I watch the mother. Her lips are moving as though she's talking to herself, but no words are coming out. She shakes her head a few times, disagreeing, losing the argument with herself and refusing it. The little girl sees me watching and is embarrassed.

I smile at her.

Suspicious, she looks away – and I don't blame her. She doesn't need an over-friendly, freaky stranger on a train adding to her list of woes. I look out the window again, and come face to face with my own reflection in the dark sky. I feel her eyes on me. I see them on me in the reflection.

135

Her mother reaches across the aisle and whacks her arm. 'Don't stare,' she says, though she too gave me a good long unfriendly look when she sat down.

'It's okay,' I say. I'm wearing sunglasses, a face mask and gloves, I suppose that's not normal. They both watch as I take the face mask off, probably expecting to see a monster beneath. The mother's colours are dark green, sludgy, not an evil black but dark enough to worry about. Inside it swirl red mists of anger, like the eyes of a creature buried in the darkness of a cave, threatening to emerge. She is emotionally unbalanced, that much is clear. I feel for both of them, a sympathy for a woman I never could feel for my own mother. How can she be expected to mother when all of that is going on inside of her? Bored of me and back in her head, the mother picks up the silent conversation with herself.

There's so much I want to say to the little girl and I don't know where to start. I want to ask her if she's okay. You hanging in there? I wonder if there was ever a stranger who looked at me this way, who may have noticed an atmosphere between me and Lily, but I wasn't aware of them looking. I always thought we did a good job of keeping it together. All in my head.

The mother stands suddenly and grabs her bags. I sit up, as does the little girl, perhaps always on tenterhooks. All the things I could have said.

'Be kind to her,' I say out loud, my heart pounding in my chest.

*

Perhaps it's an odd decision of mine to move to a huge city of almost nine million people, bustling with the very beings I try to avoid every day. Perhaps it's a kind of exposure therapy. For so long I have avoided people, I have built up a phobia of them. I don't want to get mixed up in their emotions, I want to be left alone. I don't want their problems to become mine, but I don't want to be alone either. I've got to find a way to live with people, to be among them. Hugh has told me this for years. I guess in theory it's what the academy was trying to prepare us all for, but it's only now that I feel ready. Plus it's easier to get lost in a crowd than to stand out alone, and I'd like to disappear and begin my own life.

I'm in a bar in London. The Laughing Bishop. It's happy hour from 5 to 8 p.m. and it's filled to the brim, all the way outside and onto the pedestrian street. It's noisy, people are shouting over the music, over each other, loud laughter that must hurt the backs of their throats. They've come straight from work, excited to be free for the weekend, maybe one or two scoops has become a few more. Some colleagues drink together, straight from the office; you can tell from their body language, their look of uniformity, their conversation, a little more restrained than those who have broken away from the office to meet with outsiders.

I sit in a booth alone. I've had to stop so many people from joining me and taking the chairs; in a room this busy I need the space around me.

'There's somebody sitting there,' I say of the chair with my bag on it. 'I'm waiting for someone. She's in the toilet. They're on the way. He's outside smoking.' Just a few of the excuses I use. It's okay at first, but as the place gets busier it's more difficult to keep the wolves at bay. They're surrounding the table, moving in on my turf, leaning on the backs of the chairs, bums resting on the arms. Coats and bags piling up on empty chairs. They eye up the empty booth in the busy bar, eye me up with a glass of sparkling water before me. I'm not wearing my gloves and face mask here; I'm not that stupid.

I hold my ground for as long as I possibly can and in that time I watch the interaction of the crowd. I love people-watching and I'm in prime position. The life and soul of the party, the quiet ones, the shy ones, the strategic ones, the excited, hyperactive ones. All grouped together, shooting out colours at their targets like a game of Space Invaders. Colour-wise, I focus on the predominant colour, the main mood being projected. All the other stuff is inner and quieter, the parts nobody wants to share in a busy bar during happy hour. Not with colleagues, anyway. The only exception: two women in the corner of the room, sitting close, heads together and haven't looked up once, their inner colours becoming brighter and brighter as they share, their moods changing according to what is being shared. Spilling their emotional guts out on each other. I see intestine-like long stringy tubular strands of energies. A woman sits alone on a high stool at the bar, eating peanuts from a bowl, drinking a glass of white wine, scrolling through her phone. She's wearing a grey pencil skirt and a blouse, a jacket hangs on the back of the high stool. An office job of some sort, I guess, her sleeves are rolled up, her long hair is down and gathered to the side over one shoulder.

A man who's part of a group of guys, colleagues I'm guessing, eyes her. He stands with a group of three men, half-listening to what they say but mostly looking around for something better and more interesting. He looks at the women to his left, a good look at them and away again; no, they're not to his liking. He checks out the woman to his right: no, a little too dorky-looking for him, in my opinion. He's quite cool. Slick. Handsome. Stylish. He scans the room and our eyes meet. Immediately disinterested, he looks away quickly, sips his drink and joins in the conversation, pretending to know what they're talking about. Ouch. Then when enough time passes, and his friend talks for too long about something he's incredibly animated about, his eyes start to wander again. Sends signals out to the woman on his right. She looks at him and away again. Signal blocked, it lingers there around her before dying. Then he sees the woman at the bar. It's inevitable he'd find her. She's gotten the most attention in the room and she doesn't even know it. She's perfectly happy in her own world, holding court without knowing it. He says something to his friends, downs his bottle of beer and goes to the bar to order another round.

He does an extraordinary thing. He stands beside her for a moment as if genuinely not noticing her, but he's very close to her. Slowly but surely his colours start to change, like an iguana. They become an exact mirror image of hers. A phenomenal spectacle I haven't witnessed before. When his colours have completely transitioned, she looks up as if sensing him. He says something to her then and she laughs. They speak for a short moment and then he brings the beers back to his friends. As he walks back to them his colours slowly return to normal, to be in synch with theirs and when he goes back to join her, his colours return to her colours.

She is immediately comfortable because she feels that he is like her. How many times have we thought being in someone's presence has felt so familiar, as if we've known them all our lives. Even I have felt that.

I draw on a notepad as I watch them. I draw lines as I see them, the energies they are all sending out to each other, who is sending it, who is blocking it. I use different colour pens to represent the colours being sent out. Single lines representing the rays moving in the same direction as a person, with arrows to show the direction it's moving in. I draw a vertical line at the end if somebody blocks it, if it falls short of the intended party. I draw hooks at the end of those lines where the person is possessive and manipulative; some rays are misty, and I sketch those secretive rays in pencil.

At the end of happy hour I look down at my drawing. It's a series of scribbles and lines that looks as if it's been drawn by a toddler, but to me it paints the perfect picture of the scene before me. I leave the bar as the two women in the corner dry each other's tears, and as the woman and iguana's colours begin to combine.

•

I lie on the floor of my new flat listening to the new sounds. The flat didn't come furnished, but that's okay, that's what I wanted. I couldn't sleep in another person's bed, covered by a patchwork quilt of lingering energies; twisting, turning and tangled up in somebody else's fears and excitements. I'd scrubbed and cleaned every single inch of the small flat that first weekend, then slept with the balcony door open, watching the particles of every human being who'd lived here since the place was built in the 1950s drift away.

My neighbours begin another screaming match. He seems to be the instigator of these things. There's crashes and bangs, doors slam and something smashes.

Monksrest Tower is a twelve-storey block of council housing with sixty flats. It's an ugly building, designed in the brutalist style with large sections of exposed concrete, part of a cluster of a public housing, with low rise council blocks surrounding this one, all with the names of saints. My flat had been purchased under the right-to-buy policy and is being privately rented out. It's had a fairly recent makeover, with cheap new carpets and painted walls. It's a basic one-bedroom flat and it's all mine. London is expensive, and despite my savings and my winnings from Liverpool, I will need to find a job imminently.

I'm excited.

I look out the window as sirens roar and a line of emergency vehicles race by, not for my neighbours but for some other catastrophe, somebody else's drama. It may seem a bad choice for me, to be boxed into a building of sixty flats, but it was named Monksrest for a reason. Despite the human mayhem inside the building, the land itself glows. I guess the clue is in the name. There is a quiet hum, from the generations of quiet, contemplative people who dwelled here centuries ago. This tranquillity is being tested by my neighbours, but the land is good, the foundations are good. I felt a kind of peace envelop me when I arrived for the viewing, stepping away from the chaos of the city to the calm of the tower block.

The yelling next door reaches its climax and a baby starts to cry. He yells one final time at her, not in English so I don't know what he's saying, and my wall shakes as their front door slams. I reach for my sunglasses on the floor beside me and put them on. I watch the gap under my front door as a pale light appears, gets stronger, brighter, then a hot red fills my door and lights up my room in scarlet red for a brief second before passing again. I remove my glasses. Sirens in the distance. My kitchen tap drips. I eventually fall asleep.

Clearview Academy tours are always stressful for everyone involved. Taking a predictably unpredictable group like us out needs to be highly organised and managed. This year we're going for a hike. I'm the last off the coach for a reason; I don't like the vibes and, as soon as I put one foot on the ground in the car park, I change my mind and hurry back to my seat in the back row. Even when I'm shouted at by the two teachers and talked calmly to by Gospel, I refuse to get off the coach. It's just a hike up a pretty mountain with beautiful views, and I'd been looking forward to that, but now that I'm here, I'm not getting out. I huddle in the corner, and wait for them to come back. I don't even want to be here, I close my eyes and try to pretend I'm some- where else. I have an awful feeling that something bad is going to happen. It feels like the most evil place I've ever been to. It takes them hours to get back.

'It was just a walk,' Gospel says, banging his boots so that the mud falls off them.

I shiver all the way home, Gospel gives me his coat.

I have such a confusing reaction to the trip that I research the area with Gospel as soon as we get back to the academy. It was just a walk, all right, a walk where a lunatic asylum once stood, where desperate souls condemned to live the rest of their lives were experimented on with horrific methods that look like torture devices. I could feel the fear, confusion and madness as soon as I put my foot on the earth.

Gospel shudders reading it.

It's the first time a place, the land, has shown me its true colours. It teaches me a lot about how I feel because of where I live, the energies of the houses around me, the foundations, the history of the earth that I stand on. When it's time for me to find my own home, I vow to find a place that has a joyful spirit and good vibes.

I pour milk onto my Rice Krispies and listen to the snap, crackle and pop in the silent flat until it's broken by Hugh video calling.

'He won't stop crying,' Hugh says. He dangles a pudgy-faced naked baby in a nappy in front of the camera, legs tucked up like a chicken. 'Can you check his colours?'

I grin and move closer to the screen, taking in his rolls of fat on his arms and legs. He's not crying now, confused as to why he's being suspended in the air.

'He's beautiful,' I say. 'He's full of love and joy – stop panicking, Hugh, you've done this before.'

'I'll stop panicking when he stops crying.'

He pushes him closer to the camera again and all I see is a mouth and a tongue, red gums, short little fat fingers in his mouth.

'He's teething. And he looks like he needs his nappy changed.' It's so full it's almost hanging off him.

Hugh's face fills my screen as he sniffs the nappy. He makes a face, then winks at me, 'Honey? I need to speak to my wonderful sister, could you . . . ?'

I laugh.

'Hi Alice,' Poh appears. A tired mum but still beautiful, calm and strong; their children are so lucky.

'Hi Poh. How are you?'

'Busy with these *three* children,' she says, rolling her eyes and taking the baby from Hugh. 'Oh poor baby, the smell. Hugh! How long has he been sitting in this?'

He shrugs innocently and turns back to me.

I love watching them. Sometimes he just leaves the camera on as they make their dinner or go about their day or evening and I sit there watching and listening to the utter chaos, but the easiness of the chaos, the normality of it.

'Annabelle, come here and say hi to Aunt Alice.'

'Hi!' she says, brightly. 'I'm going to be a bee when I grow up.'

'A bee? Well that's a great idea.'

'Bye!' She hops down from his lap and runs away.

'A bee, impressive stuff.'

'I don't think there's one hiving community that will have her.'

'Do you ever dress your children?'

'It's so hot here, no one needs to get dressed, ever.'

'Oh boo hoo. I'm in London, in January, all the shades of grey.'

'Do you have to clean sand out of your nose and ears every single day?'

'I have no sympathy for you.'

He leans his chin on his hand and studies me. 'How are you?'

'Survived another night on the mean streets.'

'You look tired.'

'I just woke up.'

He looks at his watch to see if my waking time is acceptable.

'Did you buy a bed yet?'

'Nope.'

'You can't sleep in a sleeping bag the entire time. You should call the landlord and tell him you demand a bed. It's ridiculous. Do you want me to do it?'

'Hugh,' I laugh. 'I'm twenty-four years old. You want to call my landlord for me instead of changing your own kid's nappy?'

'Absolutely. I know you won't do it.'

'I'm fine. I like the sleeping bag. I didn't want the bed, I asked him to take it out.'

'You could have bought a new mattress. Do you know how much beds cost?'

'Hugh,' I say calmly, 'it's okay.'

'I'm just trying to help.'

'You're picking at me.'

'I'm sorry. Subject change. What have you got planned for today?'

'More job-hunting. I've got two interviews.'

'Text me when you've finished them. Have you heard from Mum?'

'Three voicemails a few nights ago. One telling me I'm a thief and to come back with her money. The second one she was crying, saying she needs me, that Ollie doesn't do things the way she likes and was gone from morning until night, and then a third telling me I'm a stupid bitch and she should have aborted me when she had the chance.'

'Jesus,' he runs his hands through his hair, taking the insults that were intended for me but didn't land. 'Why doesn't she call me with that stuff?'

'I'm her punchbag. I suppose I should feel honoured she's so comfortable with me.' I mainly felt sad for her while listening; she'd been doing so well with her pills, with modifying and balancing her moods. Now she's drinking again, and smoking, I can hear it in her voicemails. I don't know if she's stopped taking her pills or if she needs new ones, or if they're clashing with the alcohol intake or whatever else Ollie may be supplying her with, but the balance she struggled for so many years to find has been upset by his return.

'Ollie's not up to the task,' he says. 'But we all knew that.' He sighs, the weight of the world on his shoulders. He suddenly looks old, even though he's only thirty. Greying hair at the sides, he's spent too long trying to keep it all together for everyone. I don't want him to pack his life in, ruin everything he's achieved, to go back to her.

'I'll go back,' I say.

'You will not,' he says firmly. 'Promise me you won't.'

'Promise me you won't.'

'Oh I won't,' he says, and I can see and hear the anger swelling. 'Believe me, I never will.'

I misread him. I'm surprised. I can't see his colours on a video call, but I've spoken to him on the phone and seen him on FaceTimes more than I've seen him in the flesh over the past ten years and I've always known how Hugh feels.

'I'll talk to Ollie,' he says.

'Maybe it's time to ask Uncle Ian for help,' I say. 'He's her brother, after all. They could check in on her from time to time, start acting like they actually care.'

'Good idea.'

He rubs his face tiredly, exhausted by the responsibility. He has many responsibilities: head teacher at his school, two children . . . 'Families, eh?'

'Hugh,' I say, suddenly serious. Role reversal. 'You need to let go of them.'

I realise now that I absolutely have. I have absolved myself of Lily and Ollie, of my responsibilities. They are adults, they've dug their own holes. I'll not be dragged down with them anymore. It doesn't make it easy, in fact it's harder than anything, but it's my turn now.

'Yeah,' he says, unconvincingly.

I realise Hugh will never stop caring, organising every-body, trying to keep the heavy things light. It's in his colours.

Annabelle returns and stings Hugh, prodding a tiny pointed forefinger into his thigh. 'Ow,' he yelps in faux pain and falls off the stool onto the ground, leaving me staring at the fridge covered in the kids' art. Annabelle starts crying. 'Daddy!'

Poh comes running from another room with the baby on her hip.

Laughing, I end the call.

*

I never take elevators. That's a lot of trapped energy in a small space. I take the stairs. As I lock up, I notice my neighbour's door opening and, feeling awkward and unprepared for an introduction, I hurry along the corridor.

I'm no country bumpkin; Dublin isn't exactly a village, but I know my way around it, I know the quiet routes, the back streets and alleys where I can avoid a crowd. London is alien to me and there are people everywhere. I can't do any back-channelling until I figure out where I am. I try to avoid bumping into people on the busy sidewalks, avoid their colours and magnetic fields, knowing that I must look like a crazy drunk as I weave through crowds. As the fourth person brushes against my shoulder, I stop walking and stand still in the rainbow river that flows around me. Close to hyperventilating, I escape into a side street.

I fight the sudden childish urge to cry at the realisation of the magnitude of what I have come here to do. Living alone is both emancipating and terrifying. In an effort to drum up strength, I think of Ms Mooney for the first time in a decade. I think of Gospel and of Hugh, of the people who believed and still believe in me, who invested their time and energy into trying to make me listen to them and behave. Pep talk over, I step back onto the busy pavement and continue walking among all the glowing humans.

My first interview is at a shop called Comic Geek in Covent Garden. The place is crammed with comics, statues, action figures and merchandise. It's empty of customers and it smells of dust. There's a guy in his forties with a long ponytail, an open check shirt with a Simpsons T-shirt beneath. Bart is bare-arsed and Homer is strangling him. He looks up from his work at the main desk.

I take off my glasses and my mask but leave my gloves on, knowing I will have to shake his hand.

'Hi, my name is Alice Kelly. I'm here for the job interview.'

He looks me up and down. 'Right.' He wanders around aimlessly for a moment, as if about to do something but forgetting what, then returns to the same place. 'We'll have to do it here.'

'Okay.'

'So . . . like, do you have any experience working in a comic book store?'

'No.'

He stares at me for more.

'The notice said there was no experience necessary.' I clear my throat. 'I've spent the past six years working as a full-time carer for a severely disabled and mentally ill woman.' I take joy in describing Lily this way. 'She was very difficult.'

'So you'll be good with difficult customers,' he says.

'Actually, the notice said it would mainly be a stockroom job.' I'm trying to have as little to do with people as possible.

'Yeah, yeah, I basically need someone to help out with keeping the place organised. Opening stock, labelling, stocking, keeping the place tidy. I'm not so good at that. I could tell you anything about any comic in here though, you could ask me anything.'

He looks at me as if he wants me to ask him, challenge him. I think of Gospel's collection of comics and the lesson he gave me in the academy. 'Um. Who is Spiderman's nemesis?'

'The Green Goblin, everyone knows that,' he says, disappointed. 'I recently started an online shop. Caved to the fans, so that's a job in itself. Packing it up, preparing deliveries, that kind of thing.'

'Sounds good.'

'Are you a comic fan?'

'Not exactly an expert like you, but I'm aware of them.' I look around, not recognising any of the characters on the shelves. 'Of the main guys anyway. Batman, Superman, Spider-Man . . .' I suddenly can't think of anyone else. 'You know.'

'Hey, careful who you call the main guys, around here,' he says.

He looks me up and down again. A red swirl appears over the crotch of his trousers.

I sigh.

He goes through the hours and pay. 'Sound good?'

'Yeah,' I say, trying to remain optimistic.

'I'll show you around. The stockroom is back here. This way.'

He holds his hand out for me to walk first.

The main shop window is so covered with posters, shelving and action figures it lets no light in. It's a dusty and dark room that glows occasionally in spots due to the lingering energies of well-thumbed second-hand comics.

He's so close behind me he bumps into me when I stop walking. I keep going again and notice the red is swirling around his crotch, larger, building red hot like lava as he examines me as I walk ahead of him. At the stockroom door I step inside while he stands at the door, filling it and blocking it. It's a small windowless room, boxes everywhere, no sense of order. It could be fun introducing some structure, but I feel a tightness in my chest, that warning women have had to listen to from the second we came to be.

'No,' I say suddenly, not wanting to stay any longer. 'No thanks.'

I push by him, hurry out of the shop and walk until I'm far enough away to breathe.

'So you can't work with someone who desires you?' Hugh asks, trying to wrap his head around it.

He doesn't get it.

'It's not the desire that's the problem,' an impassioned Poh speaks for me. 'I'm glad you didn't take the job, he sounds like he was a dirty, horrible man.'

'Yeah, but that's only because she could see,' Hugh says. 'My point is most men desire women, but women work alongside them never knowing. Do you not take a job because someone is attracted to you?'

Poh looks at him in such a way it makes me laugh.

'No I don't fancy anyone at work,' he answers her silent question. 'Seriously, Alice will you turn down all the jobs where you know someone's in to you?'

'Only the ones where they block the doorways and don't keep out of her personal space,' Poh argues with more bite to her tone than I've ever heard before. 'Alice isn't most women. She *knows*. And she shouldn't have to settle for working in an environment where there's a dirty little penis throbbing its desperate energy all over her every day.'

It's the way she says it; she never speaks that way.

Hugh and I start laughing.

*

On the floor of the apartment next door there's a clay dish containing a white salt-like substance. While I've never seen who lives there, I immediately concoct the story that this person is a drug dealer and this is some sort of code for letting people know there are drugs inside. I've heard people coming and going at all hours of the day, so he's certainly running a business of some sort. On numerous occasions while I'm sitting on the balcony, smoke drifts from his flat over to my side; not normal cigarette smoke but not cannabis either. I'm no expert when it comes to drugs, but I didn't want to inhale it so I went inside and closed the door.

From a young age I chose not to take drugs or drink alcohol or caffeine, and I've stuck to it. Alcohol lowers inhibitions, and while socially I could do with relaxing, after a few drinks I could easily flop into other people's energy fields, and who knows what that would do to me. At school when I didn't have a choice over the company I kept and our proximity, I changed moods a dozen times a day, felt like a different person so many times it was nauseating. I've learned from those experiences. Even if people's energies are good, they're not mine. They're synthetic and they can disrupt my rhythm and my pattern. I've also realised that I'm a highly sensitive person – and I don't mean emotionally. My body reacts strongly to anything I put in it such as alcohol, caffeine, sugar, mushrooms and truffles. My heart beats abnormally, instantly palpitates, warning my body to be on alert, that I'm in danger, that there's an intruder within.

I've wondered many times if I suffer from the same afflictions as my mother, when my moods swing as violently as I've witnessed hers, but I know the causes of our mood swings are not the same. I pick up on other people's emotions, she is buried by her own. At least I can protect myself from others, she is hopeless against herself, having surrendered to the power of her thoughts a long time ago.

There's a knock at the door. With the chain across the door, I look through the peephole. Whoever it is, is blocking it.

'Yes?'

'Dimitri. From next door.'

The angry man who fights with his wife.

I reach for a pair of sunglasses, I have them all over the place, in drawers, in a pocket of every jacket and coat. I slide the chain across reluctantly and open the door a slit. He's a ball of prickles, I've seen him in action. Anger is his core emotion, it flies from him in spikes like a porcupine's quills, stabbing at predators around him with his fierce, piercing rage.

'Hi,' I say, hoping his porcupine prickles of anger won't launch themselves at me.

'I have a petition here signed by everyone in the building for next door. You're the only one left. Here.'

He slides a clipboard through the crack. I don't take it. I won't touch that pen, not if everyone has used it, not if it's been in his pocket, next to his petulant body. I wonder how many people signed the petition at will.

'Is he selling drugs?' I ask.

'Drugs?' he laughs. 'Is she up to that too? It wouldn't surprise me, crazy old bat. No, it's about those bloody chimes on the balcony. I've had enough of them. I'm taking the petition to the residents' association to get her to take them down. You're the closest to her, do they not drive you insane?'

'That sound comes from next door?'

His eyes widen. 'Are you signing it or not?'

'No,' I say, folding my arms. 'I like the chimes.'

'Sign the letter,' he says, shaking the clipboard that's still hanging in the air, teeth gritted in anger. 'You're the only one who hasn't.'

'They're comforting, they block out the noises you make next door when you're arguing with your wife.'

I start to close the door and he moves his arm out in time. Parts of his anger fire through the crack in the door before I close it. I grab a hairdryer and blow his red porcupine needles through the air and out the balcony door. I lean over the balcony bar as far as I can without falling over to see into next door. It's decorated with potted plants, which I stupidly thought were drugs. I'm reminded to get a move on with setting up my new balcony garden. Above the door, a wind chime blows in the gentle breeze. The red rage needles from Dimitri move towards the balcony and the chimes. As if sensing his proximity, a breeze blows and the chimes swing their legs and kick it away. The red needles drift away and up, up into the air.

I think it's time I meet my neighbour.

Naomi Williams, a retired midwife, moved to London from the Caribbean when she was six years old in 1960, a proud daughter of the Windrush generation. Salt-and-pepper locs rest on her shoulders, her face and smile are warm and welcoming, encouraging you to speak, to laugh, to share, to smile. Her presence is a warm hug on a sunny day, her home is a womb-like embrace, it holds you tight and

In a Thousand Different Ways

nourishes you. There are crystals all around the place, in random spots, in the corner on the floor, balancing on a picture frame on the wall, on the rim of a flowerpot.

'Come in,' she says as soon as I identify myself. I step over the salt substance outside.

'Himalayan salt,' she says, 'to purify the air. Some of our neighbours are cloudy.'

I sniff the air and smell the familiar smoke scent.

'I was burning sage,' she says. 'My last client was . . . troubled.'

I almost laugh at the ridiculous tale that I've concocted about her in my head. She is the very opposite of what I'd imagined. I take in the room and it's hard to believe it's the same flat as mine, in the same building. There's a portable fold-up bed in the centre of the room. It reminds me of Esme immediately and, despite Naomi's warm welcome, I feel cynicism for the fake guru wash over me. If you've met one, you've met them all. I remember having such hope that other people like me existed, people who could sense more than just what you see, but I've never met one, one who isn't lying, anyway.

'Tea?' she offers.

I could always leave. I should leave. I don't need another phoney wasting my energies, but I'm curious.

'Herbal, if you have it,' I say. 'No caffeine.'

'Peppermint, chamomile, hibiscus, raspberry, ginger, mushroom.' She looks at me. 'No, not mushroom. No psychedelics for you.'

I feel like I'm standing in an X-ray machine under her gaze.

'Take a seat, wherever you feel comfortable,' she calls.

I sit in a green velvet wingback chair with large button-holes, an orange blanket draped over the back. I'm not used to being in other people's homes. I've avoided it as much as I can, but here, it feels filled with positive energy while also feeling refreshingly cleansed.

'That was my mother's chair,' she says, placing a cup and saucer on a mosaic table beside me.

'She must have loved this chair,' I say, taking a sip and watching the glow around the chair I'm sitting in, feeling it hug me.

She pauses. 'Yes. She did. It was her knitting chair.'

I rub my hand over the orange blanket draped over the back of the chair. 'Lovely.'

'How did you know she knitted that?'

'How did you know I wouldn't like mushroom tea?'

'Lucky guess,' she says. She cocks her head to one side and examines me. 'Have you settled in well? I've tried to catch you a few times but I've been . . . unlucky.'

'I'm settling in fine, thank you. I've been busy with job interviews.'

'I see, and how are they going?'

'Not very well.'

'What industry are you in?'

'I was a carer, but I'd prefer not to work with people again.'

'Limits things,' she says, sharing my smile. 'Nature, perhaps,' she says, lifting her cup to her lips. 'Not mush-rooms.'

I laugh, to my own surprise. 'I'm here because Dimitri has a petition signed by everyone in the building to have your wind chimes removed.'

She looks surprised. 'Everyone?'

'Not me. I like them.'

'Thank you.' She looks out at them and they tinkle as if sensing the attention. 'Perhaps if they're bothering everyone, I should remove them. I wonder why nobody ever said.'

'I'm guessing they just signed it because he told them to. He's bringing the petition to the residents' association.'

She laughs at this. 'Of which I'm the president. That puts me in a predicament. I'll have to call a meeting with myself to discuss whether to remove a thing I love so dearly. But these meetings with ourselves are sometimes important.' She studies me over the rim of her cup as she sips her tea.

I shift uncomfortably in the chair, nothing to do with the chair. 'Like I said, the chimes don't bother me. I'm thinking of getting some myself, so it would be pointless for you to remove yours if mine will be even closer to him.'

'Alice,' she says. 'You be careful of him. Perhaps he could do with a free session with me. I'll sort him out soon enough.'

'Reiki?' I ask, feeling the flush of cynicism again. Esme, the fake guru, has left a bad taste in my mouth.

'Among other things. Reflexology, homeopathy, crystal healing.'

It all makes me hot with anger. All nonsense. Nothing works. Delusional people. Phonies. Con artists. I've heard enough. 'I should go. It was nice to meet you.'

Surprised by my abrupt end to the conversation she rushes to her feet to catch me.

'Maybe you could sit in on one of my sessions some time,' she says.

'Why would I do that?'

'To see what I do,' she says. 'To help rid you of that cloak of doubt you wear. You're too young to be so cynical.'

'You're not in trouble,' Esme says, sitting opposite me.

Her words don't do anything to relax me. We're sitting in her prefab, in the two comfy chairs by the window.

'You think I'm a fraud,' she begins. 'But I'm not. I'm not, perhaps, as good as you are, as naturally talented as you are. You see what I can feel.'

'You don't feel it.'

'I've trained at this for years. Do you know how long it takes to become a reiki master?'

'Training to do something doesn't actually mean you can do it. I think you've done very well fooling people into thinking you are this great wise one. Maybe you've even fooled yourself. Maybe you're clever at figuring people out, or manipulating people, but you don't fool me. You scattered Gospel's energies around like you had turned a mixer on without the lid. It went everywhere. He couldn't play football because you left the orange over his knee.'

She frowns. 'Orange. What does that mean?'

'It meant he couldn't play football that day. He's a striker who couldn't trust his striker leg.'

'Really,' she says breathily, kind of excited, instead of feeling the shame and guilt I expect her to feel. She leans forward and reaches out to take my hand.

I pull away.

'Sorry,' she says. 'Perhaps we could work together, Alice.'

I laugh. 'Work together? I'm fifteen. I'm a student.'

'Yes, but here in the school you could help your fellow students and friends, or after here, after school, I can offer you a huge opportunity. You can be my eyes. We could do it together. We could make a lot of waves in the world. We could make a lot of money, Alice. I could make you rich.'

Her excitement is causing a turquoise to develop, a dark turquoise that's beginning to take over. It's about personal status and glory. She doesn't want to help people, she wants to use people for her own personal gain. The harsh magenta of the wannabe guru has almost faded against the strength of the ambitious turquoise. Her desperation is embarrassing. My disappointment that she isn't the real deal takes me by surprise. I'd really wanted to find someone like me. I get up and leave.

Saandeep headquarters is a modern buzzy office building, dynamic and diverse, the Saandeep website brags, with over one thousand employees and two hundred shops in the UK and Ireland. They're looking for talented people to help keep pushing them forward with big ideas and big ambitions. There's a ping-pong table, an outdoor seating area with colourful seat coverings on giant steps. Long tables and benches for dining, sculptured trees in fancy oversized pots. White and wood, sleek like a Miami Beach restaurant.

By all accounts it's a vibrant and exciting place to be. It's empty when I step inside. Just security doing the rounds. It's 5 a.m. and I'm part of the cleaning team before the workers arrive, young, glossy and fashionable, gliding through security like a fashion parade. I watch them after my shift from a coffee shop across the road, not really thinking of anything other than how great they all look, how smart they must be, how exciting their lives must be, days filled with dynamic talk in smart meeting rooms with high-tech and ping-pong tables. I enjoy feeling their energy, fooling myself into believing that I too am a vibrant, dynamic, smart person, part of the team. I try to keep their energy with me all the way home. I experiment with my wardrobe, trying to become as stylish as they are. That buzz lasts me a while, until I'm standing in front of the mirror all dressed up with nowhere to go and realise I don't have any smart ideas, I don't have the platform to share them or the ears that will listen. I rapidly deflate at the realisation I have an empty day ahead of me and a cleaning job that won't pay the bills. I long for the feeling I get when I'm in there, even if the staff haven't yet arrived, because their energy of the previous day has been left behind.

I'm not sure why I've joined the cleaning team exactly; maybe self-sabotage, maybe curiosity, maybe desperation, maybe because I don't know to reach out directly. I hug the walls and slither along until I find a way in. I remember Saloni's parents pulling up to the school in their silver Maybach; to me they looked like movie stars. Her mother wore a coat draped over her shoulders, never put her arms through the holes, and I wondered how the coat would stay there. Her hair was rich and glossy, with designer clothes and handbags. Saloni's dad was so handsome, dressed in expensive suits and polished shoes, always with a smile on his face, blow-dried hair with a quiff, teeth so white. They both smelled expensive. Their skin looked filtered, healthy and glowing, so you knew their insides were as good as their outsides. With hundreds of fashion outlets they were the best models for their business, and they needed their compulsive liar of a daughter to get herself straight if she was going to have anything to do with their successful business. Saloni, Gospel and I, we were a team for that terrifying first year.

The head offices are situated in a busy part of London, right off Oxford Street. It's a good way to introduce me to the underground. The night Tube is quiet and I wear a cap, sunglasses, a face mask and gloves. I ensure that my skin is covered at all times and as soon as I go home I wash everything and hang it on the balcony to air everyone else's grievances off my clothes.

I clean Saloni's office. Dust her desk and polish her photographs, including a framed collage featuring almost every landmark in the world, the many photos featuring Saloni and her girlfriends travelling the world on hiking tours, water-skiing, skiing – a regular action girl. At only twenty-four years old, with the big job as marketing director, she has worked her way up the ladder of her family's business. She works hard and plays hard, maybe finally living out the multitude of stories she used to concoct.

As I'm cleaning the sinks, a toilet flushes, the door opens and Saloni steps out in gym gear and looks at me.

'I don't really get why you're here, Alice,' Saloni says, lifting her perfect Lulu Lemon arse in the air and in my face for downward dog. We're outside the grounds of the academy in the local village's park, ten of us doing yoga on the grass.

'To be in the moment. Or whatever.'

'Not *here*,' she says, smiling.

A playground is nearby; I can see the bright colours of the equipment peeping out from behind the trees. It holds the promise of fun and innocence, along with being dirty and seedy at the same time.

I know what Saloni means. It's been four weeks and I've been relatively normal compared to everyone else in Clearview. It turns out Saloni is not here for being a pathological liar but for her biting, which is her physical reaction to not being able to lie, and Gospel is not here because of Tourette's but because he's prone to violent outbursts. I haven't been the target of either of their aggressions, but it's been interesting, and at first surprising, to watch the rather grand and perfectly poised Saloni charging at someone who looked at her the wrong way and sinking her expensive teeth into their flesh. That only happened once; the rest of the time she's turned to her own arm, or a pillow, or whatever biteable furniture is around her. I know now where the term 'spitting feathers' comes from. Gospel is less violent with people and more so with objects. Chairs, tables, whatever he can get his hands on are transformed into missiles without a moment's notice. Neither of them can understand why I'm here. I haven't told them why either, and they've had fun trying to figure out what my 'quirk' is.

'She doesn't speak enough,' Saloni guesses.

Gospel laughs. 'You don't get sent here for not speaking enough.'

'Well she barely says anything and I know she can hear me. Hello in there,' she says, reaching out to knock on my head. I snap my teeth at her and she laughs.

'Girls!' Amelia, our yoga instructor, calls mid-demonstration from the top. We're in the back row, as usual. We wait until she's caught in another yoga move before talking again.

'Alice's not a talker, but maybe a stalker,' Gospel teases me, and we smile, because he's noticed how I watch people, silently. Observing all the time, figuring everyone out. Even now, as they continue thinking of all the things that could be wrong with me, I'm distracted.

'Stop talking down the back, please, and focus. Thank you.'

There's a man sitting on a nearby bench. He's half-hidden by a tree but autumn is asserting its power on the trees and they're less dense. I can see his colours more clearly than I see him. He glows. He's facing the playground.

'She seems normal,' Gospel says, 'or at least so far. But all of us seem normal.'

'There's nothing normal about you,' Saloni bites back.

'It's still early on for everyone to reveal their true colours,' he says. I look at him, surprised by how close he actually is.

'What?' he asks innocently. 'What did I say?'

'Saloni, Gospel, Alice, pay attention, please.'

The man on the bench near the playground has a bicycle beside him. His helmet is on his lap. There's a sandwich sitting on opened tinfoil on the bench beside him. But something's not right. There's a swirl of red over his crotch, I recognise the colour of longing from Hugh when he was with Poh, but I don't like this. It's the wrong colour, on the wrong body part, in the wrong place. Black swirls slowly above his head like a Charlie Brown scribbled storm cloud of deviance and pure evil. I've never seen black before.

I stand up.

'Hey, Alice, what are you doing?' Gospel asks.

I start walking towards the man on the bench. I need to make sure I'm right about what I'm seeing.

'Alice! Come back please!' Rachel calls.

I walk faster.

There's a toddler wobbling along the soft floor of the playground, the padded nappy the largest part of her. The man on the bench watches the toddler. She's surrounded by pinks and golds, beautiful, pure, innocent, happy colours. She's singing to herself as she picks up a leaf, throws it, picks it up again. She puts it on the swing. She pushes the swing. She takes it off again. She throws it on the ground. She wobbles away, forgetting about the leaf. She pauses. Then remembers, turns and returns to the leaf.

He watches her. The helmet on his lap. The red, harsh, harsh dirty red circling his crotch. The black is pure black, it flickers, I can almost hear it. Like an untuned radio, searching for frequency. Neither here nor there, just stuck in this black obscure out of bounds place. Dirty filthy man.

'Like little babies, do you?'

He looks up at me in surprise.

I lift his cycling helmet from his lap, see his hardness beneath and I fling the helmet at his head. The hard side connects and it makes a cracking sound. He falls to the side as I swing back again.

'Alice!' Amelia is beside me now, panting from her sprint over. Everyone has followed her. 'I said stay there!' she says to them, panicking.

They ignore her and follow anyway.

'You disgusting scum!' I shout at him.

The whole class cheers me on.

The mother picks up the toddler and moves away from the scene.

With an audience, I snap out of my rage and stop myself from swinging the helmet at his head again. Instead, I throw it down at his crotch, which has lost its overexcited red swirl.

'Gosh, Alice,' Saloni says. 'You *are* one of us.'

I've prepared for the possibility of bumping into Saloni, despite the hour and the empty offices. I have a story lined up, I've rehearsed a look of surprise that I didn't put two and two together, that this is her family business. But it all falls apart when it comes to it. Not that it matters. I don't need to drag out my alibis and explanations because she doesn't recognise me. She barely looks at me, our eyes never meet.

'I'll just be a minute,' she says politely, opening her gym bag. 'I've got to get dressed. A whore's bath,' she says with a wink. 'The shower in my office is broken again.'

I look at her, waiting for her to see me, wanting her to see me, to remember me. To rescue me? She senses my oddness, looks up at me, directly in the eyes, and still nothing. I shuffle backwards, out of the toilets, with my cart.

'You don't have to leave, I won't be long,' she says, pulling her sweaty vest over her head, down to just her sports bra.

I realise I'm staring. Her working out is paying off, her abs are toned, her arms and shoulders are muscular. She is more beautiful than ever.

'Work away,' she says, chirpy but firm now, running the water and cleaning under her arms.

Heart pounding, I move away from the sinks and into a toilet cubicle while I try to figure out what to say. But a silence falls between us as she washes and sprays and applies creams and make-up to make herself appear refreshed and dewy. Too many minutes go by and I can't say anything, can't even think of anything.

'Have a good day,' she says, gathering her stuff. She's dressed in tight grey pants and a cashmere grey jumper, incredibly high heels, looking expensive and sophisticated, her hair phenomenally thick, rich and shiny.

'You too,' I say to the door as it closes.

I would have known her face in any situation. I wouldn't have needed her family business to give her away, for a hint, or a reminder. I shared a room with her every night and day for almost a year, she was an important part of my life. I listened to every daydream and fantasy she ever had, and they were plentiful and fanciful. I look in the mirror at myself. Have I changed so much?

The door to Naomi's apartment opens as I put the key in my lock.

'I have a client in here now, if you'd like to observe.'

'No thanks,' I say, going inside and locking the door, wondering why it is that I see every part of everyone and most of them never see me at all.

I'm stirring my noodles in a pot on the electric ring, day dreaming, when like a bolt from the blue, I feel anxious. My stomach does a nervous dance and my chest pounds.

Hardwired from my Stone Age ancestors, I examine my surroundings to see what has caused my instincts to be activated. Apart from the murmuring coming from Naomi's flat next door, everything appears to be normal, still and quiet. I try to shake it off, take some deep breaths and return to my noodles. As I drain them off in the sink, I continue to feel unsettled, nervous, when only minutes ago I felt safe and completely at peace. I abandon the noodles to look around again. The thing I keep tuning into is the murmuring from the flat next door, which is really not unusual. Naomi usually has about three clients a day, spread out hours apart and, while I can't hear exact conversations, I always know when she has company. I press my ear to the connecting wall. She's talking in a calm soothing voice, there's no shouting or any obvious cause to worry, but I feel a terrible sense of dread. Without really thinking through what I'm doing, emotions before reasons, I follow my gut.

I knock on Naomi's door. She takes a moment to answer it but as soon as she opens the door the disquiet I'm feeling intensifies. It floods out of her flat and almost knocks me over.

'Is everything okay?' I ask, trying to see over her shoulder.

'Yes,' she says, turning around to view what I'm so desperate to see. She takes a few steps back and opens the door wider.

A man, an ordinary looking man, sits in her mother's armchair untying his shoelaces in preparation for his treatment. He's surrounded by the blackest of black colour that I've ever seen. So dark and heavy, I felt it emanating through the wall. The floor is covered in what looks like an oil slick.

Never have I seen such a scene since the blue days of my mother in her bedroom when she was so desperately sad. Her true sadness felt like it would rather hide, this black feels like it's hunting.

My body starts to tremble.

'I'm sorry to disturb you,' I say loudly to Naomi, so that he can hear me. 'But there's a family emergency and you have to leave.'

She nods, no doubt hearing my fearful tone. 'Okay. I'm sorry Larry, we'll have to reschedule this for another day.'

He pauses untying his shoelace and looks up at her and then me. Goosebumps fill every inch of my body. There's an unsettled awkward moment. I look at the oil slick all over Naomi's carpet. It, too, has paused. The door to the flat opposite opens and our neighbour, Ruven, appears. We all say hello to each other, the spirit of camaraderie breaking the thick atmosphere, as he locks his door. I ask Ruven a few more questions than usual to make him linger longer.

'Okay,' Larry says, tying his shoelaces. He's attempting polite but I can hear the edge in his tone. He's been slighted. His dastardly plans have been scuppered and he doesn't like it one bit. Ruven heads off, and I back away as Larry exits the apartment. I watch him pull his oil slick down the corridor behind him. He takes the stairs.

'Are you okay?' Naomi asks me. 'Can I help you?'

Ignoring her, I walk straight into her home and out on to the balcony. I watch the area by the main door, to make sure he leaves the building.

'How do you advertise what you do?' I ask.

'I have a Facebook page,' Naomi says.

'Don't,' I say.

'Okay,' she says, a little intrigued and a lot startled.

After a moment, Ruven appears. I'm holding my breath, Larry, if that's his real name, should be right behind him. A moment later he appears and I breathe a sigh of relief. He looks around as if he's casing the joint, the oil spill spreads out in the car park, then he looks up in our direction. I quickly step back inside.

It's rare to find pure evil, but you have to recognise when it finds you.

I transform my London balcony into a garden of Eden. It is sublime, if I do say so myself, and most of my neighbours have commented on it, apart from Dimitri, who complains of the bees it attracts, and of course, the wind chimes. I've installed a rainwater harvesting system by running a pipe from the gutter to feed the fallen rain into a barrel. From there I can simply remove the rainwater myself or, by using the pump system and a battery-operated timer, I can set it to water the plants at whatever time I want, for however long I want. I only use it when absolutely necessary, because by now I have learned that, even though my tomatoes need water, they don't always need the same amount at a specific time. Like people, I suppose, they have individual needs. I quite like the relationship I have when watering them; probably how a mother feels when nursing a baby. A moment of nurturing, a shared moment.

Who'd have thought I'd become the crazy woman who talks to her plants – but I have. I grow herbs: thyme, lavender, parsley, sage, rosemary and mint. I have bee- and butterfly-friendly wild flowers. It's such a busy balcony I barely have room to sit out on it, but I admire the view from inside. And oh the colours – and I don't mean from the petals themselves, but the energies that throb from the plants and flowers, the butterflies and bees when they're feeding each other. The giving and receiving is phenomenal, it's probably as close to an LSD trip as I'll ever have. It's like sound waves, a radio blaring on a hot day, the bounce of the bass speakers, the heat haze, the mirage on a road. It's like an optical illusion, an absolute phenomenon where the light appears to bend, changing all the rules of this light show I have the privilege of having a front-row seat to. Yes, at times like these, I can even call it a gift.

'You have to visit me,' I say to Lily.

'Just send me photographs.'

'It's not the same.'

'A balcony is a balcony,' she snaps.

'Well, it's a beautiful balcony,' I say, determined not to let her negativity chip away at me. 'Why don't you visit? I can show you where I live. Have a few days in London. When's the last time you were here?'

'I don't know. With your dad.' I count the seconds until she adds, 'The bastard.'

'The block has a lift, you can sleep in my room.'

'And where will you sleep?'

'On the couch. I don't care.'

'And how will I get on the plane?'

'Ollie can bring you to the airport. They'll have someone to assist you all the way through. People in wheelchairs fly all the time you know.'

She snorts, and I can tell this is a wasted conversation and she'll never come to visit.

'How's Ollie?'

'Fine,' she says, shutting it down completely, blowing out smoke.

'Is he there?'

'Yeah.'

'Are you smoking?'

'What of it?'

We leave a silence.

'What if I fly home and bring you here myself?'

There's a scuffling sound, the phone receiver is rubbed against something and Ollie's voice comes on the other end.

'You're not welcome here, you robbing bitch. You set one foot in this house and I'll finish what I started before you left.'

'Don't you dare speak to your sister like that, you clown,' Lily says in the background. 'Give me that back.'

I don't believe he'd do it but hearing these words come from his mouth makes me feel ill.

'Put her back on,' I say to him.

'Well,' she says, back again.

'Is everything okay there?'

She laughs. 'What do you think?'

'Lily, what's happening, is he caring for you?'

The door bangs.

'He's not here much,' she says, able to speak more freely now. 'He didn't get the allowance that you were getting. They wouldn't give it to him – I don't know why, don't ask me. He was on to Hugh about it.'

'Hugh never said,' I say, more to myself.

'Well, he wouldn't, would he. That's Hugh.'

'So because he doesn't get the allowance, he doesn't help you?'

'He does a bit.'

'I'll come home this weekend.'

I visit Lily for the weekend. It's been longer than it should have been. I'm not afraid of Ollie, he's my brother, my own flesh and blood, he wouldn't hurt me. Would he? Whenever I ask myself that, I remember the feel of his hand wrapped around my neck, how his fingers pressed on my windpipe, crushing it. It was only for a few seconds, but it made its mark on my skin and my mind.

I walk from the bus stop to the house feeling like a child on the way home from school, butterflies in my stomach with anticipation, tightness in my chest with anxiety. I used to live like this every day. My body was always rigid and stressed, and I didn't even know it until I left.

Trembling a little on the inside, I ready myself for attack, the definite emotional and the uncertain physical. The curtains are drawn, the door is unlocked. I step inside and brace myself. The place looks as though it's been ransacked, but it's the smoke that hits me hard. Stale and fresh cigarette smoke lingers in the air. Dirty dishes and glasses fill the sink. No pots or pans, nobody has been cooking. Lily can't reach the sink, and he hasn't been doing it. The bin is overflowing with takeaway bags and boxes, and it stinks. I go into default mode: I pull the bag out of the bin, throw it in the wheelie-bin outside and immediately start cleaning.

My row of plants on the windowsill are dead. I take them outside and place them on the ground, dead in their pots. It makes me angry. The grass still looks good; at least it's being cut.

I clean, I tidy, I scrub. I load the dishwasher and clean the oven, which is so thick with grease it makes my stomach heave. Nobody comes downstairs. Assuming I'm alone in the house, I go into Lily's bedroom not knowing what to expect. It's not as bad as downstairs, she has at least been able to control her own patch. She's asleep in bed. I quietly move around, picking up dirty clothes for the wash. Then gather the cups and mugs beside her bed.

When I see my aloe vera plant next to her bed, thriving, I cry quietly.

I am tired of feeling like a shadow.

I quit the cleaning job. London has made me feel like I'm here but apart from everyone. Surrounded by people but disconnected, as though I'm watching everyone else living and they're in the light and I'm not. Working by night, sleeping by day, not really living. This is what I wanted for so long when I was at home with Lily: to just get by and be left alone, it is my default, but I didn't move here to continue bad habits. Not when the people who once knew me can no longer see me.

I get a job at a call centre, Calling Card. With better hours, from nine to five, it pays more in this ridiculously expensive city, and I can wear jeans and a blue T-shirt with the company logo. My focus is on outbound calls. Our minimum calls per hour is ten but I'm making double that, and not for good reasons. I can't seem to keep anyone on the line to listen. While the guy to my left and the girl to my right trot out the sales spiel we've learned, everyone I get is too busy, isn't interested, wants to be called back later but then doesn't take the call later.

I'm in close proximity to a lot of people, which is difficult, but we're separated by partitions to give a feeling of privacy. There are two hundred of us in the room, ten rectangular tables of twenty, ten on each side, but they've been clever about how they've crammed two hundred people into one room, creating an impression of space when there isn't. It's a trick I need to learn, one of the great tips a city like London can teach me, but for once it's not the people that are the problem. It's the machines. The room is hot. I can't remove my T-shirt, I've no more layers to lose. I feel like there's no air, like I can't breathe. My cheeks are on fire.

'Can I open a window?' I ask Paul next to me.

He holds a finger up to stop me, he's talking on the phone. I waft my T-shirt and look around, as if expecting to find air.

'Thank you very much for your time,' he sings gaily, then to me in a different tone: 'The windows don't open, it's air con. Are you feeling okay?'

'I'm so hot in here.' Speckles of dots cloud my vision, I feel like I'm going to faint.

A trickle of sweat runs down my chest, between my boobs, soaks into my bra. I've a pounding headache.

'It's the machines,' he says. He looks at me, concerned. 'Have you got water?'

I toss my empty bottle on the table.

'There's chilled water in the tank in the corner, I'll fill your bottle,' he says, one eye on me, one ear in his headphones.

I feel a little less panicked now; his kindness has settled me, even if the heat is still unbearable. I look around. Everyone is glued to their screens, having conversations with strangers, using their skills to befriend and build trust in nanoseconds. Chirpy and helpful, despite what's happening to them. The colours around the monitors are hotter and brighter than their own. I watch the girl in front of me, Parminder, and I fight the urge to shout out as the energy from her computer reaches out to her, like an alien creature trying to suck her into the machine. Over the duration of the morning the red-hot colours have emanated from the computers and reached out to heat up everybody in the room. Whatever colours these people once had, they are now surrounded by a burning red, an added layer, like insulation, that is starting to burn through their colours, as if it's melting into their heads and torsos like hot lava.

'Ozone depletion,' Mr Walker, our science teacher, reads out the words on the whiteboard.

Someone groans. Everyone sits at tables of two, but they all know that I like my own space so I sit alone, wearing shades.

Saloni is in front of me with Gospel; she's twisting her hair around her finger, winding it so tight her skin goes white and purple, as if it's going to pop, then unravels it again. I can tell she's not listening. She looks earnest but I know that look: she's far away in her head, living a different life. In a prince's harem, one of his women, she's told me about that one before, or in a skyscraper in New York, running her own company. She has so many lives in her head it's no wonder the wrong one pops out when she speaks sometimes.

'What causes ozone depletion?'

'Avocados, sir,' Eddie shouts out.

The class laughs.

'Close,' Mr Walker says, trying not to smile. 'Manufactured chemicals, greenhouse gases such as methane, especially chlorofluorocarbons or CFCs, are known as ozone-depleting substances. The ozone layer prevents most harmful wavelengths of ultraviolet light from passing through the Earth's atmosphere. These wavelengths cause skin cancer, sunburn, blindness, harms plants and animals.'

He looks at the class for a reaction.

Most heads are on the table, looking out the window. Unaffected by his words.

'Where is the ozone layer?'

Nothing.

'I'll give you a hint. It's wide enough to wrap itself around the Earth.'

'It's Sully's mum, sir.'

'The ozone layer is high up in the stratosphere. If you look here' – he points to the projected image on the whiteboard – 'the ozone layer acts like a force field around the Earth.'

Saloni turns around and tries to catch my attention.

I ignore her.

She prods me with her pencil.

'Don't touch me.'

'Look,' she whispers. 'Him, outside. He asked me to marry him.'

'Stop, I'm listening.'

'Nerd,' she says, insulted, then turns her back again and resumes staring out the window.

My interest in this lesson is surprisingly piqued. I look at the Earth in Mr Walker's image. The ozone layer is highlighted like a green haze around the planet. It's like the Earth's energy.

'So the ozone layer is protecting the Earth?' I ask.

He seems as pleased to receive the question as he is to not receive one. He has switched himself off a long time ago. This school will do that to a teacher. 'It shields us from the damaging sunrays, yes, like the Earth's bio-field.'

'What's a bio-field?' I ask.

Some kids laugh, thinking I'm messing, deliberately trying to prevent him from finishing a sentence. He looks at me to decide whether I am or not and takes their view.

'Consider that your homework, Miss Kelly. Tomorrow you can tell me what a bio-field is. If you look at the next image to see the impact of CFCs.' He presses a button. 'This is the ozone hole.'

'Not as dangerous as Alex's hole, sir.'

He ignores that too.

'How do we know the hole is there?' I ask.

'Chemistry happens in the air. You can't see it, so you have to develop intricate instruments to measure its changes. It's measured in Dobson units.'

'Boring,' someone groans.

'But maybe that's for another time.'

'Or never.'

I look out the window and up at the sky, all the way up to the stratosphere. Above all of our energies, I picture a giant green haze around the Earth, an outer layer like we're living in a snow globe. I wonder, if I ever travelled that far, could I see it and if so, I wonder what colours would the Earth have. Would it be in pain like most people, would it have joyful colours? What possible jealousy could the Earth hold? Fascinated by the idea, I more than anything want to see its aura. Or maybe I don't need to see it, maybe just as it is the case with everyone around me, I already feel exactly how the Earth feels.

'*A bio-field is an energy blueprint that surrounds living systems. It's the matrix that connects our physical, emotional and mental dimensions,*' Gospel reads from the computer later that day when we're doing our homework. 'Whatever that means.'

I write it down, then look back up to the monitor at his Google search. His question, *what is a bio-field*, has prompted more questions.

'*Do humans generate a magnetic field?*' I read aloud. 'Click on that one.'

'*Every organ and every cell has its own field,*' he reads in a mock-dorky professor way. '*Neurons, endocrine and muscles are called excitable cells, as electricity stimulates them, creating a magnetic field.*' He pushes imaginary glasses up the bridge of his nose. Twitches. Throws his head back. Grunts.

'*Can humans glow?*' I read.

Gospel laughs and starts reading. '*Scientists now say that the human body literally glows,* what the . . . ?' He drops the dorky professor voice. '*Research shows that the body emits light one thousand times less intense than the levels to which our naked eyes are sensitive.* That's some weird shit.'

'That's why I'm here,' I say, ready to tell him, my face flushed with exhilaration at this discovery. 'I can see people's light, their magnetic field, whatever it is they call it. It's easier for me to say that I see people's colours. The colours are a reflection of people's moods, like blue for sad, pink for happy, but it's more complicated than that. The colours give me a headache. That's why I wear the sunglasses.'

He takes a moment to see if I'm joking and, for some reason, he decides that I'm honest.

'What colour am I?'

'Honey,' I say, smiling.

Paul returns with a bottle of chilled water.

'Thank you.'

'No problem. Usually people are freezing in their first week. The air con is constantly on full blast. With the high heat levels from the computers, it has to be. It's not for us, though, it's so the computers don't explode.'

I look around the room, at everybody's bodies being slowly hacked at by the computer's rays, suddenly understanding something that I hadn't grasped before. Our energies are like the ozone layer, and the computer's energy, the electromagnetic energy, is like CFCs that sear through us all, like a hot knife through butter, making a hole in a person, the bit around us. The bit you can't see. The bio-field.

There's panic over climate change. Earth is in crisis, but it seems to me that no one is paying any attention to the crisis of our souls. No units to measure all the holes that are appearing in each of us.

*

In Naomi's flat, a woman is lying on the bed in the centre of the room. In her thirties, I guess. She wears leggings and a jumper, no shoes. She smiles at me when I enter, though her eyes are red and puffy as though she's been crying.

'Lucy, this is Alice,' Naomi says, introducing us. 'Lucy doesn't mind you sitting in, we've just finished our talk so now we're going to clear the chakras.'

I'm supposed to be watching Lucy, but I can't take my eyes off Naomi. She has an aura of pure gold around her, the kind of colour I've only ever seen on newborn babies. It's a golden light that moves up from the ground, streaming upward and around her like an uplighter. It flows within the bubble, like a sparkling wine, or a luxurious just-poured flute of champagne. It's so bright, like pulling the curtains first thing in the morning and being faced with the morning rays. Almost squinting against her light, I watch her at work.

The prominent colour around Lucy is black. Not a scratchy black like the paedophile in the park, or the distressing metallic streaks of someone who is sick in the head and murderous with demon thoughts. I've seen this black before, regularly, lots of people carry it with them every single day; it's the black of grief. A quiet, contemplative black of drawing the curtains so they can search inside. It speaks to me, politely and quietly, saying, Do not disturb, I'm exhausted and I'm resting, I'm trying to heal. The black is clear and transparent like a mourning veil, it covers Lucy from head to toe; in places there are darker black knots where she is clearly struggling emotionally, particularly around the centre of her upper stomach, where her ribcage ends.

Naomi needs to be careful here, if she does what I witnessed Esme doing, the only time I witnessed a reiki session, then she could send these black knots to the wrong parts of Lucy's body, to her head or internal organs, which would be dangerous. Or the knots could resist and remain where they are, becoming tighter and darker, more knotted.

I watch as, with her eyes closed and hands out, Naomi correctly identifies the problem areas. Breathing deeply, the sound of calming water and pipe music in the background, Naomi gets to work on her first knot. I hold my breath.

When the heat emerges from Naomi's hands, I almost gasp as I see it. Red and orange, warm and inviting as a sunset. The tight black knot is resistant at first, then it starts to tighten. Instead of forcing it, Naomi stops and looks around for something specific and returns with a crystal, a musky black-coloured stone. She holds it in her hands, as if warming the stone, inhales deeply, exhales slowly, then places the stone back in the path of the sun. She holds her hands out over the stubborn black knot for a second time. Slowly but surely, the knot begins to unravel. It unravels and hangs there for a moment, as if making a decision. Then it becomes a clear transparent colour and merges with the rest of Lucy's weeping veil.

Naomi does the same with the other knots. A tear trickles down Lucy's face from the corner of her eye, she lets it fall and it runs into her hairline near her ear.

Naomi unravels each of the knots of emotion, but the black veil hanging over Lucy remains untouched.

'And now we seal the chakras,' Naomi says softly, so as not to give the peaceful Lucy a jolt.

I think of the paramedic in our house who rubbed her hands together and rid herself of the blue when I was a child. I wonder if she did it subconsciously or if, with a job like that, she had learned how to leave other people's problems behind. Leave them in the house before you return home. Naomi does the same now, she rubs her hands together, crumpling the lingering black into a ball like it's paper, scrunching it up. The heat of her hands disintegrates it and she shakes them out as though she's air-drying them. I watch in awe.

'Now Lucy,' she says, suddenly bringing us back to reality, to an apartment in Islington, in a tower block of flats where the horns and sirens of the traffic outside are audible once more. The magic spell is broken.

Lucy sits up, sleepy-eyed, with tousled hair. She takes a moment. 'Thank you,' she says, and she starts to cry.

Naomi allows her her human moment. She hands her a tissue and pours her a glass of water.

'How did you do it?' I ask, mouth agape after Lucy has paid and left.

'What did you see me do?' she asks, grinning. 'Tea?'

'No. No tea. This is, this is . . . phenomenal.' I'm buzzing. The adrenaline is pumping through me. 'Do you know what you just did?'

The gold bubble from around her is gone.

'You were like a glass of champagne,' I say. 'A gold shimmering bubble, and then the heat of your hands untied every single black knot that was around her. The one over her pelvis was stubborn, I'll give you that. It was threatening to tighten, I thought you were going to do her damage. It nearly did, but then you got that black stone thing and all of a sudden it untied itself. And poof, gone – only not gone, it joined the black veil, but it was far less harmful than it had been. And the same with the other ones. It was like they watched the first guy and said, No way we'll get away with this! They didn't even put up a fight. And there's the paper thing – crumpling it up, dissolving it and throwing it away.' I do a bad basketball throw impression with an exaggerated flick of the wrist. 'And slam dunk, she's all good. Well, still grieving, but you can't fix that, right? It's natural, you just cleared the way for her to do it herself.'

Naomi sits down, exhausted.

'Does doing that tire you out?' I ask.

'No. You do.'

'Oh.' I stop pacing. 'Sorry.'

'Don't apologise. *You* are phenomenal,' she says. 'I knew it. I sensed there was something special about you.'

'Me?'

'Yes, you. Make me a tea, will you? I need something to calm me down.'

I keep an eye on her as a mini firework display of colours pops all around her body.

'You saw everything that I did in colours?' she asks as we settle down.

I nod.

'Remarkable. Did I miss anything? Was there an energy I left behind?'

'No,' I shake my head. She's the expert, it feels wrong for her to reverse it like this. Like she's a pilot who has left the cockpit for passenger advice.

'Remarkable,' she says again. 'You said I was like a glass of champagne?'

'A flute,' I say. 'All gold and shiny and bubbly. It was around you like a bubble. What was that?' I hand her a chamomile tea and sit in her mother's chair. I get a little jolt as I sit.

'It's a shield,' she says. 'I create it whenever a client enters my home for a session. It's important to protect myself and keep our energies separate.'

This is possibly the most important information I have ever received in my life.

'You can build a shield?'

'Of course. Alice, you can do anything you want with your energies. They are your energies.'

'I wear gloves, a mask, glasses, I keep my skin covered, we have dividers at the call centre, but a shield? I would wear it every day.'

'We don't want to be shielded from everything in life, Alice. Some things must be experienced, some people we must experience. The gloves, the mask, the glasses – you have been telling people to stay away, instead of figuring out how to be among them. You have decided to become an outsider instead of engaging.'

'A shadow,' I say. 'I've already decided I don't want to be that anymore, but it's the only way I know how to live.'

'I'll show you another way. I'll teach you how to shield yourself. It's one thing to be alone, Alice, it is quite another to be lonely.'

I feel another jolt beneath me and I stand up.

'What is wrong with you?'

'Your mother is feisty today,' I say, looking at the chair, which is glowing more than usual.

She opens her mouth in surprise. 'Oh goodness, Alice. It's her birthday!'

Naomi and I sit cross-legged on a rug on her floor. The scented candles are lit and relaxing music plays in the background. The balcony doors are open, a bright spring day, the surviving wind chimes tinkle in the light breeze. The oven is emanating coconut smells and, whatever it is, I want to be invited to eat it.

'We are creating a shield of gold,' Naomi says. 'Once you create the shield, you won't need to make it again for a long time. It's like a pair of shoes, you wear it until you need to repair it or make a new one. It's always there, but you call on it when needs be. Think of it like a helmet visor that flicks back when you don't need it.'

'This is so cool,' I giggle. 'Where am I flicking it to?'

'Think of it as being there, but not being activated.'

I'm confused, unsure if I'll be able to do this. It would be easier if there was an on-off button.

'It's not for everyday use,' she says, warning in her tone, as if sensing my true intentions.

I nod but I plan to wear this bad boy everywhere I go. She looks disappointed by my lie; she may not have my aura-seeing abilities but her instincts are the sharpest I have ever encountered.

'The shield repels all harm. You use it when feeling under psychic and psychological attack, to protect against people who are overbearing and threaten your aura.'

'That's everyone. Every day, all the time.'

'It is not, Alice, and you know it,' she says, as if admonishing a child.

I giggle. 'Then why were you shielding yourself against Lucy? She wasn't attacking you.'

'I miss my mother,' she says simply. 'The greatest loss in my life is my greatest weakness. I had to do a lot of work on myself after losing her, and allowing Lucy's grief to touch mine would be detrimental to me.'

'Okay. I understand.'

'What I usually do during a session is seal my aura. It allows positive energies in and filters out negative energy.'

'Cool. I need that one too.'

She laughs. 'All in good time.'

'I once watched a guy in a bar change his colours to match the women he was chatting up,' I say.

'That's called aura mirroring. You saw his colours changing? Remarkable. That's a good device. Many people do it instinctively, anyone who is good with people. You can help make people feel more comfortable in your presence, so that they don't feel like you're dominating them, so that they can relax.'

'I bet you did it when you were working as a midwife.'

'It helped the mothers, and the babies.'

The penny drops. 'You did that to me, didn't you?'

'It's not a ploy, Alice,' she says, laughing. 'People do it subconsciously and naturally.'

'But you did it to me, didn't you? I didn't want to like you, but I did.'

'How else was I going to introduce myself to you? You

kept running away every time I opened the door,' she says with a laugh.

'Teach me how to do it all,' I say excitedly.

'All. In. Good. Time.'

I want to learn everything now, but Naomi's pace is slower, as is her rhythm. Though she has an instinct for most things, what she couldn't possibly understand to the full extent is my impatience to stop sitting on the sidelines, to step out of the shade and feel the heat and the full glare of sunlight on my face. I want this *now*.

'Are you ready, Alice?'

'You have no idea.'

I approach the data warehouse of Calling Card and draw the champagne bubble around me as Naomi taught me. I feel like I float to my workspace beside Paul.

'Morning,' he says.

'Good morning,' I say with a smile, and that friendly telephone voice that they all do.

'Ready?' he asks.

I place my headphones on. 'Let's do this.'

It's my most productive day yet. The team invite me for a drink after work.

From invisibility to invincibility, this shield starts to give me a life I've only ever dreamed of. I have a new job, I splash out on a new wardrobe. Naomi's eyes widen as I sashay down the corridor in a new little black dress as though I'm on a catwalk.

I go a bit wild after Naomi teaches me the tricks – or the tools, as she prefers to call them – of the trade. I see them more as tricks, as ways to manipulate. I go out, *a lot*, eager to make up for lost time

I can get whoever I want.

I do this by mirroring their aura, or altering mine to please them. This means watching men for some time, finding out what colours turn their head. Some like meek and vulnerable, lots go for that, damaged and pliable. Some want needy, some want detached. Others like dominant and overpowering who'll chastise them for their naughtiness, if they need to be put in their place, or guide and give them direction.

They don't know what it is about me that they're attracted to. I might not be their usual type, a weedy girl in a cheap black dress, but it's my presence that gets their attention. Something prehistoric that makes goose pimples rise on the back of their necks, forces them to find me, sending out exactly the energy that they're looking for. Gives them a feeling that they want to know more, hear more, see more.

Human chameleons; they exist.

It's why con artists can rob people in plain sight, professionals who know when to fade into the crowd without moving, or cause distraction when they need to. They do it all the time, these men that I hunt. I can be one of them when I want. With my shield, my seal and my ability to mirror auras, I've now got the superhero tools and weapons to equip me for these charming men. And I know exactly where to find them.

It's funny, after trying to escape the shadows I manage to create a new hiding place by being the centre of attention and still not being seen.

The hotel room is black. The curtains are drawn, the only giveaway that it's morning is the sound of burgeoning life outside of our room. The shower next door, Sky News volume up loud, the elevator shaft whirring to life, pinging loudly every few minutes. Ordinarily, I'd never choose a bedroom by an elevator, but it was late, the only room available. We took whatever they had, grateful it wasn't a storage cupboard or a toilet or an alleyway.

His chest rises and falls and my head moves with it. It's soothing. Rhythmic. I could stay like this all day, not forever, but for today, definitely another night. My eyes flutter closed as I listen to his calm heartbeat and just as I'm drifting I feel him shift beneath me. I open my eyes and catch his expression before he has time to change it. Confusion. Disorientated. I move off his chest. The prince has woken, the fairy tale is over, I await the frog.

'Good morning,' I say.

'Hey,' he says sleepily. 'What time is it?'

I pretend to check. 'Six thirty.'

'Wow. Okay, I was flat out.'

'Yeah, me too.'

Housekeeping shout at each other down the corridor outside our room. Moldovan shatters the peace. Reminds us that we're a cog in a wheel, we're in the way, they have work to do before more people come through.

He rubs his eyes and pulls himself up, the sheets around his waist. He looks around the room as if seeing it for the first time.

'Where the hell are we?'

I laugh. 'A Premier Inn.'

'Where?' he asks as if joking, but I can tell he genuinely doesn't know.

'Bermondsey.' I wrap the blankets around me tighter. 'And I'm Alice. We met at the gallery.'

'Hey,' he says gently, looking at me. 'I remember that. I remember you. I was just hazy on the rest.'

I smile. He was magnetic to me last night. He still is now. That golden filter of light glowing in the darkness of all those people at the gallery, like there's a crack in the curtains and the light filters through. He was the light. Even if I knew it wasn't a natural light, that it was a lamp instead of the sun, it was still inviting.

'It was late, you said you have to be back at work early anyway, so there was no point going home . . .' *The markets never sleep. But they do fuck around.* And we'd laughed. It was so stupid.

'Yeah,' he says, distracted, checking his watch, then his phone, then panic on his face.

'Okay?'

It's evidently not okay, that much is obvious, because he's out of bed, naked body moving quickly for clothes, going to the bathroom. Shower on. I hear his voice through the thin wall.

She must be angry. I would be if I was her.

Gospel was right about me being drawn to my nemeses, these smooth ambitious men who want everything and seem to feel nothing. I don't know if it is demeanour or simple self-belief that they are the greatest, that they are untouchable, but it's a fantasy I want to be a part of, that I'm pulled to even if I know it's nonsense.

Cravers of excitement, risk-takers – these are the kind of men who catch my eye. Men like these are driven and focused, they pull me in with their confidence. I confuse their greed with desire, misread their longing for consumption as lust. I'm attracted to their tunnel-visioned focus and determination, their oozing charm to have everything in the world their way, where rules are guidelines and truth is malleable.

That's what they want you to see, Naomi says when they don't call me back, when I question what I've done wrong, when it all ends in misery.

It's their colours that attract me. They're shiny. Gold and silver. And I'm like a magpie drawn into their shimmer.

I don't know why, with my unique vision, why I can't see that while from far away they shine, close up they're tarnished. Addictions, compulsions, the murky greys of hidden information and half-truths. I don't know how I miss the rust around the edges and hinges, how I don't hear the creaks and squeaks of their joints. These metal shiny tin men, in need of oil, with brains aplenty but no conscience. I rely on them to help take me home, but to a home that is lasting, a home that I feel inside of me, not a Premier Inn for one night.

I walk barefoot down the corridor to my flat. My heels dangle from my hand, the back of my ankle is cut and raw from the new shoes and no amount of extra padding or blister aids helped. I dig through my handbag to find the keys. Letting my guard down is much like taking off a pair of tight heels after a long night.

Naomi's door opens and she looks me up and down, eyebrow raised, noting I'm still in the dress from the night before.

'Don't judge.'

'I'm not. You think I didn't have fun once upon a time?'

'You're still having fun,' I reply.

She chuckles. 'For as long as my heart beats. I have a client coming by at noon.' She looks at her watch in an exaggerated fashion. 'Oh look at that, just twenty minutes away. You can sit in if you like, he won't mind. He's a gentle soul who's going through a divorce and a child custody case. It's ripping him right apart.'

'As long as he's not an axe murderer I think you're fine without me. You don't need me, you get it right every single time.'

'That's not true.' She examines me, worried. 'Anyway, that's not why I was asking you. He's having an identity crisis, might be interesting for you to see what's happening.'

Annoyed by what I consider a pointed remark, I step inside and close the door. The plants on the balcony need my attention, there's a very thirsty-looking white bird of paradise watching me from the kitchen. I don't have the energy. I pull the curtains to stop the harsh sunlight from streaming through, and fall face down on the bed.

'We use predictive diallers,' Paul brags to Reynash, the guy who's chatting up Parminder. He works in a call centre too, a small one for a small company that doesn't make as many calls an hour as we do. It's like they're whipping their manhoods out on the rickety, beer-bottle-covered table and comparing sizes. Still, I've seen sadder things. 'Not only do we have automated phone-number dialling, we also use sophisticated algorithms to predict agent availability to optimise agent utilisation by ensuring we're never idle. We integrate predictive dialler with CRM applications, which allows agents to see customer info that leads to a more relevant, personalised call,' Paul says. His ability to reel off information, in comparison to my robotic reading of the script in front of me, always impresses me. He licks his finger, holds it to the air and hisses.

'Ooooh,' we all say in unison.

Reynash laughs, good-humoured about it. 'Yes but we still have to dial the numbers ourselves, so we are doing extra work . . .'

We boo him and he gives up.

'Agile fingers, Parminder.' Paul winks at Parminder, and twinkles his fingers at her. Parminder laughs.

'Anyway, there's no point arguing with me in here about who's the best because we all know I am,' Paul says, lighting a cigarette. We're sitting outside a bar, the Pig and Duck, in a narrow alleyway filled with work-is-finished-for-the-day celebrants, people are spilling out of doorways, spilling out of dresses, spilling out with half-truths, shouting to be heard, laughing to feel alive, and I'm among them, in the messy squiggle of lines that shoot across from one person to the next, criss-crossing like art gallery laser-beam security in a heist movie. The kind of scene I previously walked around, viewed from afar, the kind of place I was never in the epicentre of. My shield is up, of course, as it almost permanently is, secured in a warm bubble so that I'm defended against all alien energies. I take it down only when I turn the key in my door or when taking a walk through the park. Though it depends on the park and the time of day. This shield has given me new-found freedoms and I'm milking it for everything it's got.

'It's true, you are the best,' I agree. 'How many sales this week? You'll be running the place soon.'

He rolls his eyes, as if the idea bores him. 'I don't plan on staying long. I didn't move to London to work in a stinky call centre for the rest of my life. I have plans.' He pirouettes across the cobblestoned alley and lands side-on to a wooden table heaving with people. He extends his leg high into the air, into a perfect ballet hold. Everyone cheers, apart from the lad whose pint was knocked over. Paul spins back to us. 'I'm going to be a West End star. You're looking at Aladdin in *Aladdin* at the Swindon Theatre, Adam and Felicia in *Priscilla Queen of the Desert* in its National tour and Munkustrap in *Cats* in the South Korean tour.'

'South Korea?' Parminder wows. 'What was that like?'

'Amazing,' he says with an eye-roll, 'I can't even.'

'Fabulous,' I say, trying to sound as fascinated as I would feel if I actually believed a word he said. He's a fun, fascinating creature; seemingly shallow but with incredible layers that are difficult to unpack. There's always a part of what he says that's true, based on some sort of reality, but I'm not sure which part. He may know someone who went to South Korea to dance, he may have planned to go, he may have auditioned but didn't get the part, he may have seen the show in South Korea. There's a part of him that almost believes what he's saying, but the metallic flickers belie him. I would have avoided someone like that. Before London, before the shield, I would have seen that as a dangerous trait; someone who was unstable and unsettled in who they are could send tremors into my world, so I'd have avoided him on first sight. But not now. When I'm this other person, it doesn't matter. He can't affect me.

'What about you,' Paul turns to me. 'International woman of mystery?'

We laugh.

'I don't know, what's to tell?'

'Everything. Why did you move to London, alone? Are you on the run? Witness a murder? Are you in witness protection? Are you escaping a jealous boyfriend? Or girl-friend?'

'If she's in witness protection, she can't say,' Reynash comes to my aid.

'Nothing as exciting as that,' I say, wishing I had some-thing more exciting to tell them, but then realising who'd even know the truth? Nobody here tells the truth. Most people I've met in London aren't from London, they've come from somewhere else, drawn to this great big multi-cultural city because they're hiding from something or looking for something. Even lovely Parminder, who's wasting Reynash's time because she knows she has one year until her family start introducing her to a series of possible husbands. When you don't know anyone and no one knows you, why not be free and shake off the shackles?

'I was in university but I dropped out in my third year. Law,' I say to their oohs. 'I wanted to go travelling.'

'Lawyers can't travel?' Paul asks.

'Where did you go?' Parminder interrupts him.

'Europe, India, Southeast Asia, Australia. So now I'm here, penniless and working at a call centre.' I could have thought of something more exciting. I'll work on something better for the next people who ask.

'Hmm,' Paul says, getting off the chair, already bored with the conversation. He prefers it when it's about him. 'Shots.'

'Not for me,' I say immediately.

But Reynash thinks it's a great idea, so the two lads squeeze themselves into the crowd waiting at the bar. I chose not to drink because I was afraid of losing control, especially in an environment like this where I could get hit by different energies at least a few dozen times in the crossfires. It would be like being repeatedly shot by a stun gun, if the electric current was emotions. I wouldn't know who to be or how to be me when confronted by what everyone else is feeling. But now I have my shield, I've been using it for months and my life has changed beyond belief. I'll have my shield up. I'll keep it up. Time to join the rest of the world.

'Tequila!' Paul yells, carrying a tray filled with shot glasses.

'It's very bright in here,' I say, putting my arm over my eyes. 'Do you have any food? Something smells yum.'

'Mmm,' Naomi says, moving around the room quietly. It's as though she hovers. She removes her shoes when clients arrive, and pads around barefoot. No sounds to break the silence and calm. Apart from me, whining about being on this bed, even though I climbed up here of my own accord.

I'm exhausted. Wearing my shield so often is taking its toll on my body. While it's protecting me from others, building it and holding it up means I'm draining myself.

'You've been wearing your shield?'

'Sometimes. On the Tube and stuff.'

'Why not just seal your energy, why guard yourself so staunchly? It's a very militant way to be.'

'Because it works.'

'Does it? Let's see about that. Arms down by your side.' She closes her eyes and takes deep breaths, hands out. She frowns, says, 'Mmm,' and not in a good way. 'You need to find another way to live, Alice.'

'No,' I say angrily, sitting up and swinging my legs off the bed. 'I'm not in the mood for this. You don't say a word to your other clients. Not one thing. There's supposed to be no judgement. They come in here with addictions and weird impulses and crazy stories, and you say nothing. With me, you can't help yourself.'

'You're right. I'm sorry but I consider you a friend, Alice, it's difficult for me to say nothing when I see you hurting.'

A friend, she calls me her friend, how many of those do I have? Instead of embracing that, I leave, like a petulant child.

She suggested I lower the shield but I'm like a child with a comfort blanket. I will not allow anyone to take this from me. I will not go back to slithering along the walls like a shadow.

I listen to Paul on the phone and feel jealousy stirring within me.

It's the way he delivers it, his tone. It should be annoying, but it almost always works and they never hang up. He makes jokes, they laugh, they make jokes, he laughs. He makes it seem so easy. If I could see people, I'm sure I could do better, like him. I could be the best on the team. I could mirror their auras, I could be whatever they want me to be in order to convince them to believe in this stupid electricity bill deal. I'm irritated by Paul's greatness, my inability to connect to anyone down the line, yet I can when I'm in a room with them. Jealousy is rising in me.

A few suits enter the room and we get back to work, completely diligent and robot-like.

'Who are they?' I mouth to Parminder.

'His ticket out of here,' she says, looking at Paul, and he instantly agrees with a giant head nod.

'Magma are setting up a new sales team.'

'Outbound calls?'

'No. Outside.'

'You mean, outside in the . . . world?' Henry, beside Parminder, asks.

We all laugh, then take our calls.

'They're looking for the best salesperson,' Parminder continues after her call.

Paul gives us razzmatazz jazz hands.

'No point in any of us even trying,' Henry says. 'Hello, I'm calling from Calling Card on behalf of Magma Energy . . . okay, goodbye.'

I watch the three men in suits gathered, talking, something new and bad rising in me.

*

Crystal Palace training grounds are at Selhurst Park, an hour's train journey from Paddington. I haven't researched Gospel in a fanatical frenzy, but I've been keeping an eye on him; it's difficult not to when he's one of the premier league's greatest players. On 7 June, Tourette Syndrome Awareness day, he released his autobiography detailing his journey with Tourette's Syndrome and how it helped him to focus on the field, feel freer than anywhere else, just clear focus and precision. It was a book for the football fans really, I speed-read it, I wasn't in it, wasn't expecting to be, but still looked for my name.

Crystal Palace fans are certainly fanatical, they have fansites dedicated to each of their heroes. Gospel is particularly popular, not for his skills but for his looks. I see photo after photo of him happily smiling with fans after training sessions, as they wait outside in the wind, hail and sunshine for the opportunity of a photograph or autograph. Gospel appears to be generous with his time. I don't attend any of his matches but I do bite the bullet one day, on a day off, and I visit the grounds. I can't believe how easy it is to see the players as they walk from the training grounds to their cars. The fans stand around in a group, wrapped up in their Crystal Palace hats and scarves for warmth. It's a crisp fresh day, the sun is out, always helpful so I don't stand out wearing glasses. I wear a heavy parka, a woollen hat. If I didn't know I was me, I wouldn't recognise me. My hands are buried deep in my pockets.

They come out in twos and threes, these otherworldly type of athletic creatures. Freshly showered and glowing, expensive haircuts, and clothes, muscular and lean, rich, talented, desired, admired by men and women. The energies from the fans race towards them, like adolescent hormonal girls throwing themselves at their feet, wrapping themselves around them, and the men take them, accept them with open arms, their own energies throbbing a little more with each worship. I don't know who any of them are, but there's great excitement each time a new face is revealed from behind the magic door. The adrenaline from the groupies is hard to ignore; it's so intoxicating that I don't know if it's their excitement or mine when my heart skips several beats as Gospel steps outside. It's been ten years since I've seen him in the flesh.

Some players race through the fans, heads down while they sign autograph after autograph without really engaging or looking people in the eye. Gospel looks at them all, he speaks to them all. He is generous with his time, paying particular attention to the man in the wheelchair and the kids, asking their names and whether or not they play football. The honey colour from his teens has matured, as though a swarm of bees have been busily building his hive into a fort. He oozes warmth, sweetness, charm and, most importantly of all, kindness. His predominant colour reaches out like it has tentacles but not in a vindictive way, as Lily's did, but they are inclusive tentacles, they wrap themselves around people, tuck them in, pull them closer. He is magnetising.

I'm standing away from the crowd. As if suddenly sensing me, he looks up, over their heads and right at me. I get a fright and change my aura to a grey mist, like a cloak of invisibility. One that says, Don't look at me, I'm not here.

His eyes scan right past me, and he continues signing the poster of himself. My heart pounds.

I walk away before he has time to look up again.

I time us to enter the building simultaneously. Me and Jacob Blake, the head of Calling Card. I've never bothered with him before, never wanted him to notice me because I didn't need him to. My sales record certainly wouldn't cause me to stand out. Not shockingly bad, but certainly not in the highest ranks, I sit somewhere in the middle. A little ahead of Parminder, who can get flustered easily and give up on a caller, but nowhere near the unbeatable Paul. If it could be as simple as allowing his energy to rub off on me, I would do it, but it wouldn't work. You can let a mood rub off on you, but you can't take a skill.

I change my aura to match Jacob Blake's. Self-important, someone in control, someone to admire and aspire to. As if sensing a more important presence in the shared space, he suddenly looks up from his phone and at me. From shadow to shining light.

'Good morning, Mr Blake.'

'You what?' Paul looks at me, gobsmacked, mouth hanging open.

He heard me, so I'm not about to repeat it; it was hard enough saying it the first time. Despite the knife in his back, I was oddly looking forward to this moment, to the looks of admiration on their faces, the shock and surprise. It's not going exactly as I hoped.

'Did you give Blake a blow job?' he asks.

Parminder gasps. 'Paul!'

'But you didn't even want the job,' he says, looking at me, the hurt and rage evident.

'Wow,' Henry mouths to Parminder.

'I did.'

'Why didn't you say anything?'

'I thought everyone was going for it.' I look around, feigning cluelessness.

'No way, I thought Paul had it in the bag,' Henry says.

'I'm happy here,' Parminder says, wanting nothing to do with it.

'But . . .' I look at Paul. His shock has become pure hate, rage, jealousy. My shield is up and I feel nothing, like a mere bystander observing with interest. 'But we were all entitled to go for it,' I say. 'It wasn't *your* job.'

'They practically told me I had the job,' he says. 'You're such a liar, Alice,' he says, standing and throwing his lunch in the bin. 'Good luck, that's all I can say,' he says, his voice trembling with rage. 'Good luck in the real world if you're going to stab people in the back like that. And good luck telling them about the fake law degree,' he says bitchily, and raises his voice. 'Which never happened. Did it?'

Henry and Parminder look at me.

'South Korea tour of *Cats*,' I say to him, and appalled, afraid, embarrassed, he walks away, trying to hide his defeat in his movements.

I try to ignore him for the few weeks before the new job starts, but it gets worse. It's not that no one talks to me, it's not an American high school movie, but it's how they change the way they talk to me. Cold. Distant. As though I'm someone not to be trusted. A pariah. I put my shield up but it doesn't work as well as it used to at the beginning, I feel their disgust of me, their distrust. More importantly, their general feelings of nothingness toward me penetrate my personal space, and that travels deep into me.

'How do you make a shield stronger?' I ask Naomi in a casual, subtle way.

We're out for lunch in a Caribbean pop-up café in Shoreditch, for Naomi's birthday. She looks up at me from her saltfish fritters, and from her expression I'm sorry I asked.

'Why do you want to make your shield stronger?'

'It's work. The call centre. It's the energy from the computers. I think it's too strong for me. I just wanted to see if there's anything else I can do to—'

'There's nothing else you can do.'

I think she's going to leave it at that and I'm hoping so because she knows I'm lying and I don't want to talk about it.

'When your guard comes down, Alice, you'll feel everything, a hundred times stronger like you've never felt it before. Your body will be so used to not feeling everything, imagine. Let's take that pale skin of yours. You wear sun factor, don't you? You wear that over and over again, the sun never hits your skin, your skin will never get used to it. You need to let the sun hit you now and then, or you'll be scorched.'

This has the opposite effect on me than she intends. I swallow my food nervously, planning to never let my guard down, imagining my insides burning like tar through the heat of a magnifying glass.

Door-to-door sales is a triumph for me. My success at it and the ease with which it comes to me means I never look back. It's summertime, the team was put together deliberately for this time when it's easier to catch people in their gardens, when they can't ignore the door and when some are too polite to ask you to leave them alone. All I need is for people to see me and I've got them. I've learned from every dodgy caller we've had to the house how to earn respect. I'm the number one salesperson on the team, outselling everybody every single month. I learn quickly to stop just beyond our sales targets, saving potential customers for the following month. I receive bonuses, praise, I'm flying, but I am absolutely exhausted. For every person I meet and win over, I feel like I'm giving them a piece of my soul and soon there'll be nothing for myself.

'Fix me,' I say as soon as Naomi opens her door. I walk into her flat without an invitation and look around for the bed, which isn't in the centre of the room as it usually is. Instead, there's a table set up for dinner.

'I have friends coming over soon.'

'It won't take long. I'll lie on the floor.'

'I'm not getting down on the floor. What do you think I am?'

I hear the dangerous tone in her voice but I continue to push her.

'Can you do it standing up?' I kick off my shoes.

She views me for a moment, then walks closer to me. I close my eyes, I don't need to see her chip on her shoulder, her judgement of me. I don't care what she thinks of me. I need a band-aid so I can get back to work tomorrow.

'No.'

I open my eyes in surprise.

'What happens when you take too many antibiotics? They can weaken your immune system,' Naomi says roughly, storming around, heavy on her feet unlike usual. 'They stop your immune system from fighting infection. Or the germ becomes so used to the antibiotic they can resist it.'

'So I'm the bacteria, is that what you're saying?'

'Well maybe you are, but I'm talking about your shield. You've overused it and it has weakened.'

'Oh don't start that again.'

We've both raised our voices.

'It wasn't designed to be worn every single moment of the day, Alice; it's weakening and you're weakened as a result of carrying it, so you're even more highly sensitive than usual. Now you can keep coming in here,' she says angrily, 'but at this point it's like placing a tissue on a gunshot wound. You are haemorrhaging, girl, this is no A&E and I am no miracle worker.'

'Clearly,' I say, sarcastically.

'Out.'

'What?' I look at her in surprise.

She's pointing at the door. 'You heard me. Get out of my home, please.'

'You're throwing me out?'

'Can't just be me that does the work in this room, Alice, there are two of us in it. I deserve to be treated with more respect.'

'Great,' I say. 'Thanks a lot.' I pick up my shoes, storm out and bang the door shut.

I open the balcony door and lie down on the hot floor where the sun is shining, no energy to face the dying flowers, and I pray for the sunlight to give me energy. Next door, Naomi's guests are loud and vivacious. They don't care about being overheard as they laugh and shout over each other, her open balcony sending out the delicious Caribbean food smells into me as if on purpose. I lie on the hot rug in the full scorching glare of the sun, feeling as if I'm in a desert, parched, starved and dying.

Magma see my sales. They take me from Calling Card and offer me a job as sales rep on the road working with their best customers on their biggest accounts. A company car. A phone. Increased bonuses. A nicer wardrobe. A better haircut. I drink more. I work harder. From shadow to shining light. This is living.

'When are you visiting?' Lily asks.

'What?' I ask in surprise. She never wants me to visit. I usually just turn up in case she deliberately avoids me. 'Is everything okay?'

'Yeah. I'm fine.'

'Is it Ollie?'

'Ollie's . . . Ollie.'

'Then what is it? What's wrong?'

'Maybe I'll visit you.'

She's testing me. Pity I wasn't as smart over the phone with clients as I am with her.

'Yeah, sure. When do you want to come?'

She sighs. I called her bluff.

'Are you okay?' she asks.

'Yeah. Why?'

'I'm just asking.' She loses her temper, swears at me and hangs up.

There's a knock at the door, which is surprising as the only people in this entire city who know where I live are my neighbours, and I can count on one hand the amount of times that has happened. It's a Saturday morning, I'd planned on staying in bed until Monday morning. I'm exhausted, I can barely lift my head off the pillow. I fully intend on ignoring the knocking; if it's anyone, it's Naomi to apologise, and I'm not in the mood. She can wait. But the knocking intensifies, builds to banging.

'Okay!' I yell gruffly, pulling myself out of bed. I pull a jumper over my head and, feeling like my legs can barely hold me up, I hold on to the wall to keep myself upright all the way to the door. I look through the peephole.

'What the . . . Hugh!'

'Surprise!'

'Give me a second. Wait.'

'Open the door, Alice.'

'No, I'm not dressed, wait.' I run around like a headless chicken, not actually doing anything productive at all, unable to think about the first step of getting dressed until I stop, take a moment, pull on joggers, brush my hair and tie it back, moisturise my face, hoping I look less deathly and a little more dewy. I open the door.

'Surprise,' he repeats, with less enthusiasm this time.

Despite my size and my lack of energy I almost knock him over with the force of my hug. While I'm apparently squeezing the life out of him I hear the quiet click of Naomi's door close. When I'm finished hugging him, inspecting every part of his face that I haven't seen in the flesh for so long, and all the colours around him to make sure he's okay, I sense a man in turmoil.

'Please don't tell me you broke up with Poh.'

'I didn't.'

'Is she okay?'

'Yeah, she's fine, she took the kids to the Natural History Museum.'

'Without me?'

'We're here for two weeks. We're both on school holidays so it's a good time.'

'It's about time,' I say, knowing it will annoy him. 'Can't believe you chose London over Greece or Croatia or wherever else you usually travel around in your summers, but I'm glad you're here.'

He's given me the lift I've so desperately needed, like a sugar hit.

He looks around the flat.

'It's usually a lot tidier than this. I've just been so busy.'

He looks out at the balcony, the usually glorious balcony that's decorated in bees, butterflies and life but looks neglected.

'I haven't had time. It's usually so much nicer – oh Hugh, I wish you'd given me notice, I could have had time to prepare.'

'Why? So you could pretend everything's different?'

'Actually yes, that's usually what people do when they have guests.' I put the kettle on, awaiting the bad news that is inevitable. He didn't come here just to see me, he has something on his mind. I wait for him to bring it up. He keeps looking around as if he's picking the place apart. Suddenly I become anxious and shaky, trying to anticipate what's coming. So weak, I annoy myself. I pour myself a glass of water.

'I thought you said you were earning more money?'

'I am, loads of it.' I giggle at the thrill of it, at the sheer surprise and shock of it. I've done it, I've made it happen, but somehow it's as if it's happening to someone else.

'Why don't you move somewhere nicer if you're earning better money?'

'I like it here. Besides, now I actually have extra money for me, and not just rent money. It's a luxury. I move now and it will all go on rent again.'

'Yeah, but you could move somewhere a bit safer. I think I almost got mugged in the lift.'

'Why the hell did you take the lift? Anyway, don't worry: I pay the drug lord across the hall protection money so he keeps me safe.'

The look on his face makes me laugh.

'I'm joking. Hugh, you've been spending too long in your fancy house, if you think this is a shithole.'

'There's nothing fancy about living on an oil refinery. We're thinking of moving somewhere else. An international school somewhere. Spain, maybe. Somewhere with sun but not a desert. Somewhere with water that's not constant rain.'

'Here?' I ask hopefully.

'Somewhere we can afford to feed and clothe our children,' he adds, looking around.

'So now that we got the weather out of the way, what's up, what's the problem?'

'Why should there be a problem?

'Because you're here, unannounced from Doha for the first time in . . . how many years? And I'm not stupid.'

'How are you, Alice?'

He asks it in a way that makes my stomach churn, that makes me want to put my shield up immediately. He's here about me, and that makes me sick. I don't need anyone's help, I've never needed anyone's help, I've always taken care of me.

'I'm fine.'

I try to put up my shield. I've never had to do this with Hugh before, haven't physically been in his company since I was able to shield myself, but it feels weird, guarding myself from the person who makes me feel the safest. As I try to put my guard up, something that was as easy as changing a thought, my body starts to shake, as if I'm trying to lift the weight of an elephant. I feel a cramp in my chest, a tightness, pulling. I suck in air from the pain, and my glass falls to the floor and smashes.

He can't see me like this, not Hugh. I try to put a brave face on it, try to think of something clever, something funny, something to say to detract from what's happening, but instead I feel myself shatter like the glass on the floor and I crumple to the ground.

'Alice!' he shouts.

He holds me in his arms and I want to move, to smile, to tell him I'm fine, but I can't do any of those things. I feel paralysed, completely numb, trembling from the inside as if I'm in a million pieces on the floor.

'I'll call an ambulance. Where's your phone? No. I'll get my phone, okay? Don't move.'

He leaves me to rush to his bag and I rest my face on the ground.

'No, Alice!' he yells.

I need to close my eyes.

'There's glass.' He puts the phone down and comes to me again, brushing the glass away.

I hear banging on the door.

'Not now,' Hugh calls.

'Let me in, I'm a neighbour, a friend!'

He runs to the door and I hear Naomi enter, I feel her.

'I'm calling an ambulance. She collapsed.'

'Why is she bleeding?'

'She fell on the smashed glass.'

'Alice, darling, open your eyes,' Naomi says. 'Come back to yourself now.'

I open my eyes and look up at her.

'I'm so sorry,' I say, teeth chattering. 'I'm so sorry.'

'No cause for sorrys, you just get yourself better. Breathe in and out.'

'Sorry.'

'Stop with the sorry,' she says, smiling. 'I don't think there's any cause for an ambulance, but you do what you feel, Hugh,' she says. 'I'm Naomi – I'm a neighbour. I'm a friend. I can help her.'

'She's told me about you. Okay, whatever you think,' Hugh says, coming to the floor and sitting beside us. 'What happened?' he asks her gently as I breathe in and out slowly.

'The wall tumbled down,' she says. 'All the bricks have crumbled. And she's weak inside. She's got to build herself up from the inside out.'

I look at her.

'We all tumble, we all fall, we get ourselves back up again. Thank goodness you were here, Hugh,' she says, rocking me back and forth. 'Also, I think I kneeled on some glass.'

I start laughing. It takes them by surprise. I can't stop, it's bordering on manic. Then as quickly as it arrives, it turns into uncontrollable tears.

Gospel was right about the characteristics of my arch-nemesis. I remained wary, on the lookout at all times for the person who could take me down, the person who lacks empathy, compassion, who shows no remorse, who manipulates and charms. He warned me that my nemesis would pull me to them over and over in my lifetime, that they would be so clever, I would never know who they are. He told me, if a nemesis is a mirror reflection of you, then in a way that makes them part of you.

In all the scenarios I envisioned, all the people I watched like a hawk, never for a second did I think my arch-nemesis could be myself, that I could tear myself down so viciously while I wasn't paying attention.

*

I was overconfident. I manipulated my aura for too long, pretended to be somebody I wasn't, and every single time I altered myself to become someone I wasn't, it ravaged the real part of me. It didn't take Hugh seeing me to realise that, but it did take seeing how he looked at me, my life from his perspective, to understand I couldn't hide it anymore.

I dispense with the shield, feeling naked without my shell, but on a positive note, lighter. I accept that I must learn to cope without it. I return to wearing sunglasses because my pain has meant I can see it even more brightly than before in others. After my own troubles, other people's emotions are even clearer and in sharper focus.

I was numbing myself to the effect other people have on me, but I cannot numb myself to my own. You can't shield yourself from yourself, not without becoming ill. Ironic, that my own actions would be the thing to make me feel worse. I can't keep trying to handle other people, I need to handle me when I'm with them.

I hand in my notice at work. I'm taking my time. My savings will keep me afloat for a short time while I find my feet again, and I'm taking baby steps. A walk in the park every day feeds my soul. I start taking care of my balcony garden again, and as I nurse my plants, I nurse myself. Today is day one on the Tube without my comfort blanket. I feel weak and vulnerable, shield gone completely. I feel like my insides are shaking, that at any moment I will get off and run home. I hate this frail young woman I've become, but I need to be her for a while.

Instead of standing by the door on the Tube, I move to a seat. A teenager looks up from her phone and stares at my trainers. She sends out hateful jealous green comets across the carriage at me. A man directly opposite me is reading a rag, he's spending a lot of time on page three, where a young woman with enthusiastic boobs smiles back at him, inviting him to create all kinds of fantasies. Red swirls around his crotch, mixed with black. I've never seen it before but it's like a diseased desire. I'm reminded right there of why I hate the Tube and wish I could wear my mask again and put up my shield. But I can't, I told myself I was constantly under urgent psychological attack every day, submerged in strange bodies, but I need to wean myself off it.

A man who appears never to have seen the inside of a bath or shower sits near me. His head swirls with an ever-changing cloud of colours. A strung-out young woman listening to dance music on headphones, whose jaw is working overtime, with pupils so big they almost fill her eyes, has disco lights flashing round her head. A couple sit together, holding hands, sharing pinks. Tired and resting their heads on each other, looking as though they're not long out of bed together. I don't mind being close to them; they're not interested in sharing their colours with anyone else, if they even notice there's anyone else in the carriage. *Mine*, their pinks say to each other. A man with predominant blue colours stands up to allow a pregnant woman with a gold torso to sit.

I'm so close to chickening out and putting my shield up when I see a guy further down the carriage. He's wearing large headphones and he's reading a book. How he does both is beyond me, but maybe there's no music on or he's not really reading. He turns a page. I watch his face. He's lost in the story. He's wearing a light grey suit, with no tie, the top buttons of his shirt are open, he wears trainers and a bag across his body, which rests on the empty chair beside him.

I keep looking at him. I can't figure him out. Reading and listening, a suit and trainers with no tie. I don't know if he's enjoying the book, if he likes the music he hears. I don't know if he's tired, or lonely, or happy, generous of spirit and mind. I don't know if he's grieving or excited about something. He reminds me of the couple twisted around each other – like them, he's in his own world and doesn't seem to notice anybody else – but the similarity is striking for a different reason and I can't put my finger on it.

The Tube stops. The doors open. A crowd gets off, a crowd gets on. A person squeezes her large hips beside mine. Somebody blocks my view of the man. I lean forward. I realise now what is so different about him, I realise why I have no sense of who or what he is.

He has no colours.

But that's impossible. Maybe they're faint; some people have very insipid wishy-washy colours. I remove my sunglasses.

He has no colours.

No colours.

I have never seen anyone without colours, not since I was younger than eight years old, not unless they're on television – and he's not on television. He's right in front of me. I can't stop staring at this freak of nature. I'm probably looking at him the way most people look at me.

All of a sudden he glances up from his book, at me, then down again. No doubt he's unnerved by the intensity of my stare, but if he is, I can't tell. I can't tell! I don't know if he's rattled, irritated, or if he noticed me at all.

I examine him for colours, all over his body, but there's nothing. No hidden swirls or mists, no rolling, no fireworks, no sparks or pops, no slow sleepy spirals. Absolutely nothing.

He glances up again, and out the window at the platform. Suddenly realising where he is, he jumps up and runs off the Tube, just before the doors close. Stunned, I leap for the doors but they're closing. I press the button over and over again, but they won't open. Hands to the glass, I watch him run through the crowd on the platform, dodging through the commuters, weaving in and out of colours as though they're puffs of smoke from a steam train. As the Tube pulls away, my hands remain on the glass as I watch the lone man jogging through the colourful crowd emitting no colours at all.

I tap my fingers impatiently on the kitchen table, waiting for Hugh to log on.

'Hey,' he says, finally. 'Are you okay?'

He's worried. I'd told him to call me urgently; he was in the middle of a class, I had to wait. He had to wait. No doubt we're both blobs of stress.

'I saw someone today.'

'Yeah?' He moves closer to the screen to see my face. I see the teacher's room in the background.

'A guy on the Tube.'

'Don't fall in love with a guy on a London Underground,' he warns playfully.

'He had no colours.'

He takes this in for a moment. I appreciate this about him, that he processes the things I tell him, to see how they fit, to see what they mean, rather than dismissing them as insanity.

'Maybe it was a faint colour?' he says. 'Beige. Maybe he's really boring.'

'No, I checked. I looked at every part of him. There was nothing at all. I didn't know how he felt, who he was, I didn't know . . . anything.'

'What did you do?'

'Stared at him and freaked him out? I didn't know what to do. Then I lost him.'

I'd gotten off at the next stop and gone back to the station I lost him at. I wandered the platforms even though I knew he wouldn't be there. Then I went up to the surface and walked up and down. It's a big road, with streets streaming from it on both sides, buildings crawling to the sky on both sides, endless numbers of businesses, shops and offices. He could be anywhere.

'What is a person who doesn't have colours?' Hugh asks. 'A sociopath?'

'I've seen plenty of sociopaths: they're full of colours, they feel a lot, just not the right feelings at the right time.'

'Do you think your gift is disappearing?'

I smile. He's always called it a gift when I always felt it was a curse.

'No, if anything it's gotten stronger since you left. What do you think I should do?'

He ponders this. 'I think you need to be very careful.'

I nod, feeling my heart sink. 'Yeah, I should just leave it.'

'No, Alice.' Unable to raise his voice in the staff room, he moves closer to the screen. 'You absolutely have to find him.'

Find the man with no colours.

I had ended up in that particular carriage of that Tube due to a series of errors – deliberate errors, I suppose. I was wandering, I was trying to get lost, I didn't have any particular destination other than trying to feel better, to feel my version of normal again. I wasn't supposed to be on it, the odds of me ever encountering him were slim, but I did it once. I need to find him again. I spend the next few days getting the same Tube, as close to the time as I can remember, and then, recalling how he was running when he disembarked, I guess he was late and should have been on an earlier Tube. So I get on the earlier one too, moving up and down the carriages, fighting the temptation to raise my shield, even if I had the energy to do so. Then I change tack, I give up on the Tube and instead stand at the entrance to the Tube station where he got off, monitoring everyone who comes and goes.

I don't find him.

I then reason that the odds of me being on that Tube were so low that the same could have been true of him, and he may never be on that Tube, or at this station, or on this street ever again in his life. So after three weeks I end my stalking and obsessive behaviour, feeling embarrassingly grief-stricken.

*

I'm a regular at the local garden centre, have been since my arrival in London, even when I couldn't afford to buy anything. I enjoy browsing. I notice a table of orchids are as miserable as can be; they are alive and beautiful, seemingly perfect to the consumer, but they are sad. There's no one around and so I quickly start to move them to the next table. I had killed many orchids in my time. I would bring them home and wander around with them in my hand to every part of the house, trying to figure out where they'd have the best chance of survival.

'Excuse me,' says a woman behind me.

I'm caught red-handed. I turn around, ready to apologise.

'Could you tell me where the dahlias are. I'm going to visit a friend in hospital and I want to give her dahlias.'

I suppose I do look as though I work here, dressed in black, wearing gloves. I direct her to the dahlias, but she looks confused, so I walk with her while she tells me about her friend, who slipped and broke her knee, which is unfortunate as she was just starting to get used to her new hip. She's a pleasant woman and I guide her to the dahlias then return to the orchids, where a young guy is staring at the half-empty table of orchids and little bit too crammed table of geraniums.

'They don't like it there,' I tell him.

'Did you move them?'

'Yeah. They don't like it there,' I explain. 'Look.'

I point up at the pipework on the wall beside them with a fan and hot air coming out from the café that faces in the opposite direction. 'It's like putting them beside a radiator.'

'Yeah,' he agrees. 'I'll move them, thanks.'

I beam all the way home with a sad orchid that I had to save.

Everyone needs time to find their place, and that's also true of plants. Sad Orchid takes her time, a little bit stubborn at first, a little bit pouty and moody. But I quickly grow to love my temperamental friend. She wants to be moved continuously to have the best of everything at all times. She refuses to settle in one place when there's another corner with better light at another time. She won't settle, she always wants the best for herself. She teaches me.

I return to Crystal Palace training grounds. I have been there many times already, each time observing him, just feeding some sort of need, not necessarily for him but for something familiar, warm, comforting. I go to him to ease the loneliness, which he does without knowing it, but I always walk away. I used to change my energy so that he wouldn't notice me, or I'd leave, but I'm not doing that anymore.

He signs the posters, programmes, his autobiography and whatever merchandise the fans have for him. Again he looks up as he's signing, over their heads because he's so tall. I'm wearing my shades, gloves, a long coat. I hold his book in my hands, hugging it to my chest, actually.

His eyes narrow suspiciously.

'Alice?'

The group of fans turn to look at me.

I hold his book out. 'Sign my book?'

'Alice Kelly!' He gives the fan his book back and then places one hand on the barrier and with a light bounce, he leaps effortlessly over the metal bar and runs to me.

'Alice?'

'Yes,' I grin, his excitement contagious.

He lifts me up and spins me around and I laugh, delighted and embarrassed at the same time.

'What are you doing here?'

'What do you think? I came to see you. I didn't know how else to get in touch with you.'

'Oh my God, this is amazing,' he puts me down and studies me. 'Still wearing the glasses.'

'Yep.'

He places a finger and gently pulls down the centre of the glasses so that they slide down my nose. He doesn't take them off completely, just stares deeply into my eyes.

'Yep. There she is. Right!' He claps his hands. 'Let's go.'

'Where?'

He grabs my hand, notices the gloves, but doesn't say anything.

'How did you get here?'

'Train, why . . .'

'You're coming with me.'

'Excuse me, excuse me,' he says, pushing his way through the gang. 'This is Alice Kelly, my best friend from school. Let's go.'

I laugh as the group cheer and he brings me to the car park to an expensive black jeep.

'Come to my place?'

I look at him.

'Not like that. If we go anywhere else, we won't get any peace,' he says, referring to the fans. 'And I don't want to miss a second of hearing all about you.'

My heart skips a beat. 'Uh, there's not much to tell.'

'Shut up, get in the car.'

I laugh and climb up into the enormous Range Rover.

'Gospel, how much did this thing cost?'

'Two hundred grand,' he says with a cheeky grin. 'Can you believe it?'

We both start laughing and I feel like I'm back in school with him.

'I got two of them.'

We roll around laughing. He wipes his eyes and starts the engine.

His house is even more impressive than the jeep. An enormous house in the countryside, with a guest house, and loads of land, a long drive and a sweeping car park with a water fountain.

'Whoa.'

'You like it?'

'Like it? I love it. It's incredible.'

The door opens and a little boy comes running outside, followed by a petite blonde woman. 'Daddy, daddy, daddy, daddy,' he shouts, running straight at him.

Gospel opens his arms and scoops him up, smothering him with kisses as he wriggles in delight.

'Hey buddy, I brought someone special home today.'

'McDonald's?'

'No not McDonald's. It's even better than that. It's my best friend from school, Alice.'

'Hi there. What's your name?'

'Cassius.'

'Cassius, what a great name. Nice to meet you.'

We shake hands.

'Come on,' Cassius shouts, running back into the house.

'Hello,' I say to the young blonde standing at the door, feeling immediately jealous and glad that Gospel can't see the immaturity of my colours.

'This is Mia, his minder,' he says.

'Oh, hi,' I smile, even bigger.

'Let me show you around.'

It's like a hotel. We end up sitting in his monstrous kitchen, gleaming worktops and fancy ovens, windows that fill the wall looking out over a massive garden with a treehouse and every toy a child could want. But the energy is stagnant. I don't know who decorated the place but the energy is not Gospel's. In every single room there are antlers on the walls or tiger skin on the floor, parts of dead animals like ivories, skins, shells, horns, taxidermied and embalmed species. Gospel is so positive and full of warmth, and his son is so full of life and fun, and yet the flow is constantly interrupted by death, which looms over the place.

'What do you think?'

'Gospel, you've done so well for yourself. It's incredible. Congratulations.'

'I couldn't have done it without you.'

'Well that's a lie,' I say, 'but sweet of you.'

'It's true. I'll never forget what you did for me. That day changed everything.'

I shake my head and fold my arms, not wanting to talk about it.

'The rose bush died,' he says, eyes wide. 'Of course it worked. Look at me, Alice!' He raises his arms, their expanse so long, to indicate everything: him, his home, his life. 'I wrote to you loads after you changed your number and didn't give me your new one. I even phoned you at the school, but you wouldn't take my call.'

'Yeah, I know. I got them, I just . . . you know what it was like in the school. When you left, it was weird. I was kind of alone. Had to start again.'

'If you'd kept in touch, you wouldn't have been alone.'

I shift uncomfortably.

'You did your Leaving Cert?'

I nod.

'Yay.'

We laugh.

'Then what?'

'Then . . .' I sigh. 'Lily got sick. She had cancer on her spine. They operated on her. Removed the tumour successfully but it led to paralysis, so I became her carer.'

'What? No . . .' he says, shaking his head, not liking where this is going. 'What about your brothers. Hugh and . . .'

'Ollie? Ollie went to prison, don't ask,' I roll my eyes. 'And Hugh moved to Doha.'

'What the . . . Alice, this is awful, I'm so sorry.'

'No, it really wasn't so awful. And it's okay now, I'm here in London. Got my own place. Have a job. I was in sales but now I'm a Grow Wild Engagement and Training Assistant at Kew Gardens. It's a youth project, an outreach programme encouraging people in disadvantaged areas to get involved in plant and fungal science. So, yep. It's as fancy as it sounds.'

'You're like Mr Smith at the academy.'

'I am *not* like Mr Smith,' I say, laughing at the memory of our poor allotment teacher. 'Oh, poor Mr Smith.

Remember when Simon threw the pot against the wall because there was a worm in it?'

'He's a cameraman now with Sky Sports.'

'Simon is?'

'Yeah, I met him when I was doing an interview. Couldn't believe it when he shook my hand. He got over the germs thing.'

I laugh and decide not to mention seeing Saloni.

'You've always liked getting your hands in the soil,' he says, a smile crawling onto his lips as he remembers. 'The rose bush died, Alice.'

'I'm just the course administrator,' I say, waving the repeated comment away, not wanting to go there. 'So it's more hands on a computer than in the soil. It's a twelve-month contract and it'll be over in a few months so I need to find something else. But everything's good. I just wanted to see you.'

He can sense my loneliness and I'm embarrassed, wishing I'd come here as the success he has become, wishing I had another story.

He places his hand over mine and I feel his warmth through my gloves. Seeping into me, moving up my arm, into my chest. Like a hot cup of tea on a cold day.

'It's okay,' he whispers.

I nod, tears filling my eyes. 'Thanks. I think I should have gone with you when you asked me,' I say, laughing, and wiping the corner of my eye quickly before the tear falls. '"Come with me, Alice,"' I imitate him, laughing. '"We can live together."'

'I really wanted that,' he says.

'We were only seventeen.'

'Yeah, but I meant it.'

'And wow, look how things worked out for you,' I say, changing the mood, and lighting up. 'You're a footballer. You're a dad.'

'Yeah,' he says, pinks popping like bursting bubble gum all around him at the mention of his son. 'He's the best. Cassius is the best thing that ever happened to me. What about his colours? Did you see them?'

'Of course. They're swirling around him like mini-tornados. Hyperactive, energetic bright red, bright yellow and neon green. Bundles of energy.'

He throws his head back and laughs. 'That's exactly him. So he's okay?' he asks, relief in his voice.

'He's okay,' I say. People change, but Cassius's predominant colour is an energetic, powerful red. I think he'll be moving through life like a cyclone and may at some point have to learn to slow down; he has none of the thoughtful, focused and logical colours of his dad.

The front door opens. 'I'm home,' a woman calls.

'Mummy!' Cassius races like hell through the rooms to get to her.

The spell is broken, we both move our hands away from each other and I wipe beneath my eyes, sit up straight to see the long-legged beauty stride into her home, a yoga mat under one arm, her son under another. Supermodel limbs with skin that glows and hair that shines. If she's put out by my presence she hides it well, though she does look surprised.

'Hello,' she looks at me, and then to her husband.

'Baby,' he says, standing up, going to her and giving her a kiss. 'This is someone very special that I told you about – a *lot*: Alice Kelly. Alice, this is my wife Jamelle.'

Her eyes widen. 'Alice. Oh my God. I've heard so much about you.' She puts down Cassius and her yoga mat, and comes to me, her arms open, then pauses. 'Oh no, you don't like hugs. Wait. What do I do?' She looks at Gospel nervously, then back to me. She squeezes her own chest in a hug. 'Okay, I'm hugging you.'

I laugh. 'Thank you.'

I'm crying. Gospel is crying. He's packed his bags. The summer holidays will end soon, he's finished at the academy, he's not coming back, he has trials with Burnley, he can't miss the opportunity. We've spent the summer together, I was allowed to stay at his place, his parents became my parents, and now it's over.

'Come with me,' he says, placing his hands on my cheeks. He kisses me gently.

'To Burnley?' I laugh, crying. 'And what would I do?'

'You don't have to do anything. They're paying me.'

'I can't just do nothing.'

'Do what you did this summer. Work in a café, wherever, it doesn't matter. When I'm a massive football star I'll make enough money for both of us.'

We laugh at the dream.

He blinks, twitches, throws his head back and grunts.

'It's a nice thought, Gospel, but I don't think the host family will let me stay with you, besides I have to finish my Leaving Cert. Hugh would go crazy if I don't. Education is the only way forward,' I say, imitating him.

'Not if you're a footballer.'

'Think I have a chance at that?' I smile.

He twitches and blinks again. He's upset, anxious, he's been acting out more often the past few weeks. He's nervous. He throws his head back three times in a row.

He swears loudly, frustrated with himself, and then screams. Not at me, it's at himself for the part of his body and mind he can't control. Red bubbles burst around him like an exploding dye pack leaving him surrounded by a red mist. I give him a moment to calm down, for the mist to evaporate.

'What am I going to do when this happens to me at the club?' he asks, throat raw from shouting.

'It won't happen. It never happens on the pitch.'

'What about off the pitch?' Blink, blink, twitch, grunt. 'What if we're in the dressing room in the middle of the manager giving us a pep talk and I can't stop. . . .What do you think will happen then?'

He has so much orange around his chest.

I have always avoided touching him when he is like this – for me and for him. I've sensed he hasn't wanted anyone near him when he is highly upset and vexed, any more than a caged lion would want to be patted. The pale orange of low self-esteem, his low sense of self-worth, his discomfort and self-consciousness, brings the red mists of rage; for him they go hand in hand. He has worked hard while at the academy to manage the rage, taking deep breaths, breathing in slowly, holding it and letting it out, going for runs outside, doing laps of the pitch or yoga exercises. But those tools aren't acceptable or accessible when you're in normal life, you can't always run out of a room and race down the road, you can't always stop an uncomfortable conversation or a heated argument to breathe deeply in and out. Sometimes the tools they've taught us can't prepare us for life, but the very living of life, of finding ourselves in those uncomfortable situations will give us tools of our own. He will have to find this in the changing rooms when surrounded by his peers and his heroes. My heart aches for him, and I fear for him. How long will he last there, how will they treat him? Will they realise that his talents on pitch far outweigh the motor and vocal tics off pitch?

I take my gloves off and place my hand over his chest. It goes through the pale orange, but I leave it there. I feel his battle with himself; a control conflict, and it becomes mine too.

'What are you doing?'

'It's always right here,' I say, trying to ignore his feelings that are transferring to me. It's the first time I've told him this. We've talked before about his colours but never his colours of discomfort, I don't know if he knows there's a difference. The orange always clings to him here, as if trapping his chest and causing the tics, the blinks, the twitches, the grunts. I guide him to the floor, and we sit opposite each other.

I put two hands in the orange and move my hands around. For once I'm not afraid that it will get on me. I want to take it away from him. It moves with me side to side, but it's thicker than it looks. Sluggish, like mucus, yet hard like it needs to be broken down. I place my hands on his chest. No wonder he can barely catch his breath. It's strangling him.

'Why is it here?' I ask. 'In this place of all places.'

'I dunno.'

'I read something about trauma,' I say, swallowing, not sure how he'll take it. 'When we experience trauma, it gets stored in the subconscious, like an echo. It sits in our energy field disrupting our natural flow of energy. I think this is an echo. It's not related to anything that's happening now. It's nothing to do with now.'

He tries to move, uncomfortable with the conversation. I hold on to him.

'It's all around here,' I say, moving my hands around in it. I can't feel it, but the colour moves like thick gunk under my motion.

The more attention I give it, the more the orange grows. He blinks, he twitches, he grunts.

'What did the therapists at school say to do?' I ask.

'Breathe. Look at the things in the room I'm in. Five things, then four things, then three things . . .'

'Forget that. Just tell it to fuck off,' I say.

He starts laughing.

'Fuck off!' I shout at the orange at his chest.

'Fuck off!' he yells, joining in.

We both yell it over and over again, stronger and louder, getting all our frustrations out.

I close my eyes. I have so much love for him. I don't want him to leave, but I want it for him. I don't want him to be bullied in the dressing room, this kind, beautiful soul. I don't want him to have a day of worry. I want him to have the perfect life that he deserves, for all his wishes to come true. If anyone deserves it, it's him. I want to take it all away from him and make the world easier for him. I want it, I want it, I want it so badly.

'Alice,' he says suddenly, and I open my eyes.

'What?'

He's breathing normally. The orange from his chest is gone.

But my hands are on fire.

I stand up and run outside, out through his kitchen where his mum and dad have abandoned reading the Sunday papers to listen to us through the door.

'What's going on?' his dad asks.

'Leave them, they're arguing,' his mum says.

I run into the garden. Gospel chases me. My hands are on fire, like two flames have taken over my hands. I fall to my knees on the grass and I push my hands into the soil beside the rose bush, as far down as they can go, until the flames go out.

I fall back on the grass, exhausted. He lands beside me and we stare at the sky.

'It got on my hands,' I say simply.

'Well, maybe an orange tree will grow,' he says.

I silently doubt very much that anything will grow there anymore. But maybe Gospel will now. We start laughing hysterically.

Gospel's father tuts, watching us from the door, then goes back inside.

The old adage 'You'll find what you're looking for when you stop looking,' is nonsense. I never stopped looking for the man with no colours. Not from the moment I lost him. I looked out for him everywhere, particularly on the Tube, as if it was the only place a creature like him could live. I looked for people like him, people without colours, but he remained a phenomenon because I never found any.

Until I found him.

It's 9 a.m. and I'm standing at the corner opposite the Tube station entrance. I've been here since 8 a.m., thinking it a good time to cover all angles and all average work starting times. Of course he could have been in the area for pleasure, to visit someone, or a salesman perhaps, but that only presented a depressing conclusion that I would never find him again, so I returned to Plan A: him working in the area. I did entertain the notion that he'd been so deep in his book and listening to whatever he was listening to that he may have missed his stop. I'd spent mornings at the other Tube station, too, searching for him.

But this morning here I am at the corner, with a view of the Underground steps and every which way he could go from there, pondering whether I should risk getting a bottle of water from the shop or to stay put at my post. The 'just five more minutes' mantra is endless torture, and so I decide to stay until 10 a.m., but when 10 a.m. arrives I want to stay for five more minutes. Perhaps a bottle of water and five more minutes. As I'm having this internal argument, he appears. He steps up to the top of the stairs, navy-blue suit, white shirt, open buttons, trainers, bag over his back. I actually cannot believe it. Nine months later. I freeze in shock then realise I need to move before I lose him again. He takes a right, so I run across the road, a car beeping as I narrowly avoid being hit as it rounds the corner, and I follow him on the path, hurrying and slowing down according to my overexcited, panicked inner voice.

He walks slowly, strolls, everyone overtakes him in fact. He's like a stone stuck in a stream, blocking everything behind him and sending people gushing around him. He wears the same headphones, a suit with trainers, the same bag. I try to keep track of where we're going but I know that I'll never be able to retrace my footsteps. My eyes are on him and his lack of colour. Now that I can see him up close and examine him, I can confirm there really is no colour. After a while I start to relax, settling in to the fact that I've found him. He walks across the side streets, sometimes waiting for pedestrian lights, sometimes running across just in time. Unreadable and no rhythm. I'm enjoying myself now, watching him in the flesh after thinking about him so much.

He's taller than me. Slim build, with black wavy hair, wavy curtains, and short at the back. I want to see more of his face and I rely on the bus and passing traffic on the side streets for that so I can view his reflection.

Older than me. Mid to late thirties but I don't know exactly, age isn't my forte. He's handsome, but not in a way everyone would turn to stare. The kind of face that gets better the longer you stare, which I do. He has a button nose that seems too small for his face at first glance, but it's cute.

He looks over his shoulder at me at one point, at a side street, when a car passes. I'm standing too close. He smells clean, fresh, like he's just showered. I don't know the names of scents. Maybe there's gym clothes in that bag, maybe he's just worked out and taken a shower. Maybe he's going to work out now. There's so much about him that I don't know, least of all his inner feelings, his soul. He crosses the street and I allow more space between us.

He takes a right and I do too.

There's only one building that dominates this dead end, only one place he could be going and therefore the only place that I could be going to too.

New Horizons Youth Work Centre.

'Hi Andy,' a guy says, walking past him.

'Hey Greg,' he says in a Scottish accent. My heart leaps. Andy, from Scotland.

'Isn't your class almost over?' Greg teases, looking at his watch.

'I'm teaching them about endurance,' he shouts back. 'They'll need it.'

'Ha,' Greg retorts.

I stop walking as Andy nears the building. That's it. He'll go inside, I won't see him anymore, but at least I'll know he's in there. I wonder how many entrances and exits there are. If I should wait and follow him home or have faith and come back tomorrow. Of course I'm going to follow him home; anything could happen, he could get fired today for being late and never come back. I'd never find him again.

He opens the door and looks back at me. Then pulls the door open and steps to the side. Holding it open for me.

'Oh,' I say.

I know I should fade my aura, I don't want him to think I'm a stalker, but I also want him to see me. I can't mirror his aura, choose which would be the best and most attractive for him, because I can't see his. I can't lessen my colours so I'm not overpowering, or increase them so he's drawn to my power. I'm completely at a loss as to how to get his attention, how to please him, how to be something or someone that entices him.

I'm stuck here, as me, just myself, and I don't know what to do.

'Are you going in?' he asks, holding the door open.

'Oh no, thank you,' I say, taking my sunglasses off.

'Just . . . taking a walk?' he says with a grin. 'You have to go back the way you came, it's a dead end.'

'No it's not,' I say, looking at him, looking up. 'Hopefully it's the beginning.'

I don't know what else to say, but I don't want him to leave, I'm still standing in the middle of the road, looking at him. He allows the door to close. He remains outside.

'I saw you on the Tube,' I say, before I really have the chance to think about it, but it all comes out anyway. 'Months ago.' I swallow. 'And then I saw you again, just there. You passed by and I just wanted to . . . um, well, I know this sounds weird – I promise you I'm not weird. Actually, that's not true, I am a little weird, but not in a bad way.'

He's grinning at me, seemingly open to my ramblings.

'I just wanted to say hi to you.'

'You followed me here?' he asks.

'Um. I should say no, but, yes.'

He chuckles, takes his headphones off and wraps them around his neck. 'What's your name?'

'Alice Kelly.'

'Hi Alice Kelly. I'm Andy. It's a pleasure to meet you,' he says. 'I'm flattered.'

I smile and we hold it for a second.

'I'll see you on the Tube again, maybe.'

'Yeah.' I back away and wave, then turn around and walk back down the street, my heart pounding, fighting the urge to turn around. I lose the battle at the corner and when I turn around, with a smile ready, he's gone.

'You get on the Tube again tomorrow,' Hugh says. 'Definitely.'

'I don't know,' Poh says, their toddler asleep in her arms. 'I don't know. I need a guy's perspective.'

'Am I not a guy?'

'Yes, but we're married and out of the dating game a long time,' she says. 'In fact we only ever dated each other.'

'That's what you think,' Hugh says, teasing. 'Andy's practically said to her, I'll see you on the Tube.'

Andy Tennant, he's on the youth centre website. I like that Hugh used his name, speaks about him as if he's real now, because he is real. I found him, but how do I keep him, figure him out?

'You think? You don't suppose that he'll be creeped out that she's following him?' Poh asks. 'I don't know, Alice, this is so different, you asking us about what people want. Usually you know instinctively.'

'I know, that's what's so odd about him. It's like he's speaking a different language and I have to learn how to speak all over again.'

They both laugh.

'What?'

'Welcome to being human,' Hugh says. 'I'm still trying to figure out what she wants.'

'Sleep,' Poh says, standing up. 'His advice should come with a warning,' she says. 'Night,' she kisses him and he watches her leave.

I want what they have.

And I smile to myself because, as terrifying as this is, I've wanted to be just like everyone else for a long time. Now I have it. He's the connection I've been looking for, the power cord that can attach me to another person without me directly sticking my finger in the socket and getting a shock, the source that I need for my own quality of life. He is the only man, the only person who can make me feel so . . . human.

I attend a job interview which I have no business applying for, to become manager of a garden centre and nursery. I have no idea why they call me for an interview; maybe they're desperate.

A panel of three people face me. As I shake their hands and take my seat, I try as quickly as possible to get a feel for them. It helped that I observed them together earlier before they went into the interview room. There is a logical yellow, a rich powerful blue and a sympathetic deep green. I instantly know never to go darker than the powerful blue so as not to be seen as a challenge. It is the powerful blue that I must win over. The man with the deep green is understanding and smiling throughout, asking gentle light questions where he thinks I will shine, asking me about things I like to do, hobbies, that kind of thing. Logical Yellow asks questions to assess how I'll deal with problematic matters, difficult customers and preparing plants for a cold snap. Dark Blue, cynical and conservative, is intent on making me as uncomfortable as possible and sending me on my way.

It's been nine months since I stopped shielding myself and changing my aura colours. I think today is an acceptable break away, and even Naomi agrees. I temporarily draw the predominant blue colour over mine when she asks her questions and while I answer. It's difficult to do this while I'm so nervous at the same time as trying to think of clever answers, as well as trying to stay calm, but I have become a bit of an expert at this. I have taken what Naomi has taught me to new levels that even she could not fathom.

'Usually,' Dark Blue says, 'applicants have a degree in botany or horticulture or some experience in this area.'

It's not a question. It's a reason why I shouldn't have this job.

I draw the blue over me, slightly paler than hers, but dark enough for her to feel we're in the same club, that there's a chance we're on the same level. 'For the past year I've worked with Kew Gardens on their Grow Wild flagship outreach learning initiative, engaging with youth and community audiences across London to encourage people to enjoy plants and fungi. People in disadvantaged areas, who wouldn't ordinarily be in the position to do so.'

'Your role was in administration, was it not?' Dark Blue asks.

'I wanted to be in the botany world and I learned a lot being in that environment. My love of plants has helped me to become more educated and knowledgeable about them. I've learned about them in my own time, not in college.'

'Yes,' Deep Green looks down at my résumé. 'You were a carer for your mother.'

'Yes. We used to walk all the time, through parks and gardens. That's how I discovered my love for it. I transformed the garden at home, I felt it helped with her development and my own mental health.' It's an interview, it's almost expected you'll lie about something. 'She wasn't the easiest of people, so I think that experience will help me with disgruntled customers. She taught me to have patience.' I say, realising this isn't a lie.

'But this isn't gardening job,' Dark Blue says. Dark Blue wants to stick to the rules. She's against me. Deep Green is for me. It's up to Logical Yellow to give the presiding vote.

'I think the same rules apply to a garden centre and nursery as they do to my balcony,' I say, thinking of my bustling balcony at home. 'You must consider the scale and use of the space available, the importance of seasonality and selecting plants that provide year-round interest. Try to have something in flower every week of the year. Consider light and aspect to help select plants that will thrive. Be realistic about creating something you can maintain.'

'What do you imagine your typical day will be like here?' Dark Blue asks with a smirk.

'I imagine no two days will be the same,' I reply. 'Weather and seasonality will dictate most of it.'

Deep Green smiles supportively.

'I may not have horticulture theory and qualifications, but I have plant knowledge. Let's just say I understand trees and plants better than I understand most people. Tree roots connect and communicate under the ground, if you follow their line of communication you can identify where the problem is. Like a line or circle of handholding; when someone lets go and breaks the chain, you have to identify the problem.'

'Have you any examples of how you identified a problem like this?' Logical Yellow asks.

'I've brought a letter from Laurence Metcalf, the head gardener at the Ormsby Estate and Private Gardens.'

'Laurence Metcalf, the recent recipient of the Royal Horticultural Society's President's Award?' Dark Blue asks.

'And regular winner at the Chelsea Flower Show,' Deep Green says with a smile.

I didn't know that. I try to hide my surprise.

'I was out walking with my mum when I recognised ash dieback in the trees and brought it to his attention. As a result, the government set up a scheme to help parks and forestry with a fund to replant ash affected by dieback. I believe Laurence was the first to avail of this grant, the first to report sight of the plague.'

I hand Logical Yellow the letter. She puts her glasses on and reads.

They contact me three days later to tell me the job is mine.

I'm on the Tube, I am glowing with the news of my new job. I'm slightly distracted, wondering how on earth I'm going to pull it off, believing in myself as well as thinking I'm the world's greatest fraud, when I feel a poke on my shoulder.

'Hello, Alice Kelly,' he says.

'Andy, hi.'

I have been on the Tube every day since I met him; he did not appear. I have been disappointed but I haven't panicked; I know where he works, I can find him if I want to.

'Too bright down here,' he says, noting my glasses.

'Oh. Yeah. Kind of.'

'Hungover?'

'Oh no. I don't drink.'

'Okay. Weirdo,' he says, laughing, then immediately stops. 'Sorry, that was a joke. The last time I asked someone why they didn't drink they told me they were an alcoholic. That was embarrassing.'

I look at him, around him. Trying to figure him out. We've never stood so close.

'Don't tell me you're one,' he says, worried.

'No!'

'Phew. It's just that in Glasgow, where I grew up, if someone was an alcoholic, it meant they drank too much, you know? Not like now when it's alcoholics who say they don't drink.' He visibly cringes. 'Let me start again. Hi, Alice Kelly.'

'Hi Andy.' I smile. 'You can just call me Alice, you know.'

'Great, we do know each other a little better now after all. On your way to work?'

'Actually no, but I just learned I got a new job.'

'Yeah? Congratulations. What is it?'

'Nursery manager.'

'Babies?'

'No.' I don't know whether to laugh or not, I don't know if he's joking or not. I can't catch the tone, though maybe

I could if I stopped looking around him for the usual tell-tale signs. I've actually got to start listening to *him*, reading *him*. He looks over his shoulder to see who I'm looking at. I try to focus on him, on his face, on his button nose, on his brown/hazel eyes, but I'm so used to reading colours I have fallen down on pure human interaction. The gaps are clear, my weaknesses are revealed. I feel my body start to tremble nervously. I want to please him so much.

A man gets on and stands beside us. He has worrying, troubled colours all over him. I move Andy away from him quickly.

'What's wrong?'

'We just need to move.'

'Okay.' We walk down the carriage to the next standing area. The man we left behind suddenly vomits all over the place. People groan and move away, the stench is horrific.

'Good call,' he says, impressed. 'Let's get off at the next stop, we can walk the rest of the way, yeah?' he says, holding his nose. I agree and we don't speak again until we get off, along with the rest of the people on the carriage.

'So you work with babies,' he says, once we're in the fresh air.

He walks so slowly, the world spins around him again and he just strolls along, probably late for work but in no rush at all.

'No. Actually, it's a horticultural nursery,' I say. 'Plants.'

'Now that's different,' he says. 'Do you have a degree in horticulture or something like that?'

'Nothing like that. I didn't go to university. It's a long and uninteresting story.'

'That's the way to tee it up.'

I laugh. 'Don't worry, I'm not telling it. Basically, I'm completely unqualified. I don't know why they hired me, so I probably won't last long.'

'That's the spirit,' he says, punching the air, and I laugh. 'But seriously, feeling out of your depth – that's when you know you're doing the right thing.'

'Oh.'

'Unless you're in a pool or the sea and you don't know how to swim. On that occasion, depth is a bad idea.'

I laugh.

He watches me for a moment. 'Would you like to go for a coffee?'

'So you don't drink coffee either,' he says, looking at me clinging to my bottle of water with gloved hands.

'No. No caffeine.'

I don't offer a reason and he doesn't ask.

'You were saying: you didn't go to uni because . . .'

'I wasn't saying.' I smile.

'But I want to hear it.' He tears the top of a chocolate muffin and stuffs it in his mouth.

'I had to care for my mum. She had an operation on her spine that confined her to a wheelchair, so I stayed home to care for her full-time.'

'You've no siblings?'

'Two brothers. One is in Doha, the other was in prison at the time.'

He raises his eyebrows. I sip my water, watch his reaction.

He leans in. 'Doha? Well that's a new one.'

I laugh. 'Prison is no big deal, but Doha is?'

'Well,' he says, 'I've known quite a few people who went to prison, I don't know anyone who's gone to Doha.'

We both laugh.

I look around the coffee shop. I don't like the energies of the person closest to me. 'Do you mind if we move over there?' I point to a free table, away from everything else.

'Yeah sure.' He picks up his coffee and chocolate muffin and moves immediately. 'You don't care for your mum anymore, so does that mean she's . . . ?'

'Still alive. My brother got out of prison and he's caring for her. If that's possible. I had to go, I couldn't stay there.'

'Never good to stay in toxic families.'

'No.'

'I know a lot about that.'

'I'm sorry to hear that.'

'From the youth centre mainly. I've a great family, thankfully. I was raised by my grandparents. Didn't know my dad, and Mum was a drug addict, but despite that I had an idyllic upbringing. It could easily have gone the other way though. I think that's why I was drawn to my job.'

'What is a youth worker, exactly?'

'It's when a thirty-six-year-old man gets bullied every day by teenagers.'

I laugh.

'Nah. Most people think it's teaching troublemakers, but I take issue with that.' He licks chocolate from his thumb. 'In the mood to hear a rant? It will help me practise for when I rip the head off another teacher this afternoon.'

'Absolutely.' I grin.

'Here's what I think about troublemakers. No, here's what I *know* about troublemakers. It's a social label that I despise.

Troublemakers are usually highly sensitive people and highly sensitive people can be very conscientious, cautious, perceptive and empathetic. They can often see what others cannot and they're like sponges, absorbing all the energy and stimulus around them.'

I watch his lips, his eyes. I suddenly can't remember how to breathe. I'm holding my breath. I have to remind myself of the in and out. Is this a set-up? Did Hugh organise this? Or Naomi?

'They notice when someone is uncomfortable, sad or angry, no matter how much someone tries to hide their feelings. They understand the differences in perception versus reality, and inequality. They usually have strong values such as kindness and fairness. People who don't understand the nature of highly sensitive people refer to them as troublemakers. And that's how I feel about that. I will defend my students until the cows come home.'

He takes a final bite of muffin and squeezes the wrapper together, sending crumbs everywhere. He's very messy.

'I won't apologise,' he says, mouth full. 'You gave me permission to rant.'

'I'm glad you did. Where did you learn that?'

'I studied sociology, but mainly I learned it from being with my students over the years. Anyway. What's your favourite movie?'

I laugh at the sudden change of direction.

A man enters the café with a swirl of muddy green around his head. He sits at the table beside us; the swirling reminds me of racing bluebottle flies circling over a heap of dung. I finally have Andy here, right before me in the flesh and all I want to do is leave. Don't want to, *need* to leave, I need to get away from the man whose thoughts are attracting an infestation. I twist the lid of my water bottle tight, I'm unsettled in my seat.

'Or are you more of a TV person? I can binge an entire season of a show back to back until 4 a.m., but for some reason a movie is now too long.'

I laugh again. I could just listen to him the entire time, not say a word, but I know it doesn't work like that. And the man beside me is putting me off. I could draw my shield but I don't do that anymore after what happened, I can't return to that fragile state, and anyway, I don't want to be numb to Andy, not him of all people.

'You done?' he asks.

I nod. 'Thank you.'

'Okay. Next time you'll have to let me buy you more than a bottle of water.'

I smile at the promise of next time.

As we're leaving, the man who was seated behind me violently pushes his chair back, crushing mine, and stands up. He starts thumping his chest as though he's in church, bellowing an admission of guilt and sinfulness.

'Christ, they're all out today. You dodge the crazies like Muhammad Ali dodges jabs,' Andy remarks.

'They're always out. You just have to know how to see them,' I say.

'But why can't I touch you?' Andy says.

'You are touching me. I'm naked, you're naked, I'm on you.'

He looks at me, those eyes, and I hate that I don't know

what he's thinking. Probably that I'm a freak. A few dates in and he's already discovered it.

'If you don't want to do it like this, then we won't,' I say. I climb off him.

He pulls me back. 'I do. But we've done it your way. Now let's try it my way. Trust me.'

I find myself moving slowly down onto the bed, the sheets heated by the sunlight through the window. His lips kiss my neck, he takes my hands and folds his fingers over mine. I'm used to doing it my way, the way I've always done. The less bodily contact the better. I don't want, or need, to feel everything my partner's feeling in this moment, nothing is ever 100 per cent passion, everything has roots in everything. Sometimes I've sensed their guilt, that's a big turn-off; their hunger, greed and neediness can make me feel their desperation; their loneliness can make me feel pity. Everything can be a turn-off. I want to switch off their emotions, make it about me for just this once.

But he has no colours that I can see. He has energies that I must learn to sense and read, but so far I can't. I try it his way. I open my eyes, I hadn't been doing that. I see him. I feel him. I notice things that I haven't before, things that colours hide, that they can distract you from.

'Well?' he asks afterwards as we snuggle down under the blankets. He's spooning me and kissing my shoulder. I can feel his heartbeat against my back, the sun is starting to rise.

I concede that his way is better, but only with him.

*

He shows me his office.

There's a mug on his desk that says *There's a good chance this is vodka.* On the wall there's a small sign hanging off a picture frame that reads *Some days I amaze myself. Other days I look for my phone while I'm talking on it.* A huge pinboard is cluttered with different coloured Post-it notes filled with messages from past students: *Thanks bro, Johnny. Thanks for everything, Laura. Good luck without me, Alan B. I will never forget you, Alison. Best teacher ever, Sarah.* Stuffed teddies and weird creatures clutter his desk and decorate his computer monitor. A Mr Messy bookstand holds together paperwork in his scribbly hands. A photo of him with his grandparents who raised him, him with friends at a music festival, wearing sparkles on their faces, muddy wellington boots on their feet. A box of tissues that says *How do you make a tissue dance? Put a boogie in it.*

I look at the pinboard of Post-it notes again. A lot of people trust him. They must have liked him to scribble their notes and stick them to the board. He must have liked them to keep them there. They all left here. They must have told him their secrets and they moved on. A wall of references, a wall of voices telling me to trust.

Though I know very little about how to run a nursery, that part is actually the easiest. The people are what I struggle with most at the beginning. I open the nursery in the morning and close at the end of the day. I create staff work rosters and delegate duties. I order nursery stock, including soil, stones, fertilisers, shrubs, plants and trees. I look to the previous orders for an idea of quantities. We grow plants, trees and shrubs to use as stock. I monitor watering times, soil conditions and plant positions.

I can't afford to work exactly as I did at home in Dublin or in the flat and the balcony, allowing things to die in order to figure out where they'll flourish, but I do read the plants' colours as well as reading the instruments, and I do take some inspiration from my balcony by setting up a rainwater harvesting system, which captures rainwater on the roof. Frankly, I'm surprised the previous manager didn't do this, but there are many new things I'm surprised he didn't do, and many new things I'm surprised that I can bring to the job.

What I love doing most is creating attractive gardens and plant displays. I could spend all day doing it if I had the time. The staff are a nice bunch, but they don't all like each other, as is normal. In the first few terrifying weeks I watch the flow of colours to see who is the dominant character, who is changing the air for the worst and who does it for the best. That would be Cathy: all colours flow to her. People like her. I put her in charge of staff rosters.

Margo is like dynamite. She arrives angry, manages to have some sort of altercation with everyone who crosses her path, including customers who she considers imbeciles, and then goes home. Her anger to me looks swollen, like hot teething gums. Something is beneath, pushing up, and it's hurting her and as a result is hurting everyone around her. I notice her irritation rise when she's given long detailed descriptive orders. The less words and directions, the better. I shorten my sentences as the red starts to appear.

Umar is the opposite. Before I arrived he was working on displays, but it muddled his head. He prefers logistics, problem-solving, organising the preparation of trees and shrubs for sale and shipment.

Donal used to handle the machinery work but clashed with Terry. Jim talks incessantly about plants and flowers to anyone who'll listen, but not many people do. Donal, who lost his dad when he was thirteen, seems to gravitate towards Jim. He sends his colours out, Jim receives them and sends his back. Donal embraces them. I take Donal off power tools and put him on the ground with Jim, away from the retail part of the nursery.

I put Margo the dynamite stick in the tractor, moving stuff around, relishing the banter with red-faced, foul-mouthed Terry. Whereas Terry used to scare Donal and stress him out, his company seems to invigorate Margo.

I give Jim a phone so that we can transfer customer calls to him, but only the ones who have the time, the ones who appreciate the oversharing of information.

I notice Lucy, an outgoing girl from the garden centre coffee shop, chatting to everyone. She's young, hip and cool. I steal her from the café to work on marketing. She whips up informative social media posts and responds to customer requests, and her witty posts gain us lots of new followers. She also has an eye for what looks good on Instagram, lets the public know what's in stock, what the latest trends are. And she gives the old-fashioned, stuffy website an overhaul.

I create hampers to sell in the store and online and they're such a hit that we can barely keep up with the orders over the Christmas period. The customers enjoy browsing the tunnels and the outside areas in a quest to find the elusive plant, and I begin a new project to introduce a garden for children to get lost in while their parents browse. We're already attracting customers, mothers and buggies, to the coffee shop, it would be good to bring them out into the garden centre itself. I set up a dedicated area to the healing power of plants. The best plants for the workspace, plants for the home, the best plants for a bathroom with low light, ideal plants for a windowsill. Plants that will help reduce mental fatigue, plants that generate an abundance of oxygen and help a good night's sleep. My little corner grows and grows with the interest it receives, until it needs an entirely dedicated section of its own. The years caring for my mother have given me the experience and knowledge that's required for this, to be able to help others.

On my contemplative days, when I have time, I reflect on all of those lonely worried years when I wondered *why me*, why is this happening to me? And I now know that if you don't feel your own pain, you cannot recognise it in others. Our own suffering can cultivate the ability to help others.

When my three-month appraisal comes around, I'm nervous, but the powers that be – Logical Yellow, sympathetic Deep Green and even conservative Dark Blue – all remark that staff job satisfaction has never been higher. This nursery won't work unless the energy is flowing between my staff.

It's far from easy; I'm stressed much of the time, exhausted, often unable to sleep. I'm taking weekly, sometimes twice-weekly trips to Naomi for reiki, reflexology, everything I can do to rebuild me. Most of the time she tells me to just breathe.

But what helps me the most, the greatest tonic of all, is that I've fallen head over heels in love with Andy.

*

I bring Lily to a nice restaurant for her birthday; not fine dining, but a lot better than she's used to. I've told them about her disability in advance and so they make a fuss of her when she arrives, not in an insulting way but in a way that shows they've made efforts to prepare for her arrival. Of course she's uncomfortable about the entire thing, but not necessarily in a bad way either. I, too, find it difficult being praised; the attention seems lavish and undeserved, but it always makes me feel better. I know this from Andy.

Lily studies the menu with her face screwed up in disgust, reading silently with her lips moving, holding on to her glasses as she scans the page. I know this disgust is primarily fear; fear of the new experience, fear of the new food, fear of not knowing what anything is, of pronouncing it wrong, of not liking the taste, of looking like a fool.

'It's in Italian,' I tell her. 'It's an Italian restaurant, the English is beneath.'

'I can barely see it! Why is the English so small?' she asks loudly as the waiter pours the water and delivers the bread to the table. I take a deep breath and let it out slowly, calmly.

She despairs of the gazpacho, having never heard of cold soup in her life. What kind of idiot is running the kitchen? She goes for the minestrone, she knows that from her cuppa soups. 'Is it hot?' she asks the waiter with a bite to her words, and a snap. She's embarrassed, I know her.

After a discussion with the waiter about what is what, a turned-up nose for most of them and a look of horror when she hears the specials, she settles for a plain penne pasta and tomato sauce from the children's menu.

'Well,' she says, looking around, a little more relaxed now that the stress of ordering is over. 'This is fancy.'

Three simple words that may seem harmless to most people but to me they're loaded. It's an insult. It says, look at your life now, since you left me, living it up while I'm here at home, with nothing. Who do you think you are, rubbing it in my face, getting the run of yourself . . . All in just three words.

'Yeah, the new job is paying me well. You need it in London. Everything is so expensive.'

She studies me, looks at me properly for the first time since I arrived and found her waiting for me at the door.

'You look better than the last time I saw you. You looked like you were on the game.'

It's supposed to be hurtful, but I laugh. She's probably right, I was kind of playing a game, with myself, with everyone. She's also right about the difference in the way I look. Before I moved to London I used to hide behind my clothes. I'd wear dark colours, mostly tracksuits, gym gear, loungewear – nothing that would stand out; the gloves and glasses did that enough for me. These days my life is about more than daily trips to the park and needing to dress athletically to best manoeuvre a wheelchair. Not that I need to dress up for work; I need to be warm and comfortable but at the same time I want to be stylish. And then there's Andy. The two of us go to places: restaurants, theatre, gigs, pubs. While I'm reluctant to meet his friends, there's a wedding coming up that I'm not sure I can get out of.

'At the garden centre,' she says, reaching for bread in the centre of the table, thumbing through all the different types, examining them as if they're grenades and settling for the plainest.

'Yeah, it's a nursery too,' I say, and to explain, I add, 'We grow our own plants and flowers from seed.'

'I know what a nursery is,' she says. 'You always liked plants. I have Mr Ganguly doing the garden now.'

'Thank you,' I say.

'It's my garden,' she says. 'But you got the grass looking good, so we had to keep that. Ollie and I were sunbathing on it last Sunday.' She snorts.

I light up at this thought. 'That's lovely.'

'I got burned to a crisp, didn't I? Fell asleep and got sunstroke. Still, I got a nice colour.'

She holds out her skinny arms and turns them over.

'You have.'

Our starters arrive. I've ordered buffalo mozzarella and tomato.

'What's that?' she asks, wrinkling her nose again.

'It's cheese.'

'Cheese? Doesn't look like cheese.'

She tries her soup, the tiniest bit on her spoon as if it's poison. Her eyes light up. 'This is gorgeous.' She looks at me.

We both start laughing.

'This is the best soup I've ever had,' she says happily to the waiter as he takes it away. 'Oh my god I'm so full. I couldn't eat another thing.'

She's more relaxed now that the food isn't as scary as she thought it was. I look at the colours around her.

'What?' she asks, warily.

'Are you on new medication?'

'Yeah.'

She doesn't want to talk about it. As much as I dreaded coming here, leaving the warmth and easiness of Andy's company and bed, I have to admit that there's a comfort being with her. I can read her and this makes me feel safe. I know her inside out. I do not have the upper hand with Andy; most of our arguments have been because of my inability to feel anything until I know how he feels. He doesn't know about my abilities, I've chosen not to tell him because I don't know how to tell him. I've always been guided by others, I react to them, use them as my starting point to then decide how and who I'm going to be. I don't have that with Andy. I've never felt so happy and secure, yet so vulnerable and lost at the same time.

'Why did they change your meds?'

'Because the other ones weren't working.'

The waiter places our main courses down.

'I'll never get through all that,' is her response.

'Thank you,' I say.

'What's that?' she asks, pointing at my plate with her knife.

'Cannelloni.'

'What's that?'

'A kind of pasta wrap, filled with cheese and spinach.'

'Alice,' she says, disgusted, then concentrates on her food. She lifts the basil from the centre of the pasta and places it to the side as though she's found a hair in her food.

'Black pepper?' the waiter approaches the table with an oversized grinder.

'The size of it,' she says.

'No thank you,' I say.

'Parmesan?' he asks.

'Cheese,' I say to her.

'I'm not thick,' she says loudly.

I look up at the waiter, who gives me a sympathetic smile and leaves.

'The meds are stronger,' I say. They're heavier, I can tell. They're a different colour than the others, for a start; it surrounds her mood as though it's a bacteria, but not like the others, it crushes the mood, it's heavy.

'They make me tired.'

'Did you remember to take your old meds when you were supposed to? They always worked well before.'

'Yes, I remembered,' she says loudly, and then remembers where she is. 'Sometimes I forgot. Ollie isn't a slave driver like you.'

'I'm going to take that as a compliment.'

She shovels the pasta into her mouth. 'This is delicious.'

I'm pleased. Inspired by the positivity, I open up. 'I met someone.'

'Yeah?' she looks up, a smirk on her face.

'Andy is his name. He's from Scotland.'

'When were you in Scotland?'

'I wasn't. I met him in London.'

'Oh well, I don't know, do I? I don't know everything you do.'

Silence.

'I can never understand what those Scottish people say.'

I laugh, smile goofily at the thought of him. 'He has some peculiar turns of phrase.'

She keeps eating. For a tiny woman who said she couldn't

eat another thing, she's doing a good job of the giant bowl of penne.

'He's a youth worker.'

'What's that?'

'He helps kids who need support, teens, up to twenty-five-year-olds.'

'Troublemakers?' she asks, a grin on her face. 'No wonder you get along. Does he get paid or is that one of those volunteer jobs?'

'He gets paid.'

'Good.'

She forks the pasta into her mouth so fast I barely see her chew.

'What age is he?'

'Thirty-six.'

She raises her eyebrows. 'Is he married?'

'No!'

'Are you sure? They lie, you know.'

'He's not married.'

'Well he's old to not be married. Is he separated or divorced? You don't want what little money a youth worker makes going to another family.'

'No, he's not. Anyway, I can take care of myself.'

'That's what I said,' she says, but she's good-humoured about it because she places her fork down in an empty bowl and groans. 'I couldn't eat another thing.'

'I didn't bring your present with me—'

'Oh don't,' she interrupts, not wanting to talk about her birthday.

'We have to collect it today. It's not far from here.' Which is why I chose this restaurant.

I pay the bill and she's all thank yous and looking people in the eye as she leaves. The best food she's ever eaten, she tells them all.

We're only a block away from where we need to be and she goes silent when she sees where we're going, her head, I'm sure, filled with racing thoughts.

I won't ever forget the look on her face when the salesman appears with an electric wheelchair, wrapped in a big red bow. The bow must have been Hugh's idea.

'It's from me and Hugh,' I say. 'And Ollie,' I force myself to push out. He didn't donate a thing, but she'll know that.

Her trembling hands go to her face as tears fill her eyes.

Andy's friends' wedding is in Edinburgh at a private estate house of previous nobility, a stunning stately home from the sixteenth century that has been added to and renovated over the centuries. The actual ceremony is in a sixteenth-century chapel in the grounds, but we have use of one room in the grand house: the champagne reception takes place in the drawing room that looks out over a long lawn and the magnificent manicured gardens, which is where I long to be. Later, we'll move on to a marquee for the reception.

I'm nervous about this day from the moment Andy asks me to be his plus one. We've been together for five months and I have so far managed to avoid meeting his friends. Between getting to know each other, weekend trips home to check on Lily, weekend trips home for him, and work, we have so far made this relationship just about us, which is what I prefer. We're stepping it up a level, I can feel it, and I don't know if I can do it. I'm afraid of him seeing my true colours. I invented as many excuses as I could think of to get me out of this, from having to work, to visiting Lily; but he's not stupid, he could tell I was doing everything I could to not come. Eventually I made an adult decision. If I want this relationship to survive, which I do, then I need to make an effort and take this trip.

He's aware of my often neurotic behaviour. He's seen what I'm like on trains, in restaurants, and cafés, how choosy I am about where to sit, how I want to avoid certain negative vibes at tables and how I'm pulled to another table, asking the waiter if we can move, trying one place before moving to another, and that's okay with him because he's particular about things too. He prefers to see the door in every room, he hates having his back to it. He won't sleep if a wardrobe door is left open so much as an inch, and if he doesn't have an eye mask, he can't sleep without total darkness. We both have our quirks, and we accept them, but he does not know what I'm like at a wedding. Particularly a wedding being held in a marquee on the grounds of a field that was once a battlefield.

The sadness hits me as soon as I step out of the car. It is the saddest field I have ever walked on. He mistakes my freezing in place for a pause to take in the glamorous surroundings.

'Beautiful, isn't it?'

'Mmm.'

The reason I've driven is because I don't drink, which means we don't have to take the organised coach with all the other guests and be carted around together like we're schoolchildren, or even worse, cattle.

'You're just a control freak,' he'd said when I insisted on renting a car. 'You can't have it your way all the time.' His tone was teasing but he meant it, and he was right. I am a control freak, I have to control what I can control, because the alternative is terrifying.

'I'm not a sheep,' I tell him.

No, he does not know the reaction I will have when I set foot on the ground where so many men were slaughtered, when my roots connect with these roots and they start speaking to each other, whispering in hushed voices in condolence and fear, fear that they'll come back, that it'll happen again. I feel a whirl of dizziness, nausea, panic, anxiety, anger. A surge of bravery and courage. I feel feisty, ready to fight. Ready to charge at someone and swing an axe, ready to take off their heads. Not an ideal mood to be in to meet Andy's friends for the first time.

'Where's the chapel?' I ask, looking around.

'Invitation just said to meet at the main car park,' he says, barely looking at me, watching the people around us. 'Do you think you need to wear your sunglasses today?' he asks gently. 'It's quite overcast.'

The overcast days are worse, because people's lights are stronger, but he knows I don't wear them for sunlight, he thinks it has something to do with migraines. His comment hurts me. He's ashamed of me. Faced with his people, he wants me to be someone else.

Andy looks nervous when he introduces me to the stream of couples that we encounter. He knows that I hate touching people, he thinks it's an issue I have with germs, but I'm wearing gloves, built into the Audrey Hepburn evening look I've deliberately created, so I can shake as many hands as he wants me to but I pull away from their hugs and air kisses. There's no need for that level of closeness with people I've never met before.

When a coach arrives to take us to the chapel, which is somewhere in the grounds, Andy looks at me and grins. 'Baaa.'

We pile on the coach, in our finery, most men in kilts, women in high shoes they struggle to walk in on the loose stones in the car park, and pretty dresses. A concoction of complex characters, swirling and mixing, like the aftershave and perfumes, some that complement, others that clash.

It's pretty to look at but not to sit in. The battlefield ground is sad and fiery, the people are excited and anxious, and so I sit on the coach battling the feelings of anger, fight, anxiety and excitement. Oh how I'd love to draw my shield.

I hate how Andy's personality has changed almost instantly. We sit on the bus with the ghosts of Andy's past, as they behave like a bunch of naughty school kids, listening to childish jokes and overexcited retorts and insults flying up and down the coach. It's like he's back in school. He already had a few drinks while we were getting ready at the B&B; he's on holiday, he has a right to let loose, but it's new to see Andy behaving like this. I'm not the only person who becomes a different person in the company of others.

In the chapel the love in the room is enough to make me relax. The amount of red and pink throbbing energies being sent in all directions makes me want to sidle up to everyone I avoided on the bus. Of course there is sadness too – even when people are happy they can feel sad – and there is regret and bitterness being shared between couples as they witness a union that reminds them of the unreached potential of theirs, but the overwhelming, predominant energy in the room is love. I take off my sunglasses and hold Andy's hand, watch the aurora borealis of love energies swishing, a celestial ballet of light in the rotunda.

Andy steps up to the altar to do his reading and a surge of neon red shoots towards him from behind me. I turn around to see where it's coming from, but I can't see the source in the packed congregation. I can't concentrate on Andy's reading, my heart pounds so loudly in my ears, as the red shoots towards him like laser beams. They travel to Andy's magnetic field and they swivel around before disappearing. Colours seem to disintegrate as soon as they hit his bio-field. I don't know if he accepts them or if he throws them back. I have no idea what he does with the energies he receives and those he manufactures himself. He looks out to the congregation as he reads, and I want to know who in the room loves him so fiercely and intensely that causes their love to fire from them like from a cannon. My heart is hammering, angrily, wildly at the insult, the danger, of somebody somewhere wanting something of mine.

We mingle at the champagne reception. Ask after a lot of children and people from the past that I haven't heard of, feeling very much like a spare tyre stored in the boot, being carried around everywhere with Andy but really only required for moments that his conversation is punctured or goes flat and requires rescuing. I tune out of most conversations, looking around for the source of the violent laserbeam love.

I excuse myself from a conversation with another nice couple to go to the toilet but instead I follow the call of the majestic gardens, breathing in the calm and blowing out the stress. I take my time examining each of the flowers and plants, reading the names of the trees. I'm in a state of heightened bliss when I hear my name being called.

'What the hell are you doing?' Andy asks, his eyes bloodshot, his tie crooked. 'I've been looking for you for the past half an hour. Everyone's sitting at the table, waiting for you. I feel like a knob.' I've never quite seen him such a ball of rage. I don't need colours to tell me that.

'Sorry. I just wanted to look.'

'You could have told me and I would've joined you. Is everything okay?' he asks in an irritated way that doesn't welcome an honest heart-pouring response. Plus he's obviously had a few too many drinks.

'Yes,' I say tightly, needing his help but unable to ask for it. 'I'm just not that great with people.'

'Well try then,' he says, walking away back to the reception.

My heart is heavy. I look down at the pink rose and wish I could draw its colour. I don't want to pluck it from the bush, end its life, take away its beautiful energy colours, but it's the pink that I want. I hold it in my hands, attached to the stem, and I imagine I'm pulling it around me like a veil, for everything to literally be rosy and rose-tinted.

His feet crunch over the stones as he makes his way back to me. There's anger in his steps.

'What the . . . ?' he's about to explode and then suddenly backs down, melts a little. He lets go of the pent up energy, his shoulders visibly drop as he takes me in. 'You look so beautiful.'

I smile, surprised.

He wraps his arms around me and hides his nose in my neck and kisses me.

I grin as I twirl the stem of the pink rose between my fingers.

'As you can see, this is a magnet,' Mr Walker explains in science class. 'You all have one in front of you. Magnets are solid objects of stone, metal – Alex, get it away from your braces – or other material, which have the property of attracting iron-containing materials. This attracting property is either natural or induced, which means formed by unnatural means.'

'Just like how Eddie was conceived, sir.'

'All objects are made up of tiny particles called – what?'

'Herpes, sir.'

'Atoms. Atoms are composed of several different particles including tiny negatively charged electrons that rotate around the – what?'

'Anus, sir.'

'Atom nucleus,' Mr Walker says, continuing as if he's not been heckled by almost everyone in the class. 'The electrons in the atoms of magnetic objects are nearly all spinning in the same direction around the nucleus. This is what causes an object to be magnetic. In each magnetic object there are many different groups of atoms, each forming its own mini-magnet, but these groups are in opposing directions to each other. In a magnet, these groups of atoms are aligned so that the mini-magnets are all pointing in the same direction. The term for this is – what?'

'Homosexuality, sir.'

'Polarity. All magnets have both a north and south pole. Opposite poles attract one another, same poles repel one another. This means if the north pole of a magnet faces the south pole of another magnet, they stick together, or attract.'

'Like a sixty-nine, sir.'

'However, if you hold the north pole of a magnet to the north pole of another magnet, they push away from, or repel each other.'

'Like Eddie's parents, sir.'

'As you can see, each of you has a collection of materials on the table in front of you. Experiment with the magnet – no, not on your nose ring, Jennifer, use it on the items in the basket – and tell me which materials stick to the magnet.'

Noise breaks out the minute he stops talking, and he sits at his desk, arms folded as he watches the groups of two to each table dive into their shared baskets. I sit beside Gospel, and he gets to work.

I hold the south pole to the north pole and feel their power push them apart, away from each other, this invisible strength that won't allow them to join together. I do it over and over. I like watching the invisible power.

Suddenly Mr Walker is beside me.

'That's the magnetic field; the space around an electrical current or magnet in which the magnetic force is felt.'

'Can it happen with people?'

'Not unless you're Ironman, no. Richard, get out of the class.'

'Ah but, sir—'

'Out. I saw you.'

I keep pushing the two magnets together and they wobble against my strength but win each time and push apart. There's something familiar about how their repelling against each other feels. No matter what Mr Walker says, I'm no Ironman but I've had that feeling with people.

We find our seating through Michael and Lisa's Periodic Table of Seating. Our initials are in the middle, the table number is on top and our full names are below. I dread the thought of not being seated beside Andy, but maybe it's for the best, given the mood he's currently in. I could have guessed who the person sending the love hearts to Andy was without seeing her colours. I could have guessed by the repelling feeling I have whenever I have been in her company. Working my way around the champagne reception I'd suddenly get the sensation that I was being pushed away and there she'd be. My body doesn't want me to be near her. And if you'd asked me who I'd least prefer to sit at a table with, of any of the three hundred strangers in the entire room, I would have chosen her, which makes me laugh when we approach the table and there she is. Sitting pretty.

AK, Alice Kelly, is at table 14 of thirty. There are ten on each table. The flowers in the centre of the tables are held in test tubes. It's traditional seating and so Andy and I are not seated together, I'm between a Hamish and a Scott. My head is whirling, everyone is drunk now and I've had enough unwanted sloppy kisses on the cheek and spit flying into my eyeball to last me a lifetime. Andy is spinning, starting to get messy; he needs to soak up the drink with food. I pass him the bread. He offers me wine.

Hamish, my sweet partner to my right, works in environmental science, has a boat and spends his summers cruising and his winters competing. He and his wife Anna, on the opposite side of the circular table, have grown-up children who he says don't love them anymore, apart from when they need money and want their clothes washed.

Scott, to the left of me, is so inebriated he keeps spitting in my eye, in my food, in my water glass, and repeating the same questions about what it is that I do, while his wife Rachel watches Andy. She has calmed her declarations now that she's sitting at the same table as him; she sends out marshmallow-pink puffs like she's sending smoke signals, the transmittance of her love for him. She thinks nobody at the table notices the way she ignores her husband and focuses all her attention on Andy. But I notice.

I can't tell if he is responsive to her signals because I can't see his energies and this has never infuriated me more than this moment. I study him for secret smiles, tell-tale eyes, but after only five months together I'm still figuring him out, still learning how to speak human. Rachel barely glances at her husband and when she does it's not flattering.

If she picks up on the vibes I'm sending her way, then she's not reacting. In one way I think she'd have to be stupid not to sense my feelings for her, but then on the other hand

I don't know how she can feel anything through her own insulated layer of love and lust for Andy. Fed up with making an effort with these people, I give in and my shield goes up. I sit back, fold my arms and let the circus play on around me. And on and on it goes. If I thought there'd be a chance of him sobering up over dinner, I was incredibly naïve. He cranks it up to eleven. The messier he becomes, the prissier I seem to become. Prickly and judgemental, even with my shield up and my aura sealed. Still, she sends out her energies, all to him, and I can't do anything to stop them. All I can do is wonder, is he taking them from her, wrapping his drunken hands around them? Are they making him remember her, remember them as a couple? When he pulls me up to dance, so touchy-feely, groping me in ways he wouldn't usually in public, I wonder if it's her lust that is making him so tactile.

I feel like a limpet stuck to a rock, clamping tighter the more he spins me and wriggles ridiculously against me. I'm rigid while everyone around me is fluid. Their heads are elsewhere, in some trippy happy place with butterflies and unicorns, while I'm here seeing everything exactly as it is. I can't be swept along on their magical ride of silliness because I can see the strings on the puppet, I knew the rabbit was already in the hat. The dance floor becomes packed and I sneak off.

I move away from the marquee and the fairy lights to the darkness, listening to the swish of the trees and allowing the breeze to sweep the heat from my flushed face. At last I can finally be alone.

*

Back in the B&B I sit in the corner of the bedroom, legs tucked up against my body, wearing pyjamas, make-up already off. He's pacing and flailing around like he's made of rubber. We're having an almighty row and I'm being told all the terrible things that I am. I am cold. I ignored his friends. I didn't dance. I kept disappearing. I'm so distant.

His accent is stronger than I've ever heard it, surrounded by his people, and whisky. He's slurring so badly I can just about make out his prime points.

'You wouldn't even shake Jamie's hand. Jamie was in my chemistry class,' he says unnecessarily. 'He wouldn't say boo to a goose.'

'You know I don't like touching people,' I say quietly. I hate talking about it, I don't want to talk about it.

'You don't like touching me,' he says suddenly.

'Yes I do.'

'You won't hold my hand. You won't even fucking . . .' he slurs as he goes into an inaudible slew of my failures. 'Look, you have your reasons,' he says, suddenly with clarity of thought and surprising respect. 'But these are my friends, you can trust them, you don't have to look down on them . . .'

'I wasn't looking down at them.'

'Oh yes you were, all snooty, while—'

'While you and Rachel were drooling all over each other.'

He stops. 'What?'

'If I was going to make you sit at a table with an ex, I would tell you. I would. In fact I told you about Gospel before we met him, just so you'd know, and I probably shouldn't have told you because now you won't see him again.' I'd never make him spend the entire night guessing, feeling in the way, like a spare part and a second thought.

He looks dizzy and confused. Opens his mouth and closes it again. 'Who?'

'Uh, I'll give you a guess: I was sitting beside her husband, who can't have been too happy about it either.'

That's a lie. I don't think Scott noticed, I don't think anybody did. I don't even know if Andy did. His colours wouldn't tell me. I can't read him.

He's stopped pacing. His feet are in one place, but his body is swaying. I've hit a nerve. They weren't a couple but something happened, something secret perhaps.

I take a deep breath.

'I see energies, Andy. People's moods in colours, around their bodies. It helps me to see things that other people can't see.'

'Oh stop it, Alice. What did he say? Her husband.'

I pause. I've just revealed my biggest secret and he's leapt right over it, swatted it away. 'Did you hear me, Andy? I'm telling you something important about me, the thing I have never been able to tell you.' I stand up. 'I see energies, Andy, people's energies. As colours. It's why I wear the sunglasses, it's why I . . .'

He topples over slightly even though he's standing in one spot; he looks at me unevenly, and I think he's going to vomit. His pupils are huge, so large there's no hazel in sight. He looks like he wants to cry with the confusion this has caused his brain.

'What?'

Then he leaves.

*

We're lying in bed, it's the early weeks after we first met. It's a Sunday morning, it's raining. I'm basking in the feeling of utter relaxation and contentedness. Rick Stein is on TV travelling somewhere exotic, on a boat, talking about food, cooking food, eating food. We're talking about nothing and everything. Mostly I listen to him, I love the sound of his voice, so jovial and positive, even the deep-throat just-awake voice.

'What were you like at school?'

'Oh you know . . .'

'No, I don't. That's why I'm asking.'

'Quiet. Ish. Sometimes. Sometimes not.'

'Sounds like the weather forecast for Glasgow. Rain, with snow and a bit of sun.'

'That's me. A bit of everything.'

'What was your school called?'

'You wouldn't know it.'

'That's why I'm asking.'

'It was in the middle of nowhere about an hour outside Dublin.'

'Uh-huh, what's it called?' he says, moving a strand of hair off my face and watching me more closely now, sensing the avoidance.

I'm quiet.

'You didn't do your final exams, did you?'

'I absolutely did finish school,' I say, insulted.

'Okay,' he laughs. 'It sounded to me like you were stalling. Where did you study then?'

'Clearview Academy,' I say, placing my head back on his chest and facing the TV this time, away from him. 'It was a behavioural school.'

He tries to position himself to see my face, but I won't move.

'Why were you there?'

I think about it for a moment.

'I was very angry.'

I daydream about telling him. Have full-on conversations in my head about how I reveal my neuroses. Sometimes he takes it well, sometimes not. I know that I'll tell him some day. It just needs to be the right moment.

After our argument, he rejoins the continuing party in the B&B breakfast room. There's a sing-song that starts to fall apart at 4.30 a.m., but even though the singing has stopped, he still hasn't returned. I imagine him somewhere with Rachel, professing his feelings to her while I cry into my pillow. I can't sleep. What have I done? It's not how I wanted to tell him about my aura-seeing. I mean, I never wanted to tell him at all.

I pack my bag. A handful are still up at 6 a.m., talking nonsense, as I pass by the breakfast room and sneak out of the B&B. I hop in a cab, collect the car and get a coffee while I wait for the rental place to open, then get the first train back to London. I'm home by lunchtime, probably before he's even woken up.

I sleep for most of the trip home. It is not the joyful excursion it was on the journey up with Andy. Now I feel so sad, like there's a hole in me and I've lost something, someone exceptional, but also a great big feeling of inevitability. How could someone like me ever have thought I'd be happy and have normality with someone like him? My subconscious is screaming *I told you so* while the rest of me is huddled in a corner shouting *Leave me alone.*

At 8 p.m. there's a knock on the door.

It's him. He looks like he's been in a fight with himself, as if he's crawled from the mountains to meet civilisation for the first time.

'I'm sorry,' he says, stepping inside and hugging me tight, so tight I can barely breathe.

I'm confused. I was the culprit. I told him something crazy and then I left him there.

He breathes me in, and it tickles my neck. 'I'm so sorry.'

We hold each other for a long time and I don't want him to stop because I don't want to talk. Talking will get me in trouble again.

He pulls away and looks at me.

My eyes are puffed from twelve hours of crying. My nose is red and sore from blowing it, I've chewed on my lips, bitten down all my nails.

'Are you okay?'

'No,' I say.

'Of course not. When I woke up I didn't know where you were. I couldn't even remember leaving the wedding.' He rubs his face. 'I'm so sorry. I remember looking for you at the wedding,' he says, scrunching up his face, then he shakes his head. 'I don't know. I was very drunk. Jamie said I was a disgrace.'

'Jamie from your chemistry class.'

'Yeah, how did you know . . . ? Look, I can't remember anything . . .' he says, watching me, warily, wondering if and when I'm going to pounce. 'I shouldn't drink whisky. It makes me . . . angry and . . .' He sits down, woozy. 'I'm actually definitely not drinking again, until the weekend.'

I smile.

He doesn't remember anything. I feel quite elated. Yet frustrated too, that I had to experience all that, and he doesn't even remember, he gets to be wiped clean. I move away from him and fill the kettle with water, flick the switch and fold my arms, waiting for it to boil. Not remembering could be a convenient lie for him, but I've no way of knowing for sure. I can't read him.

'You said that I embarrassed you,' I say finally. 'In front of your friends.'

He shakes his head.

'No, Alice.'

'That I'm cold.'

'No.'

'That I'm not fun. That I'm distant. That I don't touch you.'

'I was so drunk—'

'It came from somewhere, Andy.'

'It was a load of drunken confused crap, Alice.'

I could pretend I never told him, live the lie for longer, pretend he never reacted the way he did when I told him, but I know I can't. And all of a sudden the anger is gone because he's right about all of those things he's feeling, and he needs to know why.

'I need to talk to you about something.'

'Don't,' he says. 'Don't break up with me.'

'Listen to what I have to say and then we'll see who wants to break up with who,' I say nervously, but ready, pulling the sleeves of my jumper over my hands and sitting down on the couch. He joins me.

I take a moment to compose myself.

'When I was eight . . .'

'You don't have to tell me,' he says, taking my hand. 'I think I know. You don't have to.'

'You don't know and I need to tell you. When I was eight, I started seeing people's moods and energies as colours.'

It's not what he was expecting.

He takes a moment to maybe judge if I'm serious or not, maybe see if this revelation matches up with my behaviour. I don't know, but I appreciate the time he gives it.

'Synaesthesia,' he says. 'My mate Johnny has it with music. He hears notes as colours.'

'Right,' I say, surprised. 'So you're kind of familiar. It could be explained as that, but this is slightly different. I see people's energies around their bodies, which is why I wear sunglasses. It can give me a headache when there are a lot of people, which explains the migraines. It's why I wear gloves. It's why I don't like being touched. Other people's moods can rub off on me. I'm sensitive to how other people are feeling. Moods seem to want to go to me, like anger, or sadness, or grief, or happiness. I don't want other people's moods, I want my own.'

He thinks about it for a moment. I can see his brain ticking over. Does he want to be with someone like this? Do I have a psychosis or is it real? Should he try to fix me or accept it? Walk away or stay? He's still holding my hand at least.

'But being around people is healthy. Sharing emotions is good. Your happiness is my happiness,' he says, finding a way to understand what I've said.

'I know,' I say, surprised to be having a greater conversation beyond the basics of whether it's real or not. 'Some sharing of emotions is good. Some basking in good feelings and bad feelings is good. I've learned that. I can't be completely disconnected, though sometimes I do disconnect for myself, and that's when you say I'm cold. Or distant. And you're right,' I say quickly, before he jumps in with another apology. 'You're right, Andy: I do numb myself to other people sometimes, and it's a bad habit, but now you know why I'm like that. On a busy street, or in a busy bar, or at a wedding, for example, if I bump into every person and feel what they feel, then . . . it's too much. Just before I met you, I learned how to shut it all down, but doing that made me sick. So I've had to learn how to be a part of it without being affected by it.'

'Does Lily have the same thing?' he asks.

I shake my head. 'And I don't have bipolar disorder, if that's what you're asking.'

'Sorry.'

'Don't worry, I asked myself the same thing, growing up. Even when she hadn't been diagnosed, I wondered. But no. I think I have this because of her, she's the source, but not because of anything hereditary. When I was little I hated how unpredictable she was. It made me so anxious, wondering what kind of woman I would wake up to, or if she would suddenly snap. I wanted to be prepared for what came next so I started studying her, trying to read her. I started seeing her moods as colours. I was sent to Clearview Academy because I didn't know how to cope. And then after the academy I hid at home, blaming her, because I didn't know how to cope. Then I got tired of being in the shadows and I came here. Then I saw you.'

'That's why you always look at me like that. Like you're reading me.'

'No,' I laugh. 'This is where it gets weirder. Andy, you're the one person I can't read. That's why I saw you on the train that day, that's why I followed you. You're the first person I've ever met who has no colours.'

'What am I, the devil?'

'No. I think you're the one who . . .' I try to figure out how to put in words what he does to me. How he challenges me, makes me feel real, human. 'You're the one who . . .' I begin again, completely unable to explain.

'I'm the one,' he says, smiling.

'Him,' Andy says, nudging me on the Tube.

I look up from my book to where he's discreetly nodding.

'Deep blue,' I say.

'Conservative,' he says, and I nod. He beams like a student who's gotten full marks. 'What about him? I bet he's wearing women's underwear beneath that suit?'

I snort with laughter and a few faces turn our way. I rest my head on his shoulder and chuckle.

We're outside the youth club. I wait for him and he walks out with a student. There's a man waiting for her, beside his car. I'd noticed him already.

'Hey,' the man says with a grin, dimples in his cheeks, looking like a puppy dog.

'You know him?' Andy asks, and she nods.

'Got the car here, thought I'd surprise you,' the man says. He opens the door to his car.

Her face is unreadable. To everyone but me anyway.

Andy looks at me, a questioning look.

I shake my head.

'Actually, Jasmine, I forgot something inside. Do you mind coming back with me? Sorry, man, we won't be long,' he says to the guy waiting.

'We really have to go,' the man says.

'Yeah, but this is important,' Andy says with a cheeky smile. 'Blame me.'

He goes back inside with Jasmine. A few minutes later he texts me and tells me to meet him around the side exit door.

'Bad guy?' he asks.

'Very bad.'

'Metallic-y bad?'

I nod.

'Jesus,' he says. 'He looked like a boy band member. Thank you,' he says, kissing me. 'You want to eat out tonight?'

On our first proper date I tell Andy that I've tickets to the Crystal Palace versus Aston Villa game. He doesn't support either team but he loves football, he'll go to any game, any time, anywhere. I've hooked him, thanks to Gospel.

I don't tell him that we'll be seated in a corporate box, because I didn't know that. There's a meal beforehand in the box, and when we sit outside, Jamelle, Gospel's wife, has ensured that all the seats in the box in the row in front of us, beside us and behind us are clear, just for me. Jamelle sits beside me, 'Is that okay?' A long-legged glamorous species with large sunglasses, who ignores the cameras pointed at her as she watches the game, though she doesn't actually watch the game, instead talks through a problem they're having.

'I didn't design the interior of the house,' she says. 'He was living with someone else before me. I moved in and it was like that. Don't get me wrong, it's a beautiful house, you've seen it. But it feels, I don't know,' she closes her eyes and shudders. 'Maybe it's because she decorated it, maybe I'm just being stupid. I can live with it, but it's more for him, he gets very . . . antsy, you know? Like he's got all this pent-up aggression. He needs to get out all the time. You know him better than I do, why am I telling you,' she says.

'I don't know him better than you,' I say.

'Oh come on, you're his first love.'

Andy visibly sits up at that and I wish he hadn't heard. I'd told him Gospel and I had been friends at school and that we'd dated, I'd prepared him for that just in case it came up, but I hadn't mentioned anything about love.

'Maybe I'm just being stupid,' she says.

'You're not,' I say, keeping my voice down, so Andy doesn't hear. 'It's the animal stuff, you have to get rid of it.'

Her eyes almost pop out of her head.

'It's a stagnant energy. All the skins, the horns, the stuffed tiger or whatever that was. Get rid of it. It blocks the flow in the house.'

'You felt that?'

'Straight away.'

'Oh my God, I knew it,' she says excitedly. 'He loves that stuff but he'll get rid of it if it's because you say so.' She brushes up against me, excited, then moves away quickly. 'Sorry. I want to hug you but I won't. I'm a hugger. This is so hard.'

She makes me laugh.

'I hope you let him hug you,' she says, whispering and looking at Andy. 'He's cute.'

He chooses that moment to jump up and shout foul language at the ref.

The few people in the box turn around to look at him, the foul-mouthed Glaswegian.

'Sorry,' he says, to me, not to them, sitting down again.

'What do you see in him?' Gospel asks me once, when we're out for drinks in one of Gospel's choices, a fashionable cocktail bar where he has a photo taken with everyone who asks. It's a double date. Andy and Jamelle are deep in conversation about his work. He's so deeply passionate about the kids he works with, I love how he speaks about it.

I think Gospel is jealous, in fact I know he is, I can see the colours swishing around with his honey coloured happiness like the beginnings of a washing machine cycle. It's not attractive and it's ridiculous because Jamelle is the most beautiful creature, inside and out, that I have ever met.

What do I see in him? I smile. 'He's kind. He's funny.'

Gospel's eyes narrow as he watches Andy, trying to detect this supposed kindness and funniness from him.

'What colour is he?' he asks. 'I bet he's not honey. Can't beat honey.' He puffs his chest out.

'He doesn't have a colour,' I say, to Gospel's confusion. 'That's what's so perfect. All I know is, the second I let my guard down, I found him.'

I'm home from the academy for Christmas and I'm counting the days until I can go back. I'm regretting not taking Gospel up on his offer to go to his house, but I wanted to see Hugh. Only Hugh decides at the last minute not to come home; says he has exams he needs to study for and he's working in a bar in Cardiff and can't take time off. All the excuses he can think of. I feel as devastated as Lily does about him rejecting us. I wear my blue cloak of self-pity as she does. For Christmas dinner we eat depressing packaged sliced turkey, the kind for school lunch sandwiches, buttered cabbage, carrots, mash and gravy in a microwavable meal tray. My mashed potato is burned on the outside and stuck to the tray but it's miraculously cold in the middle. She bought tubs of jelly and custard for dessert. She drinks two bottles of wine, works her way through a packet of cigarettes, we have an argument and she goes out until late. I hear her come in in the early hours and trip her way up the stairs. She stays in bed for St Stephen's Day while I plant myself on the couch all day eating from a box of Quality Street that Saloni my secret Santa gave me, watching back-to-back *Die Hard* films. Best day I've had at home in a long time.

Or it could have been if I wasn't so worried about Ollie. He'd stuffed dinner into his mouth as quickly as he could without saying a word, this man-child with chin and upper-lip fluff who I barely recognise, then went out with his idiot friends doing who knows what. A big group of them, all in puffer coats they can't afford and hoods up like they're a Grim Reaper fan club; trouble, the lot of them, the only eleven-year-old in a group of teenagers. I don't want to know what he's done or had to do to earn their respect and attention. He still sucks up her colours, charging himself off her with her negative energy before taking it out to the world with him.

Our fight had been about him going out with them.

Her response is that she's glad he has friends, seeing as me and Hugh left him, as if she's forgetting I didn't go away by choice.

'Hey, freak.'

I turn around and there he is, Ollie, walking in my direction. I've tried to find as many hiding places as possible every day so I'm not home with her or near him and his loser friends who walk around in gangs wearing coats they shouldn't be able to afford, not afraid to show off how much they're earning at doing nothing good. Ollie must have followed me. I'm at the local park. I started walking this morning and kept going, got lost on nature trails I'd never been on before, anything to avoid being at home. I find a quiet place and sit down to eat a handful of the leftover Quality Street chocolates. Strawberry Delight and Orange Crème are my least favourite but I keep going, trying to make myself like them. Ollie steps on an enormous branch, leans back and forth, back and forth, bouncing, until it snaps.

'Why did you follow me?' I ask.

'Nothing else to do.'

'I'm surprised you and your mates aren't somewhere nicking stuff.' He's been in so much trouble with the police, another stunt and he'll be landed in a detention centre, and I'm suspicious he's responsible for the Gangulys' car that was taken for a joyride, as is everybody else in the neighbourhood. It's humiliating, living with him.

He glares at me. A dark look, but it doesn't intimidate me. He steps towards the edge of a deep ditch. Water, mud, beer bottles, who knows what else is in there. I can see he's trying to work out how to get across to the training pitches.

'Seriously Ollie, you have to stop hanging out with that gang. You can't afford to get into more trouble right now.'

'From what I hear, juvie is better than where you and your freak friends go.'

'Nice. Maybe I'll get my freak friends to come and kick your ass. Maybe that's exactly what you need.'

'It wasn't me driving the car,' he says with an easy shrug, eyes searching my face for a reaction.

I get goosebumps as his colour flashes, like the flashbulb of an old-fashioned camera and then it goes back to normal as if nothing happened. He admitted he was in the car, I'm pretty sure his colour flash admitted something else too.

But why is he here? Maybe he's hiding too. Maybe he's scared. Maybe he's spending time with me because he needs his big sister and for once I need to be on his side like Hugh always is, no matter what he does.

He bounces on another branch, looking across, surveying the gap between and the branches above. He couldn't possibly be thinking about jumping. It's too wide.

He takes a few steps away from the ditch, then prepares to run.

'You won't make it,' I say.

'I will. I can do it.'

He must have a death wish, or a misguided belief that he can do anything he wants, because he'll never make that jump. I look at the determination on his face, seeing the little boy I know so well, and I let out a loud, surprising even to myself, genuine laugh.

'What?' he looks at me in surprise, a grin crawling onto his face.

'Who do you think you are? Tarzan? You can't make that jump,' I say, standing.

I take my sunglasses off and he stares at me. Maybe he sees his sister, the version of me he doesn't despise. We laugh as he makes a few running attempts before stalling abruptly, stopping just in time before going over the edge. On his next attempt he pulls me to the edge with him, pretends to pull me into the ditch but stops just in time.

My heart pounds as I look down into the mud. It rained every day this week, who knows how far we'd sink. I don't like to be touched but I don't stop him. I feel dangerous. Alive. Sparking like fire. Golden. A brother and sister having fun for once.

'You won't be able to,' I say, hearing the teasing in my voice. Do I want him to try?

'I will.'

He looks around, assesses everything. Calculates.

'What if you make it, what will you do on the other side?'

'I'll worry about that when I get there.'

I laugh.

'What?'

'That's the difference between you and me. Seriously though, don't, Ollie. You won't get away with it.'

He winks. 'I can get away with anything.'

And in the way a person would know something from a tone of voice or a look on a face, I know, I just know instantly that he was the driver of the car.

It happens so quickly. He runs, once at the edge he leaps up, a huge spring in his legs, to grab the branch of the tree on the other side that's suspended over the ditch. Two hands grab the branch, the muscles in his arms swell, ripple in his back and shoulders as he swings back, his T-shirt rises to reveal his skinny white stomach. He looks in control. He looks at me and grins.

'Me, Tarzan. You—'

There's a crack. The branch can't take his weight, it falls away from the tree and he goes straight down. He disappears below. A mighty thump of his dead weight and a sound from him as though he's been punched in the stomach and lost all the air from his body.

I feel sick instantly, then I rush to the edge. I look down at his body and the positioning is all wrong. He looks like a rag doll, limbs splayed out in all the wrong directions.

'Ollie,' I say, hearing the tremor in my voice.

He doesn't move.

The woods are silent, the breeze blows, the leaves rustle. I shudder.

I look around. There's no point in shouting, no one will hear me. I could run back and get help but he could die while he waits, he could be dead already. I don't have a phone; he has one but it's in his pocket. I need to get down there.

All of a sudden a light swoops out of the top of his head, like he's a tube of toothpaste being squeezed. The light

– bright white, like I've never seen it before – remains in the air, hovering over Ollie's body. I can't move. I feel frozen, terrified by this light that's like a living, breathing organism.

'Oh God,' I finally come to my senses and clamber down the side of the ditch, ignoring the blob of white in the air. I slip and slide down. Branches scrape my face. I land with a splash up to my shins in bog and water and mud. 'Ollie!'

He's dead. I know he is just by looking at him. I can feel it. I've never seen a dead body before, and that's exactly how I know.

I shake him. Tap him. My body is trembling from head to toe. I look up at the white light that's just there, hovering. I'm annoyed with it, as if I expect it to help me. It moves closer to me and I freeze, afraid to breathe it in, afraid it will touch me, trembling by its very existence.

'Go back in,' I whisper. 'Go back in. Please.'

What the hell am I doing? I need to get help. I search in his pockets for his phone, it's smashed to pieces. I swipe the screen, but the broken glass slices my finger. Both sides of the ditch tower above me, I start climbing, clinging on to roots and weeds that are pulled out from the soil as soon as I climb. I slide down time and time again, splashing into the mud. It's in my eyes and mouth and all over my face. The white light moves again. It moves towards Ollie's head. Then it goes straight in the crown of his head and disappears.

His eyes open. He looks at me.

Then he grins and sits up with a pained grimace.

'I saw you,' he says. 'I saw me. I was up there, just around there, looking down. I saw you. You saw me, didn't you?'

I shake my head. 'No, no. I didn't. I want to get out of here. I want to get out of here now.'

'You did. You did. You looked right at me, freak, you said to go back in. You saw me. Jesus Christ, what the . . . I saw myself.'

He's on a high, trying to scramble to his feet, but his shoulder looks limp, as do his legs. He's like a scarecrow that's lost its straw trying to stand up.

'You're terrified of me now,' he says. A flash of silver, a flash of gold, both of them tarnished.

He's not wrong. I look for somewhere to place my foot. I kick it into the mud wall, lodging it, and climb, but I slide back down as the wall falls away. He stands behind me thumping his chest like he's King Kong, thinking he's unstoppable, unbeatable. I know that from this moment on his appetite will be insatiable. Meanwhile, all I can do is desperately try to climb my way out of there. I feel like I'm buried alive in a grave with him, smelling rank, mud dripping from my clothes.

It's the first but not the last time that I witness somebody die.

It's the only time I see them come back to life.

Lily rings me just as I'm getting ready to go out with Andy. I'm happy, I've the music blaring. It's a Saturday evening, I've the day off tomorrow. I'm in my new underwear, dancing around and singing aloud when the phone rings. I see her name and want to ignore it but I can't.

I shut off the music, stand in the kitchen in my bra and thong.

'It's Ollie,' she says. 'He's dead. There was a fight at the prison. They just called me. Oh God, Alice, they killed him. He's gone, he's gone.'

When I end the call I don't know what to do. There is much to be done, to organise, people to contact, arrangements to be made, Lily can't do it on her own – but I can't move. I feel so sad.

For a time he thought he was invincible, but Ollie ran out of lives.

rose gold

ONE MORNING I WAKE up and the colours aren't there; for the first time in twenty-two years, nothing has a colour. Andy is sleeping, his aura is still colourless, but the plants around us are emanating nothing. I walk around our small flat looking at all the plants; it's like they're dead on the inside but with a lush and healthy facade. I look out the window and watch people walking by, no colours, as if the dimmer switch on Earth has been turned down. I feel so odd, discombobulated, dizzy and unbalanced, as if I've lost my stabilisers. I have to feel around in the dullness for a moment to settle myself. I try to think back over everything I did differently over the past few days.

Then my heart pounds as I have a sudden thought. If the source of this light is Lily, as I believe it to be, then what if the source is no longer around. I ring Lily. It rings and rings.

'Hello?' Michelle answers, my cousin who moved in with Lily when Ollie was sent to prison again, and she ended up staying.

It's a long wait while she goes to check on Lily, who isn't up yet. She won't appreciate being woken but I need her to be able to wake. I feel sick.

'She's all right,' Michelle says. 'The same as normal. Told me to get lost.'

'Oh, thank God.'

I hang up and run to the kitchen sink to vomit.

I lose my aura-seeing for exactly nine months.

In pregnancy I am so consumed by myself, by the life that's growing inside me and how my body is adapting to assist the life, that I don't see, can't see what's happening in the others around me. It is only afterwards that I discover what people were going through: a colleague secretly going through a marriage break-up, a friend in a dark place. The colours have always taught me that there is a hive of activity beneath people, that no one can ever see or know, but it is only when I lose the colours that I realise how well people bury it, how they conceal it, how they continue to put one foot in front of the other so seemingly effortlessly and gracefully that I realise how truly phenomenal we are. They all managed to fool me. When the colours return, I tell myself to be kinder, more compassionate. It is not enough to just see these things in a person and quietly understand, I need to actively understand too.

Despite the practice I've had, thanks to not seeing colours in Andy, I'm like an alien that has dropped down to Earth from another planet. For the whole time I'm pregnant I have to learn to navigate life and human relationships without seeing colours. I misjudge moods and moments. I mistime my comments. I'm not successful at work, I'm not successful at home. I'm sure everyone around me is quietly counting down the days until I have my baby.

*

Nine months later, arriving in an avalanche of gold from between my thighs, is my daughter. It is a moment of absolute euphoria, the delivery room lights up in brilliant gold as though the gates to another world have opened and shone upon us. I know I'm in the presence of someone precious who has passed through the gateway of some other realm to grace us with her presence here.

We name her Joy.

Her name is Joy but I call her Nugget because she is a rose-golden nugget in colour and nature. I drink her up, breathe her in, I fill my lungs with her marshmallow-and-powder-scented wonder. She smells of sweet urine and bacon in the morning; a sweet and salty roly-poly package of smiles that makes my exhaustion fade to nothing on first sight. Her wrists are lost in folds, every inch of her a ticklish doughy delight. She is medicine, she is light, she needs me, and she is everything I never knew I needed.

I'm not a nervous mother but I have a problem with people holding the baby. The pass-the-parcel culture of a newborn brings the mama bear out in me. Especially when I'm around Lily.

'Let me hold her,' Lily says, reaching out, when Andy and I visit for the first time.

I grip Joy tighter. I don't want Joy's golden beam to be swallowed up by the purple-tentacled monster.

'Go on,' Andy quietly assures me.

I slowly hand her over, not wanting to look at the transfer

of colours, but not wanting to look away in case I miss something important, some lingering colour on my child that she'll keep forever in her core colours.

'Hello there,' Lily says in a voice I've never heard before. 'Hello, beautiful girl.'

I feel Andy's supportive hand on my back.

I expected the worst, but what I see is a dance that brings tears to my eyes. An ethereal display of shimmering colourful lights being shared by grandmother and granddaughter.

When Joy is eighteen months old I stop seeing colours again and I instantly know that I'm pregnant with our second child. We celebrate before taking the test that eventually proves my theory. I'm planting strawberry trees in the nursery at 11.30 one morning when all of a sudden I start seeing colours again. It takes me a moment to process what has happened, and then to notice the warm sticky wet between my thighs, to realise that my sudden gain is also my loss. The baby was fourteen weeks old.

The time in my life where I wished and prayed I'd stop seeing colours is now a distant hazy memory. Now there is joy in seeing the colours of my children, in getting to know them inside and out. What a delight to watch their shades change as they learn and grow, as they develop and form their prominent colours. I watch the colours change from one end of the rainbow to the next, until the right colour finds the right fit. Two girls and one boy, the pinks of puberty, the metallic flashes of teenage life, I examine them, study them hard, while they're not looking. While they're watching television, I watch them. While they're playing on the street with friends, I watch them. Who are they, how do they cope, how do they adapt, how can I help them, what can I teach them? I watch how they interact with each other. Will they be okay? They fascinate me, they teach me.

Joy's head never stops. Something is always stirring, in the best way. Colours slowly spin above her, moving round and round like an imaginary wooden spoon is stirring her thoughts. A sprinkling of orange appears, as if it's been thrown into the pot, added to the mix like a spice, and then it starts to bubble, as if in a cauldron. Stirring and bubbling, my little one concocts dreams of the people she wants to be, the places she wants to visit, the adventures she wants to have.

Billy, the baby, is sensitive, kind and understanding, more of the empathy of his father, and not like mine. He prefers animals to people, prefers singing to talking, reading to speaking, he stops eating meat at the age of twelve, finding it all too cruel, debating with Andy during barbecues, can be feisty when he wants to be, when life is unfair, where there is injustice, when he feels he must represent those who don't have a voice. But despite the love for animals, can be the coldest with people and the hardest to win over. Funny really, from the most silent one of my three.

'What colour am I?' he asks during one dinner conversation.

'The colour of hummus,' I say to everybody's laughter, and thankfully his own.

Izzy is the middle child. I see something of Ollie in her: the neediness. I do a lot of work on her so that I stop seeing Ollie. I smother her with love and affection, hold her hand so that she knows she's not alone, that she's loved. I don't want her to go a single moment without feeling like someone has her back. She's the type to sit in a room filled with people and still feel lonely, to have sudden feelings of home-sickness even though she's still at home, the type to forget, you see, that she's not alone, that there's a circle of love and healing around her if she'd just look up from herself.

'You're mollycoddling her,' Andy tells me. 'She won't know how to do anything on her own.'

He's right of course. Perhaps I do this too much.

The sun is shining. Andy has set up a paddling pool in the back garden for the kids. They run around in their bathing suits, Billy is nude, jumping in and out of the water to annoy the girls with his boy bits.

'Eww, drippy penis!' Izzy yells, and Joy laughs hysterically as Billy shakes his little bum.

Andy's top is off, bronzed from the past few days of the heatwave. I watch him working around the garden, doing the bits and pieces we never have time to do, sanding and varnishing the furniture, sorting the weeds from the plants, cleaning the barbecue, gathering the scattered bits of toys. I sit back in my sun chair, with a glass of ice water and a fresh squeeze of lime, listening to their shrieks and watching their colours shoot across at each other like water from water pistols, feeling like I'm a queen on her throne and I'm so very lucky to be so very happy. To have people to give love to, to be in love, to feel loved, to be surrounded by love. I love life, I love my family, I love me. I love, I love, I love.

Colours get brighter and migraines intensify in certain climates, usually before thunderstorms. When the day is heavy and humid it feels like the clouds are crushing my skull, surrounding me as though I'm a mountain peak. There is little to feel positive about this aspect though it does come in handy for one thing.

'I was thinking of asking Greg and Sarah around tonight for drinks,' Andy says, spearing a potato and popping it in his mouth. 'Weather's good.'

It's so humid I feel like I can barely breathe. All the windows are open but there is no air.

'Can Alva come too?' Joy practically jumps out of her chair with excitement. She loves people. She needs to be around people.

'Why isn't Becky coming?' Izzy asks with that whine, always the victim, as though we are plotting against her to remove life of all fun.

'Of course Becky and Alva are invited,' Andy says.

'Yes!'

'Can they bring their dog?' Billy asks, and Joy and Izzy roll their eyes.

'Who cares about their stupid dog?' Joy says, and the three get into an argument about animal cruelty which leads to a debate about who walks and loves our dog the most.

I feel a shot in my temple, in the side and back of my head, as though Andy has stabbed his fork through my skull and left it there, skewering my brain like a kebab. It's been happening for a few days, not as intense as this, but it's been building gradually.

'Stop.' I say it quietly but there must have been an edge to my voice because they stop and all look at me. 'Not tonight,' I say, looking out the window.

They moan and groan. I ruin their life, I ruin their fun, I yada yada yada.

'Weather isn't due to break until tomorrow,' Andy says. 'We should do it tonight while we can. They had us over last time.'

'It will break tonight,' I say, barely able to hear my words over the sounds of the kids and the pain in my head.

The kids' colours rise and mesh in the centre of the table as they squabble. It could be pretty, a rainbow above my dinner table, if only my head didn't hurt so much.

We continue eating. I poke at my food, push it around the plate, watching their plates so we can hurry up and get this all over with. A dark room on my own calls me.

'The steak tastes like feet,' Joy says, and I don't even bother to argue with her. I take her plate and bring it to the sink. It falls in and clatters loudly. They all turn to look at me and it's as if someone suddenly pulls the skewer from my brain; my head feels like it's bleeding and I feel dizzy and faint.

'Mum?' Billy asks.

There's a crack, which silences the kids. They look outside, and there's a flash.

'Lightning!' Joy screams with delight, running to the window.

'Thunder!' Izzy follows her.

'Did we take Betty in?' Billy asks.

'Betty! Here girl,' Andy calls.

Betty, our Dachshund, comes bounding in as fast as her little legs can carry her. Then the thunder rolls dramatically, the kids whoop and holler, and Betty halts and scrambles in the opposite direction. The light outside looks purple. I feel like my head cracks with the lightning. My head tightens and tightens, then suddenly the sky opens up and it lashes rain; heavy, fat, determined drops bucket down relentlessly, soaking everything in seconds, and I feel the tension slowly start to ease from my head, like a screw being loosened, easing the pressure.

Joy turns away from the window with a dark and mysterious look on her face. She slowly raises a finger and points at me. 'The wise one has spoken again. Barbecue tomorrow night.'

And we all dissolve into fits of giggles.

To think there was a time when this haunted me, and when it can still haunt me, but now I have all this. I once thought it would be one or the other, but I can have this and still live. They have the power to make what's heavy and all-consuming so light and unimportant. They make the tiny joyful things so phenomenally everything to me. They don't even know what they do for me. They have loved me into shape.

It's a crisp autumn day and Joy and I are bundled up in coats and hats, walking through the woods. We hike together, it's how we talk. It's how she prefers to communicate anyway, through movement. Her predominant colours are and always have been vibrant, energetic, full of mischief and adventure. But today I can't help but notice how they've dulled.

Joy is a talker, the type of person who thinks aloud in order to figure herself out. She talks about everything that happened leading up to the bothersome event, everything surrounding the event and then finally we get to what actually happened. She has always been an exuberant child, never one to shy away from the details, she must get it all out in order to make sense of anything. To see if the unrelated is related, if the feels match the thinks, and it all must be aloud and in circles and repeated, until it's gone. Andy gets swept up in her tornados, feels dizzy in the eye of it, but I must be the calm in her storm. She too gets motion sickness from herself, too much too fast, but I know to stop her, steady her, direct her gaze to a still spot on the horizon. Maybe that spot is me. I've learned to be patient, and understand that the preamble is important on her amble.

The woodland floor is spongy beneath my hiking boots with soil, leaves and moss. The trees' roots reach far beneath like a web under the surface, popping up occasionally to threaten to trip me, or offer a step up. Walking in nature continues to nurture me as it did in the early days of caring for Lily. It's a habit that never left me, one of the few good habits I learned during those days. And like everything else with my aura seeing as I've aged, my experience with it has intensified. Today the floor is ripe with mushrooms, incredible looking fungi, some that look like they're lifted straight from a cartoon, others from your worst nightmares. While I want to stop to examine them, Joy is intent on motoring on, not really seeing anything around her but enjoying the adrenaline that motion gives her.

I don't just see the colours of the fungi, I feel the connection of the trees beneath my feet, as they communicate with each other, using the mushrooms as messengers. I can see the thread-like colours running beneath the soil, millions of them shooting in different directions in a complicated network, like the hectic London Underground.

'So it's over between you?' I ask, when Joy's finally reached her point and finished describing the main event. I try to hide the hope from my voice. I never liked him from the start. I didn't get to know him, a decision that I'm most certain was his, but I soaked up what I could in the short appearances he made in our lives, and from the times I watched from afar. Too much murky orange revealed his territorial nature and controlling sensibilities.

'Yes,' she cries, dissolving again, but manages to speed up. 'And now I can't go back to the gym anymore, I'll have to find a new job and I really love working at this gym. I've built up all my clients. He's such a prick; he's already making life difficult for me. What will I do?'

Hub trees, also known as 'mother trees' are the older, larger trees with roots that are deeper in the soil, giving them access to more nutrients to pass on to the smaller trees. They take the distress signals from their fungal connections and send help. Complex symbiotic relationships. Secret signals, silent distress calls. It happens below the surface and above.

That's motherhood.

We reach an intersection in the woods, we can take right for a shorter journey back to the car, or left. Joy sniffles beside me.

I choose left.

*

Billy, a teenager, returns home from school surrounded by black. It terrifies me. His face dissolves into silent tears as soon as he sees me. He tries to escape to his room but I won't let him.

'What's wrong, love? What happened?'

His body heaves as he sobs in my arms, crying like a wounded animal, a little boy who has fallen over and cut his leg, if only it were so simple now. It's so raw it comes from the depths of his soul. I feel his pain, his deep unhappiness, a huge tragic hole in him.

'Oh baby,' I say, squeezing him tight, wrapping him in my love. The aches and pains of growing up, of living, the horrible things that people do to each other.

I spent most of my early life avoiding anyone and everyone's colours, but what I learn when I have children is that I'd take every single colour away from them, every single shade, and give it to myself, to make life easier for them. For a moment at least, his pain is shared with me as we sit on the couch, entwined bodies and energies, the way it was when he was a bud inside me. I'd take all the pain away from them in a heartbeat if I could. I would live with it all if it meant they didn't have to for a single day.

It's not always welcome, my aura-seeing. The first meeting with a boyfriend or girlfriend, for example. I somehow always seem to be the last one to meet anyone they care for deeply, the first one to meet somebody they're not sure about. My viewpoints are not always believed or respected, my vision is questioned, depending on what I see, depending what their involvement is. I don't ever tailor it to suit their requirements.

'Don't,' Andy snaps at me in the car as we drive home from a visit to his sister in Glasgow.

'But don't you want to know? She says these things and yet—'

'Don't,' he says again, louder, dark and brooding, eyes disappeared beneath his eyebrows and frown. 'Keep it to yourself.'

The weather, he wants to know about. Other insights I must learn to keep to myself. People don't always need or want to know everything.

Izzy drops by unannounced. I happen to be looking out the upstairs window and see her car.

'I'm not here!' I call downstairs to Andy.

'What?'

'I'm not here!'

'Why?' he appears at the foot of the stairs.

'Izzy is outside. I don't care what you say – tell her I'm in the bath or somewhere – but I can't talk.'

He laughs.

Izzy has always been a complex child. The middle child, she's difficult, was jealous of everything: time with others, other kids' toys . . . She needed and still needs to be handled, treated as though fragile, tiptoed around like she's living in the centre of a labyrinth made of eggshells. She's heavy and she loads her heaviness on others. She misunderstands situations, misreads people, she is the victim in every circumstance, but with love, she can keep the darkness at bay. We couldn't rescue Ollie, but as a mother I can make sure Izzy stays afloat, doesn't drift and doesn't drown. As a six-year-old

I brought her to Naomi. Her chakras would be cleared only to be clogged almost instantly. Naomi laughed when I enquired about a chakra stent, anything for the child that could help her. Or perhaps a shield for me that could protect me just from her.

'Alice!' Naomi had laughed as if I was joking, but I'm not sure if I was joking.

I'm the one who understands her the most, and I realise the importance of the work that I do on her, that I make her do on herself but, as much as I love her, not even a mother can take it all the time. I lie in the bath with my eyes closed, feeling only slightly guilty as she and Andy talk downstairs. I don't hear their words but feel the low gravelly vibrato of his deep voice drifting up through the floorboards. It's soothing to hear father and daughter talking, it perhaps should occur more often, but they have always done an elegant dance around one another. Despite his gift with his students, he has sometimes lacked patience with his own daughter.

The front door closes and Andy comes upstairs.

'You owe me,' he says, sighing heavily with exaggeration, and we share a laugh.

'I'll be ready next time,' I say. 'Just not today.'

Our poor daughter. If only she knew.

I let myself into Lily's flat. After Ollie died, she moved to a wheelchair-accessible ground-floor flat. Watching her move around I can't help but think how much easier my life, her life, our lives would have been if she'd done this when I was eighteen. But that was then. Her carer has just been, has cleaned and tidied the flat. Lily is sitting on the couch watching TV, drinking tea and eating chocolate Digestives, looking fresh. New pyjamas and slippers, fluffy hair just washed and dried. It would appear on the surface that everything is fine, but I don't trust surfaces.

'What now?' she says as I stand, frozen, in the living room.

She hates when I visit because I analyse her. I scan all around her to see what's going on with her. She knows what I'm doing, and it makes her uncomfortable. It's not so much that I don't trust what she tells me, though I don't, but more that none of us can truly know what's going on in our own bodies anyway. My meddling makes her change meds, make new doctors' appointments. I uproot her life every time I fly home. She hates it, even though it's always for her own good.

Right now I liken her to a skyscraper at night, when they switch the lights off, level by level. Hers began powering off from the ground floor. Now the lights are out from the knees down. The last time I saw her it looked like she was levitating, but now it's like she's been amputated.

I haven't told her about it because she asked me not to. She said she could never face cancer treatments again, no more surgeries; she'd rather die than go through it all again. But how can I ignore this? She's closing down. Shutting up. It's moving up towards her head. Five months since I last saw her. Longer than usual, but time got away with me. From the ankles to the knees in five months; I look at her, trying to calculate time. How do we do that? Find a Dobson unit equivalent for calculating the amount of time we have left? Count the grey hairs, the lines on our faces, the scars on our body, the holes in our energy fields, the pains in our hearts, the aches in our bones, the grudges, the people we have loved, the people we have lost, the people we have culled . . . I'm so very tired, I could lie down now and—

'For feck's sake, Alice, what?'

'What happens, Alice?' Lily asks.

It's been a while since she's spoken and she's taken me by surprise. She's sleeping in a hospital bed in our front room that used to be the kids' den. She's been living with us for three months. She has a view of a cherry tree covered in blossom; she watches it all day, every day, remarking on its transition. She wondered if she'd live to see it bloom. Now she wonders if she'll live to see the petals fall, every transition a shared miracle.

I look up from the television. We're watching a makeover show, lost in the soft silliness of which couch to put where, as we await the end of her life.

'What do you mean, what happens?' But I somehow already know what she means, have always known exactly what she means all the time, like a parent who understands the babbles of her toddler. She means what happens at the end of life.

'It comes out the top,' I say.

'What does?'

'The colour. The light. When a person dies, it all comes out through the head. I've seen it. It's a white, bright brilliant white. Like all the colours that make us up have mixed together. No matter what your mood, it all makes white in the end.'

No deviant blacks, sludgy greens and browns, the suspicious mustard, the vanity of oranges, the self-pitying blues. No matter about all of that, it's white. Maybe that's because we're all inherently good.

'Gold in the womb, pink in the pram, then we leave white.'

'So we're the light?'

All of my nonsense, she had no time for it. She thought there was something wrong with me. That Andy had married somebody with something wrong and there must be something wrong with him, she couldn't understand it. But over the years she has sat with us while we've talked about my aura-seeing. The kids have spoken about it as if it's normal. *What colour is he, Mum? What's up with her, Mum? I'm guessing she's jealous, Mum, what do you think? He looks happy but is he, Mum? Is he lying, Mum?* So normal and everyday, nobody else that loved me thought it was weird. She started to see it differently. Not that she ever said, but now, now she needs peace, she needs it to make sense.

'Yes, you leave the body through the head, you're the light, and then you're free.'

'Where does the light go?'

'Anywhere you want.'

This part I don't know for certain, but I'm hoping there's will involved. I feel that there is for those who are gone but not gone.

She's quiet for a moment. 'Who did you see die?'

I've seen a few things die; rats on the side of the road, roadkill, a pigeon attacked by a magpie, more than a few dogs, flowers, plants, trees. I was too late to get to my dad's bedside. But there's only one death worth sharing now.

'Ollie.'

'You weren't there. He died in prison.'

'When we were younger. He made some stupid jump, fell down a gully. I saw him leave his body. He said so himself.'

'He never told me that.'

I shrug, not about to argue over it.

'So he had his second chance,' she says at last, having thought it over. 'I didn't do everything right,' she says, looking back out at the white apple blossom. 'But I did my best.'

The lump in my throat only allows me to nod.

The fragility of final moments.

But God, the weight of it.

The caretaker, the caregiver. For a moment, at least, care sharers.

On a windy night in late spring, the cherry blossom petals are taken out almost all at once.

Lily leaves on the same night, the wind whisking her colours away.

I visit her gravestone on her one-month anniversary. The graveyard floor has a low emerald green fog hovering above. It kicks up in a gentle wisp as I move through it, unafraid; it's peaceful, settled, not hurting anyone.

I place an aloe vera plant down by her headstone.

*

Andy's latest episode at work has upset him. Left him shaken. All the time and respect he has given his students over the years, he has been nothing but dedicated, but there is no bringing him back from this. He was shoved up against a wall by a student, a hand to his throat, and feels that even though it was just one student and there have been altercations and scuffles before, the trust is broken. The spell that the dream job had cast over him has been broken. I know what that's like, I tell him, remembering Ollie.

'Why didn't you ever tell me that?'

Anyway, he's sixty-five years old, only a year away from receiving his state pension, and he doesn't ever want to go back.

'Jeffery's dad is looking for a driver,' Izzy says at Sunday lunch when Andy makes the announcement.

'Dad's not driving vans,' says Joy. 'He's sixty-five years old.'

'Excuse me, I'm in the room, I can hear you. I'm not so old that I've lost my hearing,' Andy says.

Though he has a bit, in his left ear, I have to say everything at least three times. It makes me impatient and he accuses me of constantly being in a grump.

'Dog rescue,' Billy says. 'We can set up our own. I'll work there with you.'

'Plants and animals,' I say, thinking of what Naomi told me when I first met her, God rest her soul.

It's not the first time Billy's mentioned it; he's been talking about it for years. Andy buys into his dream and suddenly everyone is very serious about this. It's a big change and we sell the house in London and move our life to Lincolnshire. A house with land to house the dogs. Billy and Izzy work there too. Billy prefers animals to people any day. Izzy is a little lost and I'm keen to help her in any way I can, even if it means working with her less patient father. Considering Andy's previous job, it's ironic really, but we keep them apart, Izzy driving the van that transfers the animals.

One day I find Andy at the kitchen window, watching Billy in the courtyard outside as he gathers the dogs for their food. There is a curious expression on his face.

'What is it?'

'Do you not worry?' he asks. 'About Billy? That he'll never find a woman. That he'll be lonely. And don't give me that "you don't need love to be complete" rubbish,' he says, predicting my response.

'I've never said that. You don't need a man or woman to feel complete, but you certainly do need love,' I say, going to him at the window and resting my head on his shoulder.

I feel his kiss on the top of my head.

'He's always alone, he rarely goes out. He hasn't any relationships that I know of. Apart from with you,' he says with a smile. 'Maybe if you stop being everything to him, he'll start looking elsewhere.'

'No mother can be everything,' I say gently, but it's true. I blanket my children and every aspect of their lives because I never had a mother who did that.

'Do you see anything? That would explain why he always wants to be alone? You can tell me, you know. You keep too much to yourself.'

'Andy,' I say with a laugh. 'You used to tell me not to tell you.'

'That's when they were teenagers, I didn't want to know. But now I'm worried about him.'

'Billy's never alone, he's always with the dogs.'

'Exactly my point!'

I watch him. Jim, our veterinarian, works alongside him. I smile at the rosy pink passing of colours to each other.

'No,' I say simply, then move away, gathering my paper-work.

'What do you mean, no?' he asks. 'No, what? No, you're not worried?'

'No, I don't think he'll ever meet a woman.'

And on that response I leave him, with a wink, to mull over my words.

Andy isn't the only one for me. Not in the way I believed when I first set eyes on him and felt the instant magnetic pull. Before we're married we travel to New York for a short break. It's not a surprise trip, he knows I hate surprises and I've prepared myself for it. If I can survive a city like London, surely I can survive New York. The colours and the people are different and it takes me a moment to feel the altered energy that flows and throbs but it is essentially the same experience for me. We are in FAO Schwartz buying toys for his niece and nephew when I feel someone looking at me, that tingling feeling I get when eyes are on me. I look around and lock eyes with a man in the queue beside us, a young man, my age, handsome, and we hold each other's gaze for a moment, a moment longer than we should, before I look away, feeling a large silly smile unable to leave my face and a desire as great as the children's in the shop who want, want, want everything on the shelves that they touch.

I try to pull myself together and not attract Andy's attention when I realise, after a delayed reaction, what is so very different about the man. He has no colours. I instantly look back at him and our eyes meet again. This time, he's caught and looks away again, but I don't. I can't take my eyes off him, as we shuffle along the queue, some-times him going ahead of me, sometimes him falling behind. I have the same physical reaction as I had with Andy on the train. My body responds in the usual way it does when it wants something, in a surge of adrenaline. I can't stop looking and nor can he. A ludicrous back and forth staring competition, catching each other out, looking away again, grinning stupidly.

'Alice?' Andy asks, snapping me back to reality. 'What's that about?'

'Hmm?'

'What's his deal?'

'Who?'

He glares at me then.

'I was day dreaming, sorry.'

I could have told him the very big news that I'd just seen another man with no colours, but I needed time to process it. When I saw Andy on the train with no colours, I felt, as did Hugh, that I had to find him, that he was someone who could hold the key to something for me; unlock my caged future happiness. I thought he was the only one of his kind. I even believed, in my greatest throes of falling in love during the honeymoon stage, that this entire colour skill was in fact a gift given to me in order just to find him. It was a sentimental belief that has since passed, but who's to say there isn't a colourless person in every village, town and city in the world waiting for me? A special mutant group of humans sprinkled throughout the earth whose sole purpose it is to accommodate my life journey. Perhaps they are a map of how and who with to live my life and I can see the way. Am I to follow these people like a trail, hopping from one to another throughout my life like stepping stones until I reach the end? A kind of monkey bars from person to person, legs dangling wildly, while hanging on to one to await the next. And can you truly hang in there tightly, one-handed, when the other is grappling around in the air for the next? Which man do you stop at, which relationship do you invest yourself in, when do you say this is it...and so on go the great looping thoughts.

I do a lot of soul searching on this trip, while simultaneously looking out for the man that I never see again. My distraction is understood to be down to my general weirdness and awkwardness when faced with any new people, places and scenarios. After days of forensic studies into each inch of my body, mind and soul, I reach a finding that turns out to be more liberating than initially feared; Andy is not the only one for me, but he is the one I'm choosing.

No marriage is perfect but we work hard at it. We are fortunate that one of us has the will to keep it alive during the moments that count, that at no time when things get dark both of us want to give up. A marriage requires two people doing their part, yes, but not necessarily always at the same time. At all times it needs at least one. Sometimes one on the ledge and the other to talk them down. Someone to stay awake at camp to make sure the fire doesn't go out.

I realise over time that even though I've never been able to see Andy in the same way as I see others, I've learned to read him as well as I can read everyone else. I know Andy's soul as deeply as I know a stranger's, and though I can know a stranger on first glance and scan them like an X-ray, it has taken me years of hard loving to get here with him. Perhaps it's having to work harder with him that makes the results more rewarding, the understanding of him deeper.

My love, my best friend, my flawed and loyal lover.

white

I SEE ANDY'S COLOURS ONCE.

They drift up from his body, up, up, up from his roots and out through his head, as he lies in my arms, his wrinkled skin, pale skin and bone, with mine. He is wrapped in a blanket in my arms, like a baby, when his breathing starts to change, and his colour appears for the very first time.

A wonderful white. The rarest colour of all. Pure light. A higher power, a soaring spirit, the defender of all.

'Oh darling,' I whisper. 'Oh darling. I see you.'

The brightest white of them all. My angel.

I tell him this.

I kiss his lips and watch him leave.

But he stays around in places. I catch his brilliant white around the house, on the children and the grandchildren, especially Louis, who is so like him. I see him when I'm not expecting to sometimes, in our favourite holiday destination, his brilliant white around a rock that was his favourite place to perch and watch the sea, or at places and things I didn't know he held so dear. On a sweater I often wore, in his favourite corner of his favourite bar, around the dog he walked every day, who remained his faithful friend by his side until the end. I learn even more about him in his death.

'There you are,' I say now and then, catching sight of him. 'There you are.'

Days that are too short, nights that never end. I have too much time to think,

About him,

About everything,

That we did together,

And every moment that we spent.

Every look,

Every touch,

I have too much time to think about how the only person who had no colour,

In his departure has drained the most colour from my life.

They're all around me now. I can't see their faces, my eyesight has faded, but I can see their energy colours. I come in and out of the room without sense of time. All my family, my three children and their spouses, even Charlie, Izzy's ex-husband, is here. I'm grateful for that, setting bitter disputes aside to be here for me. Torn apart by love, brought together by a different kind of love; everyone here is bonded by the only thing that ever truly counts in the entire insane journey. My eight grandchildren are here. Izzy is holding my hand, dear sweet Izzy who has always been afraid to let go. They say newborn babies don't realise they are separate people to the mother or person that is feeding them. I used to feel it with her the most, so attached we were practically one, a physical and mental closeness that never really went away. I hear her sniffles as she tightens and loosens her grip on mine.

I won't be leaving on my own, and I'm glad of that, but I don't want to leave them behind. I cannot sever her grip; when you hold on for so long for your children, all your life, for them, it is impossible to leave for yourself, not when they hold on so tight. But we can't all linger here forever, somebody has to leave first, and I don't want to be alone. With all that I have witnessed in my life, I don't know where I'm going. I have watched so many others leave and parts of them stay behind, linger in the places and the people they love best. I wonder whether I too can be with the people in this room and the people who have left. If that is why we scatter, some of us here, some of us there, one foot in this world, the other foot in the other world. In life, I have felt pulled as a mother, a wife, a friend, a daughter, a sister, a colleague. Perhaps it's only in death that there is enough of us for everyone and everything.

I long for my Andy. Ten years without him. I long for my brother Hugh, gone five years now. It has been a long time since I saw dear Ollie, killed so young in prison, but I want to see him now, the little boy who played quietly at the playbox of broken toys, longing for love and connection. Naomi, who opened my eyes, helped me remove the shades and the barriers, helped me to live in the light. My dear dad. Long gone Lily.

Her colours flash before me, like a kaleidoscope montage of everything she was, a woman so trapped and a woman so lost. The colours aren't terrifying as they once were; she was so very lost, trapped in a fog, on stormy seas and needed guiding to a safe harbour. It's been so long since I saw her colours, and yet they are so familiar, they offer comfort to me for the first time. Maybe she is my lighthouse now, guiding me in. She put me in this world and she's on the other side like a beacon.

'Mammy,' I say, suddenly feeling like a child again.

Izzy gasps, and I'm back in the room again.

'Leave her be, Izzy,' says a voice, gentle now. 'Let her go.' My Joy. I don't want to leave my Joy. My rose-golden nugget who brought my world to another place, to a level I never knew existed. All my babies, who now have their babies, whose babies will have their babies. All in this room, curled up together as if in a womb, a family fortress. The levels and layers of living. The underground webs, the symbiotic relationships. The ones we can see, the ones we can feel. Transitional colours. Transitional rooms. I drift, I come back. I drift again.

'It's okay, Mum,' Joy says, beside me now. Izzy is holding my hand, she won't let go. Billy is by my feet, rubbing them gently, rooting me to him. Joy kisses my cheek, brushes back my hair, whispers in my ear. 'Go to them.'

Yes. I must do that now.

And suddenly I am so light, weightless, and I can't see them anymore, no bodies, just their glorious lights, reaching out to each other and filling the room.

All they are, are light, as all I am is light.

*

I have had a life-long relationship with colours. Enduring them, confronting them, accepting them, surrendering to them. Our bodies act as a prism in the light and all the colours shine through us like an ever-changing light show. At times I felt like I was trapped in a prism prison, but light gets through the cracks. I learned to find the cracks that became my connections to outside. I have seen and felt them all; all the shades, tones and variations of every colour in the spectrum.

I have experienced others' pain and I've experienced my own.

The colours of rage,
Of hate, envy and greed.
The colours of confusion, frustration,
Of betrayal and fear.
The colours of lust, of longing, of loneliness.
The colours of happiness,
The colours of hope,
The so many colours of love.
Insipid, vibrant, vivid and sharp,
One by one and all at once,
I have seen and felt,
All the colours of living.

ACKNOWLEDGEMENTS

It takes a lot of people to publish a book, and so enormous thanks to HarperCollins UK, particularly:

The wonderfully artistic and clever Claire Ward for coming up with the perfect title, which is derived from the Oscar Wilde quote, 'Mere colour, unspoiled by meaning and unallied with definite form, can speak to the soul in a thousand different ways.'

My long-time editor Lynne Drew for the encouragement, support and guidance, Kimberley Young, Kate Elton, Charlie Redmayne, the indomitable Anna Derkacz, Lucy Stewart, Hannah O'Brien, Abbie Salter, the sparkling Liz Dawson, and all the whizzes on the wider team. Team HarperCollins Ireland: Tony Purdue, Patricia McVeigh, Jacq Murphy and Courtney Fitzmaurice. It's an honour to work with you all and I cherish it.

The fantastic visionary team at the think tank headquarters that is PFLM: Theresa Park, Abby Koons, Andrea Mai, Emily Sweet, Kat Toolan, Ben Kaslow-Zieve, Charlotte Gillies and the team.

To Anita Kissane, Howie Sanders and Kassie Evashevski at Anonymous Content, and Chris Maher.

In a Thousand Different Ways is entirely fictional, though of course even pretend things grow from the seed of real things. I read *A Little Bit of Auras: An Introduction to Energy Fields* by Cassandra Eason, and while I interpreted it in my own way for the sake of my story, this research book was part of the story's building blocks.

Sending thanks and love to the people at the centre of my world; Mimmie, Dad, Georgina, Nico, Rocco, Jay, Gia. And all my wonderful friends for the chats, tears and giggles.

Thanks to my tribe; my David, my Robin, my Sonny, my Blossom... my everythings...

About the Author

Cecelia Ahern is an Irish novelist whose work was first published in 2004. She is read around the world in forty-seven countries, in over thirty languages, and has sold over twenty-five million copies of her novels. In addition to her novels, she is also the author of a highly acclaimed collection of stories, *Roar*, which is now an Apple Original series on Apple TV+.

Cecelia Ahern lives in Dublin with her family.